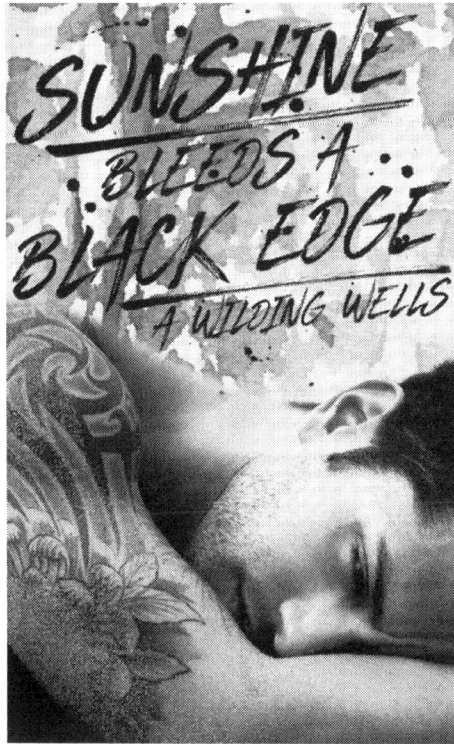

By

A. Wilding Wells

Copyright 2016 A. Wilding Wells
All rights reserved.

For more information, please contact A. Wilding Wells at aw@awildingwells.com.

www.awildingwells.com
www.instagram.com/awildingwells
www.pinterest.com/awildingwells
www.facebook.com/awildingwells
www.goodreads.com/awildingwells

HYP NOTIC PRESS

VERBA POETICA

Table of Contents

Chapter 1 1
Chapter 2 5
Chapter 3 9
Chapter 4 21
Chapter 5 29
Chapter 6 37
Chapter 7 45
Chapter 8 53
Chapter 9 65
Chapter 10 69
Chapter 11 81
Chapter 12 91
Chapter 13 97
Chapter 14 103
Chapter 15 109
Chapter 16 115
Chapter 17 121
Chapter 18 125
Chapter 19 133
Chapter 20 141
Chapter 21 147
Chapter 22 151
Chapter 23 157
Chapter 24 163
Chapter 25 169
Chapter 26 177
Chapter 27 181
Chapter 28 185
Chapter 29 187
Chapter 30 193
Chapter 31 197
Chapter 32 203
Chapter 33 207
Chapter 34 211
Chapter 35 215
Chapter 36 219
Chapter 37 225
Chapter 38 229
Chapter 39 237
Chapter 40 243
Chapter 41 247
Chapter 42 253
Chapter 43 263
Chapter 44 269
Chapter 45 273
Chapter 46 277
Chapter 47 281
Chapter 48 285
Chapter 49 289
Chapter 50 291
Chapter 51 295
Chapter 52 299
Chapter 53 303
Chapter 54 307
Chapter 55 315

Chapter 1
Coming Undone

Ruby

(Paris, France)

As I peer at the contents in the tiny open box resting on my shaking hands my stomach flips.

Bile rises in my throat as I try to make out the partly smudged postmark. Snowvale, Wisconsin. My hometown. Shoving the box into my bag, I nestle it next to the paperwork for the house I recently purchased in Snowvale. A home on the lake for my mom and younger brother, Echo.

"He's waiting for you," Florence, the receptionist says. "And, Ruby, congratulations! *Vogue* tweeted about your new makeup campaign this morning!"

Breathe and speak. You cannot come undone in the lobby of the biggest modeling agency in the world. I lift my head and look at her, certain I'm seeing triples of everything. *Someone in Snowvale knows what happened to me?* Air is suddenly scarce, a mere whisper passing my lips. "Oh. Thanks, honey," I say softly.

"Are you all right?" Florence asks.

"I'm going to be…sick."

I hurry down the hall and duck into the ladies' room just in time. *How can this be happening?* I want to flush the box contents down the toilet along with my vomit, make everything go away.

Staring in the mirror while washing my hands, I see fragments of the girl whose life was forever changed in minutes on her high school graduation night.

Emerald eyes glow back at me, then tears follow, rivering down my pale cheeks. Threading my trembling fingers through my long blond hair, I hear his voice. Rebel Field. I see him standing in front of me on the shoulder of the highway the day I ran away to save my soul. And the sad expression on his face when I told him not to follow me to the airport. Rebel. My best friend, my lover. And, the one man I've never forgotten.

"Ruby?" Teddy says from the other side of the door. "Are you okay, darling? Florence says you're ill." The door squeals when Teddy pushes through it.

"I'm—

"Ruby…Jesus. What's wrong?" He wraps his arms around me, his warm, sexy scent enveloping me.

"It's nothing. Just nerves about going home." Though I love and trust Teddy, I can't tell him about my past. Can't tell anyone. It was enough just thinking about seeing Rebel again when I fly home next week. But now this?

Teddy kisses my wet cheeks, his azure blue eyes wandering my face with concern. He not only founded the agency, he was its biggest grossing model for years. He owns the words mysterious, dark and sexy. "Shorten the trip, go for a week instead of two. Meet me in Cannes, maybe you'll accept my proposal this time?" He waggles his brow.

That would be his *third* marriage proposal. Maybe I should accept it and move on. I know all love is not the same. Not all people reach inside you, searing themselves to your memory. I know because I've mourned for years the soul-filling love Rebel gave me. "Teddy." I huff out a breath. "It's not going to happen with us. I love you, but—"

"I know. Are you sure you're okay?" He brushes my hair aside and places a soft kiss on my temple. "Hate to see my girl cry. I know we've been off for a while, not seeing each other, but still…I love you and I need to know you really are okay."

"I'll be fine."

Fine? Yeah. But will I find out who sent the box? And if it's linked to the murder?

Chapter 2

Snowvale

Ruby

(Snowvale, Wisconsin)

"Mom, you're going to throw your back out." I clutch my mother's rail-thin arm as she tucks her pet swan, Lake, into the back seat of her rusted-out Wagoneer.

"He goes everywhere with me. He's suffered enough loss." She nestles next to her bird, double belts them, smooths her hand down her skirt, and lets the list of deads roll. "Opal and your father. God bless…"

"Goddamn, Mom. Are you going to go through the whole deads list every time you bless anyone?"

She slips her rosary out of her purse, works her fingers over the beads, and continues chanting her list of deads. It's one of her many lists. And one of her many quirks. She's list obsessed. The deads, the gays, the riches, the poors, the outs, the down-and-outs. She's a little different. Always moving sideways. Read: beautifully batty. And, after my sister, Opal committed suicide, she dipped deeper into the buggy pot. Then she had a nervous breakdown and took one more dive. After Dad passed, our long-distance phone conversations took on all kinds of new eccentricities. Opal and Dad sometimes joined in on calls.

The deads were not going to be disregarded, according to Mom.

I slam the car door—too hard. Nerves. I still haven't seen him. Rebel Rifle Field. Maybe I'll find the courage to seek him out today. The one guy who stole my heart. Could he still own every beat of it?

Maybe it's naïve to think he might still want me. And what if he does? What about my life and career an ocean away? Could I ever live here again? Could I leave Paris and my career? My whole life is there now. And this town is the opposite of Paris.

I toss a bag of clothing headed for Goodwill in the back of the Jeep and then ease into the driver's side.

"Don't take the Lord's name in rain. God and damn are not like peanut butter and mayonnaise."

In rain? Yup, that's another new thing with her, word mix-ups. Mom clears her throat three times. It's always three times: one for the Father, one for the Son, and one for the Holy Ghost.

"You must have picked that sass up while you were gallivanting around the world."

"In vain, Mom, not rain. And, my gallivanting bought the house you and Echo are moving into." I back the car out of the driveway and head toward town, a sweet-and-sour taste on my tongue as we pass the high school.

Mom clucks her tongue and yells, "Stop correcting me!"

I swing a right on Main Street as Mom waves her errands list, catching my attention.

"I need a hair trap. Stop at Field and Farm first."

Maybe a tongue trap too.

I break out in a rapid sweat. "So…Rebel's hardware store? Is that it?" I ask, knowing the answer, my pulse racing.

"That's it. S'pose I should've told you more about him...but…" Mom clears her throat three times. "Was a shame. She got clocked at the Stop-N-Go. One of the deads now. T-boned, don-cha know. Boy lived."

Mom travels in and out of thoughts so recklessly that it's impossible to keep up without acting like bumpers on a pinball machine.

"You're speaking in tongues. Please, Ma. Use full sentences and names."

Confused and annoyed, I pull over, jam the shift into park, and process the mind dump she's unloaded. "What are you talking about? One thing at a time. Start with Rebel." I twist to face her.

Her eyebrows rise as she makes the sign of the cross. "Wife died in a car accident. Went through a Stop-N-Go on red. Has a sixteen-year-old. Name is Rifle, he lived. Paris died."

He has a sixteen-year-old kid? My heart thumps hard. He was married? *I hate this.* Foolishly, I'd tried to imagine him single all those years. I made myself believe he missed *me*. Needed *me*. I'm as delusional as my mother. *"I'll wait for you," he said.* I guess not.

I huff out a breath. "Paris?"

"Paris was Rebel's wife." She smiles. "Bless her soul."

The list of deads rolls off her tongue while I tap my fingers against the unraveling braid of pleather on the steering wheel.

"The ladies at the salon thought that was droll since you left him for Paris, and he off and married Paris." Mom laughs and laughs. She laughs so hard that she has to dab the corners of her eyes with a hanky.

The reality of Rebel's situation screams at me as I hold on to the truth and ramble off a, "Holy fucking shit."

"That tongue of yours ought to be—"

She was going to say slit. She always said that—until Opal's tongue was slit by the Kline boys as a warning the night my life fell apart. Mom doesn't know who slit it. I was the only one who knew everything. Or so I wanted to believe, until that box arrived and changed everything. Except this. My sister died because of me. I'd thought I was saving her by being a martyr. There was never a choice. But I'd thought someone was going to come and save us. I was betting on God or Rebel. Neither showed. I needed Opal to survive. One of us had to. I was willing to die on the inside to save her life. She never would have survived what they did to me.

It never crossed my mind it would kill her to be a witness.

Chapter 3

Gossip

Rebel

(Snowvale, Wisconsin)

In a town this size, you know everyone's business. Every affair. Death. Facelift. Stomach stapling. Marriage and miscarriage are gossiped about between grocery aisles and church pews alike. Rumors are spread as easily as manure on the fields. So, the second I heard Ruby bought a place on the lake for her mom and her brother, I knew she was coming home. Call it premonition or faith. Call it cocky. She was coming for me.

I really have no right to stake claim to her after all these years. Even though I told her I'd wait. But then I saw it happen twice in recent years at school reunions. Past lovers reunited. And some of them weren't much more than a high school fling as I recall.

Ruby and I though… Do we have a chance like that? Can we take what we had back then—magic, love, and lust—and turn it into a future?

She might have gone on and become a famous star to the rest of the world. But, to me, she was it.

My universe.

She's been back three days. And I have counted every second of each of them. Three days and I'm out of my mind because I haven't seen her. My Ruby Mae. She's going to have to come to me. That's how this is going down. Find me, show me the necklace and the promise ring I gave her, and tell me the real reason she left and wasn't wearing them when she did.

I tug the back of my son's collar. "Rifle, help Father H. find electrical tape."

He leads the pastor toward the tape aisle.

After turning the corner, I crash into someone. When my nerves feel the first jolt, I laugh. "Hey, sorry 'bout that."

Soft curves fill my grip. Ample breasts splash against my chest. Familiar laughter sparkles like a cache of crystals. And sweet memories hit me hard. Things I still crave: the flesh of her waist, which is now in my hands. Things I need: her love. Things I wanted: stolen.

I quickly drop my hands from her, and immediately clasp the back of my neck, optimistic my fingers won't move on their own volition back to her. But Jesus fucking Christ, look at her. Ruby Mae Rose. All grown up, a worldly, knowing grin on her face, which I have no business admiring if it's not gracing a magazine cover or TV commercial. Green, flirting eyes meet mine and punch my gut.

"Hey, Wishbone."

Her syrupy, deep voice always got me.

"Ruby." I swallow hard, trying to look away. Good fucking luck.

"Fancy meeting you here," she says. The grin on her face would make any man do handsprings for her attention.

Is her heart pounding like mine? An intense throb that aches like it's trying to get to hers. My tongue thickens as my brain—which is consuming itself with what to say—trips over miles of knots forming inside me. She's here. My girl is front and center, and fuck if I'm not starstruck.

It pisses me off, the way my feelings collide in a muddle of lust, need, and frustration. The necessity to consume her and push her away wars in my mutilated heart. I want to yell at her. I want to love her. Awful as it sounds, I want her to hurt the way she hurt me.

Then she digs into her purse and knocks me flat when she retrieves a clown nose, places it on my nose, and squeezes it singing, "Honky birthday, Wishbone!"

"Thanks. It was last week." I had wondered if she forgot.

"I know when your birthday is. You look good, Rebel."

I yank the nose off and stuff it into my pocket. Ruby's eyes lock on mine, a certain vulnerability in them.

"So, this place is yours?" She looks away and scratches her elbow, where she has a bacon Band-Aid.

She's still in there.

"I kind of have a thing for hardware stores," she says. Then she bites her bottom lip, which holds the sexiest smile I've seen in seventeen years.

"I meant to come and find you earlier…but Mom needed me to help her with packing."

"Earlier?" I ask. I'm tongue-tied, unable to say what I ought to be saying. I've had years to sort through this shit and all these feelings, and now that I have the chance I've got nothing.

Ruby grips then yanks various lengths of thick rope hanging from wheels next to us. My dick twitches as her hand slides up and down the rope.

Words finally surface and they're angry. I glance around, making sure no one will hear me. "Like seventeen years earlier?"

"Ouch," she whispers. "Let's try this again. Hey. It's nice to see you. I know it took me a while, but I'm home for a couple of weeks. How are you?" She shoves her hands into her jean shorts, her slow gaze traveling from my legs to my eyes. Measured and easy, her tongue rims her lips like she's tasting every inch of me.

"How am I?" I take a wide stance, hands planted on my hips so I don't do something else with them. Like punch my fist through the boxes to my side. "Is this the first time you've wondered?"

"Well, no...I..." Ruby's gaze darts away from mine.

Maybe she's feeling the same way. Nervous, edgy, and anxious to figure out how she can make up for lost time. How to bundle all the highs and lows racing through her heart and turn them into something. But what?

The only thing stopping me from berating her is a matching need to scoop her into my arms, take her to my bed, and lie with her all afternoon and deep into the night. To strip her down and make her understand she could still be my girl. The battle, though, is hell sitting in the middle of my personal tug-o-war.

Rifle nudges me. "'Scuse me, Dad. Father H. wants something wider and stronger. That Ape Tape come in yet?"

I drive a hand through his chaotic mess of hair. "Gimme a sec."

He nods, stepping a few feet away.

"Is that…" Ruby's gaze jets between me and Rifle. One side of her lips rises, her tongue poking out.

I want to drive myself onto her and kiss that mouth. Those pouty lips I haven't tasted in years. People can't change that much, can they? I shouldn't have kept her in my heart, but some people climb inside you and never leave. They mark you with their charm. They melt into your crevices—the parts of your soul you didn't know existed until that person abandons you. And then those phantom bits linger deep inside. They hurt like steel splinters pounding into your raw heart. They make you ache and crave; they make you angry one second and hopeful the next.

Like now.

They make you stupid. So dense you forget things that happened to you when that person left. That's me. So senseless that I want to promise her a future within a minute of us reuniting. Tell her she won't escape me again. Though, first, she needs to hear how she almost killed me until I woke from the dead when my kid was born. I had to survive. I had to know there was a future before me when all I wanted was to give her one.

"My kid. Yeah." I gesture Rifle to introduce himself.

"Rifle Field." He puts his hand out, eyeing Ruby up with approval.

Christ, he's becoming a man. Licking his chops over my girl. *My girl?* Pulling my head out of my ass, I assume the position of survival—my arms crossed over my chest—hiding the festering soreness buried there.

"Yes, you are." She impales me with a need-filled stare. "You look like the same boy I knew back in school. You two share the same muscular build, and black hair and dark eyes…my goodness. He looks exactly like you."

My fingernails dig into my palms, my rigid fists pinned at my thighs. "What d'ya need, Ruby?" I need processing time.

She's more than I remember. More everything. And she has more of a grip on me than I thought she could in such a short amount of time since coming home. I want to tell her she might have been a star to the rest of the world, but damnit, she was my life.

"Of course." She glances away, her face reddening. "Mom needs a hair trap. You know, one of those…"

"I own a hardware store." I stride away. "I know what a fucking hair trap is." Jesus, I sound like a dick.

Why does it feel like she's still mine? And still feel like we're seventeen? I'm sure she's going to spin me around any second and ask me to join her in a Cool and the Gang dance-off. Or tell me she wants to race her horse against mine through the cornfields to the abandoned red barn and make out until our lips burn. Or tell me that she bought a bunch of postcards and wrote random love letters on them so we can stuff them into arbitrary mailboxes after midnight to make some sorry sucker feel loved for a fleeting moment.

"I'm sure you know all the traps, Rebel." There's a sureness in her voice even though it's soft. It's not smug, but it holds a little jab.

When I stop, prepared to slice into her, Ruby slams into my back.

"Holy shit, you're a brick wall, dude. I mean…" She presses her hands on my back then slaps my ass. "Wow. Rock hard." She's never been shy. "Come on, Wishbone. You can at least laugh."

I don't want to look at her for fear of what I might do. Namely, kiss her in a way that should only be done in private.

"Okay, then. Maybe if I talk to your back, we'll get off to a better start." She giggles nervously while I gather my nuts up.

So far, she's slammed into my front and my backside within minutes of seeing me. Some divine force is trying to tell me something.

"I didn't mean like *get off* get off. Shit. What am I saying?" She mumbles something I can't decipher.

I walk two more steps and locate a hair trap for her mom.

"Um, Rebel? Sorry about your wife," she rushes out when her hands press against me again, causing another stir in my groin. Only Ruby could illicit a feeling that angers and turns me on. "I didn't know you married. Mom filled me in."

I turn to face her. "I didn't know you gave a shit about anyone but yourself."

Ruby exhales slowly. I turn it into something sexual. A little five-second scene in my head: her gasping then breathing out gradually as I fill her with my rock-hard cock, like I've been dreaming about since I was sixteen.

"What's up, Rebel?" She cocks her head. "Am I your enemy?"

"You're nothing," I bark out. They were heartless words, a wall crashing between us—where one needs to be. For now. For my protection.

My heart pounds when I take long steps down the aisle. Ruby's footsteps pitter-patter behind me; she still walks on her toes? That one little thing pulls me into her undercurrent. *Fight it.* Fight it until she gives her truth up.

But what if she never does? What was she not telling me about why she stayed away for so long? I feel like an asshole for being mean, but the reality is she'll need to break down and spit it out. Spit out the whys. The this-was-what-happened, the I-left-becauses. Maybe she needs more time—not that she hasn't had enough already.

The one thing I know about me and Ruby? The piece of hope I've hung on to all these years? We were meant to be together somewhere along the line. I just hope to hell it's in this lifetime and that I can get over being so pissed at her.

"I wasn't expecting you to be so angry toward me," she says. Her eyes hold an intense stare and lock onto mine like she's injecting my soul through her gaze. Pleading me to open my mind and see her. "I guess that last thing you said about how you'd be here waiting was just teenage lust talking. I get it. Too much time has passed. You've moved on. Maybe we can be friends along the way." She shrugs and takes the trap from me; our fingers brush for a scintillating second. *Friends? Fuck that shit.*

"See you around," she says. Her small pained smile disappears as fast as it forms.

"Not likely." Worry punches my stomach, even if I am channeling my inner asshole. My defenses are so high that I could block a flock of cupids.

But then her eyes… Well, goddammit. Sorrow sinks into them. And the way that one side of her lips lifts into a but-what-if expression takes me back to our last goodbye. And my last question.

I will never forget asking her, *"Why don't you have my promise ring on?"* Dipping my fingertips inside the collar of her shirt, I felt around for the necklace and the ring I'd given her. Nothing was there but her fitful heartbeat.

"Nice welcome home." She spins, charges toward the checkout, whips a few bills onto the counter, and then disappears through the door—my gaze planted on her gorgeous round ass.

And on her ass is blood.

She's not gonna like this.

I jog out the door, my fingers flying down my shirt buttons. "Ruby." I grab her elbow.

She snaps toward me, meeting me in a stare, her eyes rimmed in red and tear-filled hatred.

"Wrap it around your waist. You uh…you're bleedin'." I hand her my shirt then yank my T-shirt down when her gaze latches onto my abs.

A rich blush scoots into her cheeks. "Nice. Well this is embarrassing." She closes her eyes. "Thanks. I'll get it back to you."

Her mortified-sounding tone makes me chuckle. I recall doing this same thing in high school.

"Fucking period was done two days ago!" she says softly, almost to herself.

"Don't worry. Got plenty of 'em."

She works my shirt around her waist and knots it while I study her ringless hands.

Someone would have told me if she'd gotten married along the way. I never believed she didn't.

"Of course," she says. "Why would you want it back? That would mean seeing me again." Her voice cracks, reaching into my heart for another strangle. "I'm not in town to get in your way. I'm here to move Mom and Echo into a house. I'll be gone before you know it."

Gone again. I want to believe her—that I'm not part of the reason she's here. But I don't. Chemistry doesn't lie. Kindred spirits twine, and once they do, there's no unraveling.

"Good," I lie.

"Fuck you, Rebel," she says softly, but there's a bite behind her words. Ruby always did have a spark that could easily burst into flames.

I bite my tongue from telling her, *I will, woman. I will be fucking you. It's not gonna happen soon, but it will happen. You will feel me inside you. All these years of imagining it? They will come to fruition.*

"Not me, Ruby." I grip the back of my neck as my jaw tightens and I imagine who she's been with. "You never let me have it, remember?"

Her eyes widen, then she glares at me.

"I'm sure you've had your fair share of French, Italian, and every other man-sausage across the pond."

Fuck if that wasn't the meanest thing I've said yet. I'm a douchebag with a capital D. How the hell do I think I'm going to get her back this way? Good fucking question.

Chapter 4

Wishbone

Ruby

I know what I am. Dented and scratched, cracks filled with enough glue that I can mostly hold myself together. I might not have been honest with myself about everything I'd come home to, and how it would feel each time I turned a corner in this town and ran into something unexpected. Like him.

"Yes, Rebel. The Italians are my favorite. Long, girthy cocks a girl can ride for hours." I rim my lips, my tongue playing at the edges. "Not that the French aren't masters in the sack. All those stereotypes are true."

Rebel's eyes blacken, if that's possible, his lips taking the form of an I'm-going-to-spit-on-you scowl. I mimic his look and raise his hate with a lock-down stare and no-talking contest as I step into his space. Bring it on. I can play the game too.

One more step. Then another. We're close. Too close. His six-foot-three, broad-shouldered frame packed with muscle and a few tats is towering over me. Damn! I look up and glare at him, his short black messed-up hair and dark stubble add a certain depth to his angry sexiness. But no, I'm not backing down. Both of us breathe like we've been running mountains. His black eyes gauge mine. Then they arrive at my lips a second later, grabbing my need and riding it hard. Rebel Field live in the flesh isn't the man I expected. Can he feel the heat coming off me and swirling between us and the vibes my whole body is shelling out even though he's being an ass? My urge to slap his rugged face is tamped down when he steps close enough I can smell him. Maybe he's about to apologize. Or lay those plump lips on mine for a long, slow welcome-home kiss. And, as I recall, the man could kiss.

But he's pissing me off with his angry-man performance. He wants a bit of war by the way he keeps poking at me. And my inner smartass never could refuse a good spar with my wishbone.

"Ruby!" My mother's screechy voice hovers behind me. "Ask me a stupid question."

I turn my back to Rebel and hand the hair trap to Mom through the wide crack in the window, where she and Lake are watching us like a train wreck. "Are you ready to go, Ma?"

"That was stupid, all right."

Lake nibbles on Mom's earlobe.

"My wig is itchin' in this heat," she says. "I need some talcum from the five-and-dime."

"One sec." I look over my shoulder and hold his stare as I wave a finger at Mom. "Say hey to Rocket. Unless that's too much to ask."

He grunts. "She'll appreciate you give a shit about one of us."

"She?" I whirl to face Rebel.

"Rocket is Etta now," he says.

"What are you talking about?"

"Yes. While you were getting cocked in Europe, Rocket became Etta." Rebel smirks.

I suck in a revolted breath… *getting cocked…*? "I swear to God, Rebel. If you say another thing about me getting…"

God, he's transparent. Jealousy is something he never did well. Never hid. And it might have added a bucket of fuel to the Kline boys' lust and hatred for me. And likely why they did what they did on graduation night.

Try as I might to tamp them down, my emotions flare, and tears well in my eyes then fall. Now, he'll see my wall come down. Not all of it, because there's a massive height of damage holding it up. But enough that he'll dig in and make it hurt without much effort.

"Those are pretty big tears for a girl who told me how much she loved European cock. Wasn't your phrase 'ride 'em for hours?'"

After dragging my sleeve across my eyes, I step toward his immense frame and shove him with the force of an ox. He doesn't falter. Not one step. Mr. Stoic As Fuck. Like he's rooted to the center of the earth.

You want more? Get ready, Rebel. I've got plenty of fight in me.

"Yeah, they were great." I clench my jaw. Words scrape through my teeth. "Great big dicks." I throw my arms wide and moan out a sexual sound. War is ugly. Noisy. Graphic. Time to kill. "But not as big of a dick as you are." I climb onto the hood of the Wagoneer via the rusted bumper then clamber to the roof while Mom protests. While turning in a circle, I shout, "Biggest dick in the Midwest, ladies and gentlemen. Rebel Rifle Field!" I clap my hands, add in a horse whistle for more attention, and then dance a goofy jig and scream it all over again.

War is bloody. He might hate me right now, but somewhere inside this war, there's a man who cares. He wouldn't be fuming like red embers if he didn't give a damn.

Numerous people stop. I hear some, "Oh my gods," a few "Holy shits," and one, "Who's the hot chick doing the jig?"

Rebel stomps toward the Jeep, one fist shaking at me along with his head. "Get the fuck down here, Ruby! These people are my customers." He swipes at my leg, causing me to scream and stumble back until I land on the hot asphalt.

Dammit, war hurts.

I stare at my pain-riddled right wrist, which is bent at an obviously wrong angle.

Rebel jogs to my side. "That's broken, baby." He takes my arm in his callused, beautiful hands, his thumb brushing across my racing pulse. His gaze meets mine, his eyes soft and concerned.

"I didn't mean to hurt you." His words come out in a gentle tender whisper that I repeat in my heart, hoping it reaches him.

His effect on me might be worse now than it was in high school. I figured I'd get butterflies, though I hadn't anticipated breaking out in a sweat and not wanting to linger in his deep chocolate-drop eyes.

"We gotta get you to the hospital."

I wince, then push myself up with my other arm. "I made my way around the world." *I survived that night you never arrived.* "I can get myself to the hospital."

"You aren't driving anywhere." He hauls me up, his hands gripping under my arms.

"Now you're interested in helping me?" I chuckle. "Don't worry about it, I'm a big girl."

"I'm not worried. I'm just doing the right thing. That might not make sense to you, Miss Euro Cock."

I wiggle out of his grip, tuck my wrist into the crook of my elbow and kick his shin. Twice. He doesn't wince, though. The man is pure steel. Impenetrable.

"I hate you for this," I whisper-yell.

He nods. "I hate you for an assload more." His hand encircles my arm with a firm squeeze, and he drags me toward him, his face now one second from mine.

My need skyrockets. Hate and love live so close that I can't tell which one I'm feeling. Christ, this is confusing. Maybe if I'd stayed here he'd have helped me heal. But I couldn't do it. Sometimes, even a love like ours isn't enough when one hurts inside and can't tell the truth about it.

"Get in my truck." He points to a giant, black dually parked across the lot like a dark horse. "Get going." He edges me forward, his gruff, cracked voice acting like a little mating dance.

I take one pace away from him then backtrack to the Jeep.

He steps in my way. "I'll have one of the guys take your mother home. Now, go!"

I elbow him in the chest. "Give me a sec, all right? Fucking brute! Jesus, you are bossy!"

Mom works the rosary with her shaking hand. "Is your wrist okay?"

"I'm fine, whatever." I wiggle my wrist around, certain it's broken. But still, I've had worse pain.

"Okay, good. Ask me a stupid question," she says.

I think for three seconds before I ask, "I think he hates me. What should I do about him?"

"That is a stupid question." She smiles then tilts her head to the heavens.

I stare at her, knowing she's about to talk to one of the deads.

"Lenny, she needs him, and she doesn't know how much he needs her. I knew this would happen if she came home."

I'm not convinced he needs me. Maybe if I had come home sooner, but I didn't understand there were no rules to healing. I tried navigating my pain in any way I could, knowing I wanted to be healed fully before I came back to this town.

Year after year, I tried. And, now, I know. Healing is a funny word that means something different to everyone. To some, it means done and over, mission accomplished. To others, it means move around that mountain. To me? It means coming home and trying really hard to understand where I'll fit into the town I ran from all those years ago and the man I love.

Maybe I won't fit in at all.

And so begins the reunion of us. It has all the makings of a first-rate mystery. Blood, hatred, need, love, secrets, clues... Maybe even a solved murder or two.

Chapter 5

Hurricane

Rebel

Ruby Mae is home, and she's a hurricane. I need to love her. But first, I have to get over hating her.

"Don't wait for me. Don't follow me." She had the gall to say those words to me the day she left. But I knew she was lying. She always sucked at lying. Her tell was the same every time. She'd pull on her earlobe then twist it. And that's when I told her I'd be waiting. But the wait has been hell, and my anger is burning like a blowtorch on raw flesh.

Calm now. *Be calm.*

"I'm sorry I hurt you," I say after I've helped Ruby climb into my truck. I press my palms onto the cab's hot roof and watch her fumble with the seat belt, which she'll never figure out.

Along with her likely broken right wrist, she has two trigger fingers on her left hand that don't bend. Nerve damage from high school when she ran the jigsaw into her palm in shop class under my father's tutelage. I always liked that Ruby was the only girl in shop. She was tough and smart as a whip, unafraid of the all-guy electives and their tendencies to intimidate most girls. Even when the Kline twins tried to mess with her, she stood up to them. Ruby was a bomb of spice and confidence. Hell, not even my dad stood up to the twins, and they were his godsons.

"Sorry, my ass." Thankfully, she chuckles. "Just get in and drive."

"Let me," I say quietly. I step onto the running board and lean over her lap, my jean-clad thighs pressed to her slightly parted, bare legs. While working on the stubborn buckle, I glance down at the creamy skin between her legs, wanting her white jean shorts to be shorter. Or off.

Then my gaze drifts across her breasts, then to her throat—which might be bumping up and down as much as mine. Finally, I look into her eyes. Unyielding, though bursting with questions, they soften. I try to imitate that sentiment. But I fail.

She looks away; maybe I've scared her off. Inhaling to calm myself, I get a whiff of her. This isn't going to help the twitch in my cock. Or the ache in my heart. She smells like memories of us, and maybe after a hurdle or three, she'll smell like my next fifty years.

"You smell the same," I tell her. I need to press my lips to hers and steal the kisses I've missed. Years of kisses.

"Is that good?" She bites her lip, inhaling a shaky, long breath when she tugs at her top, maybe realizing how much gorgeous cleavage is on display.

"It's like yesterday's smell. Familiar and sweet."

She tries to hide her watery eyes. But I don't miss one sign they're sending. She's back for me. She can call it what she wants. I'm calling what I see. Calling how it feels. Kind of right with some wrong. Yeah, maybe we're going to figure this out, after all. Maybe.

I move strands of long blond hair from her eyes. Then I touch the tiny scar on her eyebrow that I gave her one day when we were roughhousing while fishing.

"You okay?" I ask, wrapping my hand around the back of her neck.

She huffs out a breath—something between a gasp and a sigh—a miniscule whimper of lust at its core.

My face is inches from hers, so close we could kiss with minimal effort. More striking than ever, Ruby is the kind of woman who makes a man feral. Makes him want to rip her shirt off with his teeth because his hands are busy elsewhere on her body. She makes my need turn inside out and boil to the surface. She's the kind of woman you would promise everything to even if it meant she'd tear your heart to shreds, leave you in the dust, and forget about you while she sought…what? Fame and fortune?

Was the grass that much greener on the other side? Did the sacrifices she made to leave me and this town amount to much in her heart? What else was she seeking? And what pushed her to seek it? You don't just up and leave like she did. There's always something else buried inside the truth.

"I'm fine. This is going to make the move a little complicated." She holds her arm up, shifting her gaze from her wrist to my eyes and then my lips.

I can't stop swallowing; my mouth waters like a leaky hose in her presence.

"I'll help. I'm the reason you broke this." I trace a line across her wrist. Her baby-soft skin snags my memory bank. "I didn't mean to scare you and make you fall. I…" *I'm just so madly in love with you. Still. I missed you. Needed you.*

"Everyone was looking." She sucks her bottom lip through her teeth as her eyes rummage around my face. "You never liked that kind of attention."

"I'm not like you, Ruby."

She edges her face away as I move in. "Not like me," she says softly. "Don't like me. Don't want to see me. What else *me*?"

Damn, she irks me. I thought we were going somewhere. "Nothing you." I slam the door, stomp around to the driver's side, and get in.

"You've made that clear," she says.

As we pull out of the lot, Ruby reaches for the radio and pokes at the buttons on my disc player.

The second the music begins, I grind my jaw. She chuckles and skips the first song. Then the next, which is followed by another laugh. And then the one after that. Of course, I have *her* mix in. I dug it out of an old box of crap when I heard she bought that lake house and knew she'd be coming home.

"You still have it?"

All I hear when I stare at her is, *You still want me?* I take a right turn, glancing at her from the corner of my eye. She strokes her throat then follows her collarbone with one finger. One of my favorite sexy habits of hers. One of many.

"Looks like you *something* me." She shoots me a smirk.

"It's not about you," I say.

She watches me for a few seconds. What does she see? A man she wants? Or a man she left forever?

"You're a lying sack of shit, Rebel Field."

"That makes two of us, Ruby Mae."

We laugh for the first time in years. I think the last laugh we shared was when we graduated and whipped our hats into the air post-ceremony. Those sharp, black angles cut the crisp blue sky like knives as they flew up then rained down on us. Fuck if it wasn't a sign of something to come.

It doesn't seem possible that we can hold so much love for someone we haven't laughed with for that many years. Perhaps love doesn't have a clock; maybe it can span time.

"I need a favor," Ruby says.

"Another?" I chuckle because that one word did come out dick-like. I'm wearing asshole like a second skin today.

"What did I do to make you so hard?" she asks.

Is she kidding? How does she have the balls to pose a question like that?

"You haven't made me hard in years. Moved on. Remember? You told me not to wait. Over you." Up goes my wall of lies. It's like I have no control over my defenses with her.

"I'm not sure I believe you." She glances at my key chain, the gold rock, scissors, and paper charms she gave me in high school still dangling there like a Welcome Home sign flashing bright in a dark night.

She touches the charms. When she grazes my knee while moving her hand back to her lap, I snag her wrist.

"I'm dead serious. Over you." *No, I'm not. I'm dead afraid you're going to leave again. A little dead inside. That you left in the first place. Dead serious? Okay, sure—that I've never wanted or needed you more. So this fight I'm putting up? Yeah, it's me working hard to break you down so you let out everything you should have told me forever ago.*

"Good for you." Hate coats her voice and seeps through my veins like acid.

"What was the favor?" I dial the air conditioning to high and adjust the vents.

"I need to stop at the drugstore before I ruin your shirt."

"Wouldn't be the first thing you've ruined." I smirk.

Her mouth drops open. "I'll be sure to buy you a new one if the blood stains. I know the last thing you want is anything from my pussy since you're so disgusted by my presence. I thought my period was over, so don't worry, it's unlikely I'll ruin your precious shirt."

"Keep the shirt. Don't want it back."

We pull into the drug store, my white-knuckle grip on the wheel working to calm me. "I'll run in," I tell her. "Tampons as I recall."

"Don't bother, I'll run in. I need to use the restroom anyway." Ruby pokes at her seat belt. She'd barely be able to get the buckle open if she had two good hands.

"Need help?" I inch my fingers toward her.

"I don't need anything from you."

"Okay. I'll meet you back here in five. I'm going to run across the street and grab a dog. Want one? Or d'you get your fill with the Italian and French?"

"You really hate me."

"Something fierce." I grin, and wink, but there's some truth in my words.

Yes, Ruby. I hate you for so many things. For leaving me when all I wanted was you. For giving yourself to other guys after I waited years for it while we dated. But, more than anything, I hate that I need you more than the next fragile beat of my broken-to-shit heart.

Chapter 6

Black Edge

Ruby

I really did a number on him, though he has no idea how hard it's been for me. Or why I scrambled out of town feeling like I was being chased by a mob of murderous clowns. He doesn't know what happened graduation night when I went for an early evening run on the stairs behind the football stadium with Opal before attending graduation parties. He doesn't know why I never showed at the Klines' party.

Every inch of sunshine bleeds a black edge. Rebel told me those exact words the last time we were together. It was the day I left town. The day I ran. He was right. It wasn't a random observation; I knew he meant me.

I was forever sunshine at my core. Pure and silly. An uninhibited, sassy cuss. He'd called me that on more than one occasion. And my brash self-assurance made certain individuals want to disgrace me. I didn't understand the hatred some people carried around for others. Didn't understand it until I lived in a world of hate.

Back then, though, not understanding it but feeling the shame of it were two different things. It began with the girls at my new high school who secretly hated me because I was pretty, naturally athletic, and—worst of all—tall and thin. I stood my ground and wore my sunshine like a protective sheath when they snickered at me under their breath over a sweater I'd bought from the Goodwill store then readapted to fit the current trends.

"Tacky," they said. "Who sews their own clothes from another person's throwaways?"

I smiled and marched past them.

I always played the nice card. It felt better inside. But they hated me even more because I was pleasant. It was easier to join the bitch-n-moan club. It was cooler to be dark and mean. Plus, the cloak they could hide behind was bear-fur thick. Happy people annoyed them.

The cheerleaders ruled that club in my high school. They bitched and moaned about everything. Mostly in the bathroom, where the boys wouldn't hear them. I could have hated them because they received pricey sports cars on their sixteenth birthdays or had credit cards with no limits to buy the perfect prom dress, which cost thousands, while I had to sew my own. I didn't criticize when they ate half a pizza then washed it down with Diet Coke and diet pills. But, when I walked down the hall with my textbooks and a *Vogue* magazine—which I had splurged on—tucked under one arm and a milkshake Rebel Field had bought me each day on lunch break to spoil me, they pitched hissy fits with tails on them.

Worse yet, they were even meaner to my little sister, Opal, who attended the annex school next door with her twin, Echo. Both of them were intellectually disabled, which is why Echo still lives with Mom. Opal was adorable. Short, curvy, and soft everywhere. She was perfect in every way, especially since she had no idea how beautiful she was—mirrors scared her. She was also physically the opposite of me, so you would think they'd be okay with her. Instead, her disfigured face and perfect doughy curves became their personal dartboard when she'd meet me behind the track to work out on the backside bleacher stairs every night.

Why did looks and status matter so much? Why couldn't we all be okay with being different in lots of ways?

But their immaturity knew no bounds. Opal and I would run the stairs, and the wicked peanut gallery would lob criticism and never-ending hate. There was no winning with them or their nastiness. Even the boys they dated joined in. They had their own club of affluence and antipathy. They could afford to hate the less-thans because they would always have more.

Money was power in our small town. And they had it by the bagload. The Kline boys were kings of that club. The Preston girls were the queens. Both sides had their minions.

Then there was me and Rebel. We danced across our sunshine, avoiding the black edges. But, on graduation night, the edges curled and closed in and everything changed.

Sweat buckets from my pores. Why the hell didn't I let him help me? Now, I'm stuck like a dog whose owner forgot about her in the car on a one-hundred-degree day. Frustration needles my nerves as neither my left nor right hand can jiggle the buckle open. I close my eyes and inhale Rebel's scent, which hangs in his truck like a provoking potion.

I wasn't prepared for his pure Rebel-ness. I was going to ease my way in. A phone call first. An easy hello. *Hey. I'm back. Miss me?* I planned on asking him if he wanted to go out for a beer or maybe dinner, though I kind of figured that might be pushing things.

A knock on the window startles me. Rebel's dad. But not in man form. Holy shit. Rocket really did go for it. Etta?

Her coifed curls soften the hard edges of her heavily made-up face. Shades of pinks and plums accent her cheekbones, her eyes, and her lips. Her fitted dress opens low at her abundant cleavage. My leer must be apparent on the Ds, because she places a hand there to shield them.

She gestures for me to roll the window down.

"I can't!" I yell and hold my right arm up. "Broke my wrist. Can you open the door?"

She nods. A heavy whiff of oriental perfume wafts up to my nose as she pulls the door open.

"Hey, Mr. Field."

"Etta." She smiles, leans in, and pecks me on the cheek.

"Mrs. Field," I say.

"Etta, sweetheart." She rubs the spot where she kissed me then stares at the bright stain of color on her thumb. "Mrs. Field is Posey. She doesn't like people calling me Mrs. Field." Her powdery, pastel skin squishes into perfect miniature accordion folds when she smiles. "I heard you were back. It's nice to see you," she says, looking me over.

I don't want to be obvious, but I love the sight of her too. She's so strangely beautiful. Even her voice has changed from all male to caramel-drizzled sweet and womanly.

"Your son isn't so pleased I'm back. He even shoved me off the roof of my car and I broke my wrist."

"He what?" She cringes then gasps. "Ruby, that's awful."

I tap my front tooth, alerting her to a smudge of lipstick on her teeth. She licks it off like a pro. How long has he…she…been a woman? And, for the love of God, how did Rebel Field, Mr. Rough-And-Tumble, deal with his dad becoming his…Etta?

"I'm kidding. I fell after making an ass of myself and embarrassing him. Don't tell him I said that. He wants nothing to do with me."

"Don't let him fool you." She pats my hand as I stare at her hairless arm.

"He's not fooling me. He's made it clear how much he hates me and how displeased he is that I'm in town. His town."

"It's your town too." She shakes her head then makes a squishy mama-loves-you face she must have worked really hard to perfect. It's not anything Rocket would have done.

"I'm proud of you, Mr.…." I clear my throat three times. Then add one. "Etta."

"Thank you. I needed to be honest with myself. I hid from the truth for too long." She pats droplets of sweat off her upper lip. "I was afraid of what others would think of me. What does it matter what others think?"

Hid from the truth, yes. It's like she's reading my mind.

I take a second longer than seems comfortable to gather my thoughts. I've wanted to tell someone about that night, anyone. But I couldn't. My parents' tiny home had been in foreclosure until Mr. Kline gave them a loan from his bank when my father approached him. He was your classic cock-sucker-banker type to everyone, but they had gone to high school together and used to be hunting buddies, so that helped. I wonder if Dick made him beg.

My family had more to lose than I did. No one could find out. I couldn't go up against the KIines. I thought karma would get them at some point. Though I didn't think it would be the week I left town. What happened that day in their basement? I wish I knew what words they spoke before they were shot and killed.

Funny thing is, apparently, there were few signs of a struggle. Just two dead boys along with their hunting rifles placed at their sides like it had been staged by God. It made no sense. But it was all printed in the paper. A nice tied-up story with no room for holes. And that was gospel in this town. It was murder-suicide per the sheriff. Two boys who had full-ride football scholarships to Northwestern University? Seemed crazy to me.

Etta taps me on the shoulder. "Did your brother tell you he's in the scrapbooking class I teach at the community center?"

"He didn't mention that. But Echo doesn't say much unless it's pulled out of him. Or unless he's talking with Mom. They babble at each other like two squirrels bickering over nuts. Now that they'll be living on the lake, he can't walk to town. I'll bring him by for the next class."

"He and I get along well."

"That's nice to hear. He needs stimulation outside of Mom."

"I made a housewarming gift for Monday. I'll have Rebel bring it to her."

"You should bring it over and see the house."

Etta's face brightens into a crimson blush. "I'm not sure that's a good idea. Your mother thinks I'm gay and doesn't seem keen on the gays. Isn't that what she calls them?"

"Yes." I nibble on my thumbnail, so many questions I want to ask. "But you're not gay."

"No," she says in a soft tone, a twinge of irritation lining it. "I'm all woman."

"I'll have a talk with her and explain."

"Keep it simple. People get very confused about the truth."

Boy, do they ever. "Of course."

"What really happened to your arm?"

"A little accident, I swear. I'm fine. Probably a break, but no biggie."

"Most people wouldn't say a break is no biggie. But you've been through more than—" She gasps.

I almost miss it. Then she smacks her mouth with the back of her hand, faces away from me, and utters something I can't hear.

"Etta?"

When she turns toward me, her face is wet with perspiration, her lips trembling. "I was just going to say how you've seen the world and… Oh, never mind me. I've got things to get to. Stop by the farm sometime. We're out at the old Finch place." She fidgets with her dainty, gold ladies' watch that seems oddly placed before her wrist bone.

"I don't think Rebel would appreciate that."

"I wasn't talking about Rebel. You and I can visit and catch up on your life."

"And yours! I'll do that, and thanks." Not a chance would he want me stepping foot on his farm.

The Finch place no less. How the hell did he score that hunk of land? Lottery win? They never had money like that; almost no one in town did. Only the Klines, the Prestons, and a few others.

"You've been missed, Ruby. Missed by many. Don't let what happened ruin anything."

Does she mean my leaving? Or Opal's death? Or what the hell? Why is she acting so weird? Must be a woman thing.

But I have to ask. "What do you mean?"

"The… Oh." Her face blushes crimson again. Maybe ten times redder than the last time. "Just this town. That's all."

So, why am I imagining it's not all? Maybe I do need to visit Rebel's farm. Even if it's only to talk more with Etta.

Chapter 7

Cherry Pie

Rebel

One of my favorite things about Ruby Mae was her silliness. She was the opposite of me, and I loved her for it. I was serious, gruff, and rough around the edges. I could have been a hardcore asshole, but she softened me. Made me a better person. She walked the line of playful-goofball-meets-goddess. And, while her beauty was the first thing that had caught my eye, her silly side and keen sense of self locked me in for life. Even as a teenager, she had depth. And it was the sexiest thing I'd ever seen in a girl. Her emerald eyes were as loud as her soul, both playing my insides like I was her personal instrument.

The year we began dating, Ruby had just turned sixteen. And, while everyone else was getting their driver's licenses and buying or being gifted cars, Ruby was saving her money for world travel or a black stallion. Always walking to her own tune, she made me laugh the way she joked that she'd someday join the circus if her scholarship to Northwestern didn't score her a job she loved. Then, for my sixteenth birthday, she gave me a honking clown nose. Something no one wants or needs a collection of. I loved the goofball she was.

It might have been frivolous, but it never stopped. Every year on my birthday, except this year, I'd receive a clown nose in a gold box with the same note.

Honky birthday, Wishbone.

But that's all I've received in all these years. That's the only communication we've had. I've followed her illustrious career as a model. And, crazy as it sounds, I've always had faith she'd come home to roost. From the time I met her, she'd had her heart set on a cherry farm on the outskirts of town. We'd ride our horses out there, pick cherries… Then she'd make me a pie. Ruby's cherry pie was heavenly. I'd give her all kinds of shit about her other "cherry pie" and how, one day, that too would be mine.

When I arrive back at my truck, Ruby's gone. Houdini? I ease onto the road that leads to the hospital, hopeful I'll find her somewhere along the road.

One mile in, I slow my truck, chuckling at the sight of her. My flannel shirt, flaps across her small ass as she jogs on the gravelly shoulder like a broken-winged duck.

I roll the window down. "You still hold the mile record at the high school."

She flips me the bird. Her version, which is pathetic considering her current hand predicament.

"After all that time traveling the world, I'd think your manners would be more sophisticated," I say.

"Are you planning to follow me all the way to the hospital?" She winces then presses her arm against her belly, which makes me cringe because I caused the pain.

"Yep. I told you I'd take responsibility since it was my fault you fell. See how that works?"

"Is this how we're going to be now?" She glances at me then focuses on the road. "You rubbing shit in my face every five seconds? Your inner asshole is a big cocky man these days."

"These days." I grunt out a laugh. "You know nothing about these days. Or any of my past days, either."

I ought to watch the road—and the filth coming out of my mouth as well. But I can't help myself. I could stare at her gazelle-like frame running all day. Her perfectly shaped tits bounce with each step. Her graceful neck elongates when she eases her shoulders back with every deep breath.

"After this, we won't be seeing each other," I tell her.

"Oh, really?" She glares at me and laughs. "Didn't you say something about helping me move Mom and Echo since this was your responsibility, Mr. Smart-Asshole?" She holds her arm up.

"I am going to move them. By myself." I smirk. I suppose this is us flirting our way back to each other. It's a little weird but maybe it'll get her to share the truth. "You won't need to be there. You'll get in the way."

"Pig!" she yells and picks up her pace, her long stride free and easy.

I press on the gas to stay next to her. "I'm no longer Wishbone? I'm a pig?"

"You were Wishbone for one reason." She's sweaty. Snarling. Sexy. And mine.

"You remember that, huh?" Fuck if talking about it doesn't make me hard.

She stops and bends. I bring the truck to a halt and wait. When she straightens, she leans into the window and drops her purse on the seat, an open box of tampons falling out.

"How could I forget the way you begged and wished you could put your cock inside me every time we lay naked? Wishbone." She skims the bead of sweat traveling down her neck with her fingers. Then she licks them. "You wanted nothing more. 'Please, Ruby Mae. Eight seconds is all I need. Please, baby. Let me put it in you.'"

"Enough." I slam my fist into the seat.

"You sure?" She glances at my crotch, the outline of my hard cock evident as a bulldozer at a baby shower.

Not that I had any idea how it would go the first time I saw her again...but this is not it. Us fighting an endless war. Me getting hard and wanting to toss her into the bed of my truck to make things right once and for all.

She turns away, breaking into a jog after a short stretch of walking. I watch for a bit, soothing myself. Damn. I creep the truck alongside her.

"Don't you have a hardware store to run or some other girl to wishbone with?" she asks.

"Ruby fucking Mae." I thrust my elbow against the back of the seat. "I swear to God."

She was always full of sass, but she wasn't quite as spiteful. Something besides world travel has made its way inside her heart. That slice of good girl I used to love and want seems stained. Time and age can do that. Perspective, as great as it is, can often hold its own net of debris collected over the years.

"What're you going to do, Rebel? Yank my shorts down so you can paddle my bare ass with your big callused man hands? You used to love getting me naked to do that. I'll bet you'd like to know if I still go commando, wouldn't you?" She grins, and my resolve vanishes further. "You think you're so tough, but inside, you're mush and boy and ache. I can see it in your eyes."

"What are you fucking talking about?" I'm hard again. I haven't been hard twice in five minutes since…when? What is she doing to me?

"Don't pretend you're ignorant of what I said. I know what I used to do to you. I know we have chemistry. I'll bet you're happy as shit I'm jogging instead of sitting in that cab where I could see you. I can tell by your face you're hard. Again."

"You are filling your big shorts damn well these days, woman. The hell you think I am? A puppet?"

"No!" She clears her throat three times. Then she growls and clears it one more time. "So I broke up with you and went to travel the world. Big deal. You went on and got married. Had a kid. I don't get what's got you so worked up."

"You!" I slam on the brakes, drop my head back, and shove my hands through my hair. "You do. Give me what I want. Let me know you have the ring and necklace. Tell me why you took them off in the first place and left. And tell me, why the fuck did you stay away so long?" My racing heart is about to suffocate me. Does she have any idea what being near her is doing to me? Killing me all over again.

When she left, I bottled my hate for her and drank it down like venom. But then I'd be at the grocery store checkout and there she was. Ruby Mae Rose on the cover of every fashion magazine. And, when I'd go home and pop a beer open, kick my feet up, and watch sports, there she was again, on every fourth commercial, riding in some sports car, kissing a guy, smiling and laughing. Living a beautiful life across the globe while I pined for her. Even when Paris died, the woman I needed most was Ruby.

I know what that makes me. But I can't help it. It's only ever been Ruby. Some men fall in love over and over with a string of women throughout their lives. Not me. I fell once, for one girl. It was a deep forever kind of fall, one I'm still tumbling into, one that'll never stop. There's no bottom to this descent. No end. And that'll make me either the luckiest man on Earth at some point or one sorry sucker hoping something can break my fall before my heart breaks all over again.

"Get in the fucking truck already," I tell her. "Shouldn't be jogging with that arm the way it is. Knock this shit off and do as I say for once in your life!"

I open her door, move her purse, then take hold of her upper arm to help her in. Then I fasten her seat belt, but not without grazing her upper thigh with the back of my hand. My mouth waters.

"Okay, Wishbone. Don't worry. I'll stay on my side."

I can't stop myself when I slide my hand between her legs, onto inner thigh, and grip it hard. Then I feather that spot in a tender, shared moment as she inches toward me. Onto my side.

Chapter 8

Murder

Ruby

I could swear he was going to kiss me. I believed it. And, Jesus, I'm not sure what I would have done. Would I have let him? His massive hand on my inner thigh, his mouth so close that I could feel his breath on my lips. But his eyes said something else. A story of hurt and pain. And I wrote that story he's wearing—every word. He may never forget or forgive me for the day I left, and he'll never know what happened to me because it'll hurt him more than anyone.

Finally, in the hospital parking lot, we walk side by side toward the ER doors that open as we near. I glance at Rebel upon entering, and chuckle at the way he's carrying my purse in ownership.

"Hazel?" I yell, striding toward the desk in the emergency room, where one of my best friends from high school is wearing a white coat and a stethoscope around her neck.

"Oh my God! I heard you were home!" she says as she scoots past the receptionist and scurries out the door. Her arms surround me in a hug seconds later.

"You live here?" I ask.

"Moved back a month ago."

I finger her stethoscope and smile. "My girl is a doc?"

"Proctologist." She glances at Rebel, who has a grin that takes me back to high school on his face.

"A butt doctor?" I ask.

"You won't be seeing me." Rebel chuckles and shakes his head. "Ever."

"You never know, Rebel. I'm the only ass doc in town." She wiggles her fingers and laughs.

"Wow. Must be weird since you grew up here," I say.

"It's no biggie. So I see a lot of ass."

"Drinks soon?" I ask Hazel.

"Yeah. We have years to catch up on. You fell off the face of the earth then landed on every cover of every magazine I subscribe to!"

"Hey, Wishbone. I need my purse." I shoot Rebel a big grin and hold my hand out.

"Your legs broken too?" he asks.

"Hang on, Hazel." I march to him and snatch my purse from his side. "No, Prince Charming. I just figured, since you're… Never mind!"

"Nice to see you guys together again." Hazel waggles her brow while I fish my phone from my bag.

"We're not together, plug your number in, babe." I hand Hazel my phone.

"We're not anything," Rebel confirms, sounding annoyed. He muddles through a pile of magazines on a coffee table.

Okay, then. We're back to this.

Hazel cringes. "That would be me removing my foot from my mouth."

"We'll talk over drinks." I lower my voice. "He drove me here because he broke my wrist."

"I didn't break your fucking wrist!" Rebel shouts from across the room. "Jesus, Ruby."

"I mean, shoved me off the roof of the Jeep." I twist and eye him up while smiling like a goof.

"Ruby!" He exhales a long sigh. "It was an accident. I would never hurt you."

"Oh, relax," I tell him. "I'm just messing with you. You look like I accused you of murder."

"Get over here." His voice drops low. Angry low.

I feel like a dog who shit in his kitchen.

"I'll call." I wink at Hazel, a nervous twist in my gut. Then I make my way to Rebel.

I stop a few feet from him, his steely eyes holding a mix of annoyance and hunger. It's a force field I'm not entering. But, then again, I could be wrong, because I swear it's starvation I see beneath the surface.

He crooks a finger at me. I take a small step. Being close to him is almost too much for me. He's a magnet. Then he proves it when he hooks his hand behind my neck and presses me to come closer and we bump chests. What now? His Adam's apple juts up and down, my breath faltering when he leans to my ear.

"Don't ever say something like that to me again."

Our stare is intense. A buildup of things gone by.

"That I accused you of murder?"

He nods, inhaling a deep, slow breath. Sweat beads on his brow, and his eyes narrow into irritated slits. Something about it makes him even sexier. Like he's about to devour me.

Yes, please.

"I was questioned after you left town," he says. "Bet you never heard that, did you?"

My heart stops for a beat, a jolt of pain shooting through my belly. "For the Kline boys?" My voice falters.

"Yes. What the hell else would I have been questioned for? Surely not your disappearing act," he says, then hisses as his upper lip rises and shakes.

His hand remains behind my neck, his thumb stroking up and down, making my knees weak, which is crazy considering the topic we're discussing.

"Why?" I ask.

One eyebrow lifts, his head tilting, his gaze wandering over my face. It feels like an accusation and an answer rolled into one.

"Because one of my baseballs was found in their basement." He licks his lips while staring at mine.

My heart pounds in wild accord to his answer and his nearness. And that tongue... The way he's rimming his lips. God help me. I look away.

He cups my cheek, steering me back to him. "And everyone knew that me and the Kline boys didn't exactly get along."

I know the answer, but I ask anyway. "The ball I gave you for your seventeenth?"

"Yes. The one with my initials."

"Right…so, do you want to talk about it?" I don't know what else to ask. Mostly because my mind is racing as fast as my heart.

Is there a chance he might have been involved in their deaths? God, no. Not Rebel.

"Nothing to talk about. Go check in now." He grips my shoulders then gently twists my body toward the receptionist desk.

Well, that was awkward. And what the hell? I had two of those baseballs made, and I gave one to Opal. She loved Rebel so much and playing ball with him was her favorite thing. Where is her ball now? And why was his ball in the Klines' basement?

Nothing to talk about? Does he know something about me and the Kline boys? Is that why he's so angry with me? But, if he knew, he wouldn't be mad. Unless he blamed me. Blamed me and thought I brought that hell on myself? Jesus.

The receptionist helps me fill out the needed forms. Upon my return, Rebel is sitting in the only single chair in the room. Sort of a You're-Not-Welcome-Here sign. I sit on one of two couches, as far away from him as possible. It seems, based on the spot he's chosen, he's looking for some distance from me.

But then he stares at me for a minute while I push my cuticles down. And he's still staring when I'm finished, so I move to the couch closest to him.

There's a weirdness between us. Of course there is. You can't go away for years on end and think there wouldn't be. I want normal back. Greedy? Yes. Normal might be as far away as China. Still, I'm pushing for it.

"I saw your dad, I mean…Etta. He looks—shit. *She* looks good. Happy." Well, that was smooth. I roll my eyes, dropping my chin to my chest as my face heats.

Rebel nudges me with his elbow. A sign of hope? I rotate to face him. Calm eyes and small crinkles at the edges somehow offer an invitation to linger in his gaze.

"She is happy." He crosses his arms over his chest, his muscles bulging like he and his sexiness have a pact to fuck with me at every turn.

"And sorry for my stupid question, but is she—"

"A she? The whole operation and all that?" He grins a proud look of approval. "Yes. All the way through. She's all woman."

"You're a good son, Rebel." I trace my finger along the seam of his jeans until I realize I might be making myself more at home with him than he's ready for. "You're a good man."

Jesus, he has been through some shit. We both have.

"Thanks." He grins this adorable Rebel-from-high-school smirk that makes my insides knot. "Etta's great. Never been happier." He smooths his hand over the section of his jeans where my finger was tracing seconds ago.

"That's nice to hear. I'll bet you played a big role in all of it, supporting him with his choice. Couldn't have been easy." I shake my head. "That's a big change."

He doesn't respond. Maybe I crossed a line, said too much. I tap my fingers on my kneecaps, willing him to keep the conversation going.

"He almost took his life before he came out as her and decided to live his truth," he says just above a gruff whisper, his voice cracking at the end.

My heart breaks for Rebel and Etta.

Our gazes meet, an understanding in them. A hint of history meeting thoughtful newness.

"Shit, that's intense." I touch his knee then quickly pull away when he drops his gaze to my hand.

He looks back to my eyes as if I'm toying with him.

My face heats when I remove my hand. "What stopped him?"

"Dunno," he answers.

"So, out of nowhere, he gets a sex change?"

"Wasn't that simple. Not even close." He scratches his jaw then grips the back of his neck. "It's not like he had money lying around with that crap teacher salary he was making. It was that weird June you left, when all that shit went down."

I work to avoid his gaze, focusing instead on his hair-dusted knuckles. He pauses for long seconds as I study him. And, when he clears his throat, I catch him smiling the tiniest bit. Maybe I was a little obvious when I was checking him out.

"After Kent and Kyle died, Mr. Kline invited me and Etta to the bank for a meeting. Since I'm Mr. K.'s godson and the twins were my dad's godsons, Mr. K. assigned their trusts to me. It was a lot of dough. Enough for me to buy the hardware store and the farm and pay for Dad to have his operation."

And reason number what-ever-the-fuck that I can never tell him what they did to me. My heart skips five beats then races. Thankfully, a nurse calls out my name so I don't have to address my sudden state of freak-out. I can never ever tell him one stitch. It would ruin him and his family. Perpetual guilt. Yeah, I know what that's like.

Why would Mr. Kline give Rebel so much cash? Why not keep it? Something about this whole mystery just got a little crazier.

As I rise, Rebel taps my arm. "You want company?"

"Look at you getting all warm and fuzzy. You want to hold my hand while they fix my broken parts?" I chuckle. Though I'm blown away that he offered.

"Just trying to be civil. You want me back there for distraction in case it hurts when they set it?" Our eyes meet and we both smile. It's kind of sweet and a little old-fashioned too. Maybe we're not as disconnected as I thought. Maybe the wall he keeps putting up is a temporary façade. Protection. Sort of like modeling was for me. Like staying away was for me.

"I'm good," I tell him. "Go back to work. They need you more than I do."

Rebel stands, making a lazy line down my cheek with one finger. Simple. Endearing. "Liar." His honeyed voice and his wink catch me off guard. "I'll be right here, sassy thing. I'll be waiting for you."

Oh, the feels when his eyebrows dip as if he's worried about me going back there for this silly broken arm. What would he do if he knew what I went through?

An hour later, with my broken wrist in a short cast that allows my fingers total freedom, I stroll out to the waiting room and find Rebel asleep in his chair. After ogling him for an obscene length of time, I lean in toward his ear.

"Hey, Wishbone."

He mumbles something filthy about wanting his mouth between my legs. Waking him suddenly seems foolish.

"Come on my face, baby," he says.

I glance around the waiting room, pleased to see no one else is enjoying the view and the one-way conversation.

"Ruby…I need you."

I giggle, taking immense pleasure in his arousal as the outline of his cock comes to life in his jeans. I want to stroke it. Dare I touch him? I take another gander around the room. Empty. Gotta love small-town hospitals. Why not cop a harmless feel?

I kneel between his spread legs and place my hand without the cast on him. Maybe there is a God? I am touching Rebel Field's hard-on. I press down then stroke his length, my hand finding its way by rote as butterflies flit through my insides.

"Fuck, Ruby. Put me in your mouth... Do it for me." His hands land on mine and his hips tilt as he presses himself to me.

I bite back a laugh, my pulse skyrocketing, my desire ratcheting up. Rebel slides a hand in his pants and starts stroking. And, now, I believe in Santa Claus. Santa and God are in cahoots. It's about time. Rebel would be horrified if one of his customers walked in or Hazel saw us. Hell, he'd probably kill me if he knew I was enjoying the show as much as I am.

"Wishbone, hey." I tickle his neck. "Wake up, naughty boy."

He opens his eyes. "Why are you kneeling between my legs?"

"I was watching… That's all." My sneer breaks into a grin when he realizes he has a hand down his pants. "I was listening too." I waggle my eyebrows.

He shakes his head, yanks his hand from his jeans, and runs it through his messy hair. Sleepy, sexy Rebel. "What'd I say?"

"Plenty."

He scoots back in his chair, that wall coming between us again. "Don't believe any of it."

"Not even that part where you said you hated me so much you wished I'd never come home?" I bite back a smile.

"Believe that." He glances around the room then pins his gaze on me.

"What about when you said you'd never ask me out on a date?"

"Believe that too."

Liar. Your sparkling, smiling eyes are giving me a whole other story, tough man.

"Okay." I giggle. "Should I keep going?"

"No. Believe everything I said. It was all true."

"Good to know you want me to suck you off and come on your face."

"Liar."

I fish my phone out of my bag. "I recorded it. You want to see?" I work hard not to laugh at my lie.

"You shittin' me?" He swipes at my hand as I wave my phone around, teasing him.

"Nope."

Rebel slides one hand behind my neck, grips my hair, and pulls me forward. "Give me your phone. Right fuckin' now, Ruby."

"Not a chance." I scoot backward. "I'm using this."

"Using? What are you planning on doing with that?"

"Bribing you." I snicker and squirm around. *Oh, Rebel, you are so adorable when you get pissed.*

"What do you want?" he asks.

I stall for a few seconds while making a mental wish list. What do I want? Oh hell, there is so much.

"Take me out on a date and I'll delete it. Just a friend date. Nothing more. I need to know we can at least be friends," I say. "Don't and it'll be on my Facebook page this week."

How can he think I'm telling the truth?

"Bitch." He laughs. "You little fucking bitch, Ruby Mae."

Oh, how that makes me smile. "Per your sleep-talking, you wish I could be your bitch and then some."

One side of his mouth slides into a smile. "Fine. One date. A friend date. My choice of place and time."

"Deal." Now, this is progress.

So maybe it was coercion, but still. A date's a date. We should at least be friends. But could we be more? How would that ever work with my crazy life? And what if we became us again? Worse yet, what if nothing happens between us on this date? No friendship, no anything.

Rebel rubs his chin, shaking his head as he grumbles under his breath. Standing, we bash chests, and a box falls out of a paper bag he's holding. We reach for it at the same time, but I beat him to it.

Once I've flipped the box over, I laugh. "Edible candy underwear?"

He snatches the box out of my hand. There isn't one ounce of embarrassment on him. Just an all-out ballsy look that says he has something I don't.

"For my girlfriend," he says.

Chapter 9

Sassy Little Cuss

Rebel

Did I really say that shit in my sleep? That sassy little cuss. Apparently so, and there's proof on her phone? Blackmail. God, I love her. Nice play, Ruby Mae. And the candy underwear I bought for her. Shit! How the hell am I going to take her out to dinner as friends and not kiss her? Touch her? I can barely keep my hands off her now. This whole hate thing is a tough one for me now that she's home. She is not making this easy.

Ruby's hair whips around her face as she stares out the truck window. We're halfway to her mom's house when she says, "What's your girlfriend's name?" She doesn't look at me, though her voice holds a certain heaviness when she speaks.

"You don't know her."

"Did she grow up here?" she asks.

I glance at her thumbnail, which is making deep tracks down the skin on her thigh. "No."

"Do you love her?"

I wish she'd look at me. "Like crazy."

My answer is for her; doesn't she know this? Even though we're both messing around in this getting-to-know-you-again game, doesn't she know she's it for me? Only my perfect Ruby.

But you took everything when you left. My heart, my dreams, my favorite person in the world. Are you here with all those things? Did you bring her back for me?

"She's the one, huh?" Her voice drops deeper, and it's wrapped in the saddest tone.

"Yup." *You are the one.*

"You think she'll be jealous? If we go on a date? Even as friends?"

"Definitely. It's going to take some explaining." I nod and wait for her to call me out on it. Wait for her to crack some joke. Some silly Ruby goofball thing that breaks through all the seriousness. Or punch me in the arm.

Nothing comes but awkward silence. And, just as I'm about to out myself that I have no girlfriend, she clears her throat.

"I don't want to ruin anything for you." She digs in her purse, messes with her phone for a few seconds, and then dumps it in her bag. "Sounds like you found the one. You're lucky. Most people never do."

It makes my heart ache that I might have said something to hurt her. Christ, I'm all over the place with my thoughts. Now, I'm worried I messed up. I'm never going to be able to do this fighting thing.

I turn the air on high. But there isn't enough air in the whole world right now. I draw in a long, reassuring breath. Then I remind myself I have a duty. Get her to tell me the truth. Even if it hurts.

And she has a duty too. To give it. *Come clean, Ruby Mae, tell me what happened.*

She clears her throat. Then, through a cracked voice, she says, "Hey, Rebel?"

Her hand lands on the seat, half an inch from mine. I shift my fingers a bit, until our pinkies touch. It's simple. Sexy. And so tempting to pull my truck over and get down and dirty about everything. Every last thing. How did I not know she'd have a stronger effect on me now?

"Mmmm-hmm."

"There was no video, I was just messing with you." She slides her hand under her thigh, and it crushes me. "Don't worry about the friend date. I don't want to ruin a good thing between you and your girl."

I chuckle, but it's caustic. "Not this time, huh?"

Chapter 10

Miles And Miles

Ruby

Maybe I waited *too* long to come back. Running away made the most sense. Far away. So far that I wouldn't have a chance to bump into anyone I knew. Sometimes there's safety and the opportunity to evolve more freely in anonymity. I thought, if I escaped this town, I'd escape the pain.

It partly worked, though I had no idea pain could travel miles and years. I didn't know pain could embed itself in your bones. God, I was naïve. But dealing with pain and healing isn't something you learn about until it springs its ugly self on you then lives inside you. It's a one-on-one thing when you're living with it. Especially when sharing what you went through would hurt your family and your true love and cause them more angst than they were already dealing with.

In my heart, I hoped I'd heal and come home to find Rebel waiting for me like he'd said he would. Such a selfish thought. *Don't wait for me.* But, in my silly head, all I wanted was for him to wait for me.

Sort of like when Rebel and I would have a fight and I'd tell him that I didn't want to talk about it. Well, of course I wanted to talk about it. I just wanted to be handled with kid gloves and make him do all the work. I was too immature to understand that relationships take more than that. I was such a confused girl. My insides were a mess. My guilt nearly suffocated me. And everything became my fault.

When someone violates you on that level—taking things that aren't theirs—life turns into something else. Something you never imagined. It takes years and years of coaxing your mind to open and let someone touch you. Then those touches flip-flop and collide in a mix of emotions that chase each other. Then they evolve into something you climb to help you heal.

Or so you think. I guess it's different for everyone.

I was dealing with that hell and missing Rebel. My saving grace was my career. If I hadn't become an overnight success, I might have wallowed so deep in my cement-shoe sorrow that a stick of dynamite wouldn't have set me free. Then, a year ago, I popped my head up and realized my friends were getting married and having kids. They'd fallen in love and formed unions while I had my blinders on, keeping the pain of what I had gone through—the nightmare—so far out of my peripheral vision I might not have noticed that the rest of the world kept moving along.

Then there was Teddy. I waffled so much about his marriage proposals. But why? Why didn't I marry him if I really did like the idea of settling down? It would be so much easier since he lives in Paris where my life is for the most part. But I don't want him. Then that box from an anonymous person arrived and blew my mind. In it were the promise ring from Rebel along with the broken necklace and the crosses the Kline boys made me wear the night they raped me. Their crosses on my heart had clinked against my ring while they did what they did to me.

Rebel can never know that that's why I can't wear the ring. Those boys are dead, but that Pandora's Box that came in the mail created a new mystery. Someone knows something, because someone sent me a message I need to decode.

"Thanks for the ride." I offer a smile to Rebel as we arrive at Mom's house. "Sorry if I ruined your day." I linger for a second, insecure and a little hopeful that Rebel might fess up about the girlfriend bullshit and ask me out. He can't think I believe that crap, can he? My mom would have known if he had a girlfriend. She would have said something. You can't hide a needle in this town.

"Sorry 'bout your wrist." He looks genuinely regretful.

So, I dip my toe in a little deeper. "I'll be fine. Bones can heal faster than—"

"Goodnight, Ruby." He unfastens my seat belt then hops out of the truck. When he opens the door, and helps me down, there's no warmth radiating from him, only a niggling, nasty feeling in my belly.

Hearts… I meant both of ours.

A bolt of electricity shoots up my throat when he leaves me standing on the sidewalk. Alone. No hug. No walk to the front door. Ouch. That hurt more than the broken wrist.

"G'night, Rebel."

Okay, then. That would be the steel toe of his boot kicking me. He hasn't hardened; he's become tamperproof. And that's my doing.

After dropping my stuff in the kitchen, I grab a beer from the fridge then hunt for Mom and Echo. The house is mostly packed up.

Thank God, considering my wrist. It'll be nice for the two of them to get out of this dilapidated hellhole.

For years, I offered to buy Mom a house after Dad passed away from a heart attack just a week after I'd left town. I had a realtor dragging her, Echo, and Lake around to see everything for sale. Nothing. Not one beautiful home piqued her interest. She liked living on her one acre on the river, where she and Echo could float around on rafts while Lake swam nearby.

Then a small ranch on the lake, with an orchard in the backyard and rose gardens bordering a picket fence, came on the market. I bought it after Mom had agreed that it was time. Who knows why it suddenly made sense. But I jumped at the opportunity. I'll admit, it gave me the perfect excuse to come to my senses and return home for the first time since I'd left. Not to mention the nudge from box.

I slump onto the couch then guzzle half of my beer, seeking a small buzz to lighten my mental load.

"I made tapioca," Mom says. She shuffles through the room, sets a tray with multiple bowls on it on a box, and edges it toward me while examining my arm.

I place my beer on the tray and stare at Mom's wig, trying to decide if she knows there's a necklace of Barbie shoes—surely of Echo's doing—wound around her black Amy Winehouse-esque bouffant. "Thanks, Ma."

"You're welcome. Made some for Opal too." She raises a bowl and smiles at the ceiling. "Nice that you girls can share dessert together again."

It shouldn't feel normal that Mom talks to the deads, but it's beginning to. So normal that I scooch over a little, making room for Opal, when Mom gestures.

"What about Dad?" I ask.

Mom clucks her tongue. "If you recall, he was repulsed by tapioca."

"I don't remember that." I pat a spot on the couch for Mom to sit.

She slides her bunny slippers off and nestles next to me, quickly hiding the hole in her panty hose under a pillow. "Called it 'pearl necklace in a bowl.' Said it belonged on a woman's chest." She fingers the fat strand of pearls dangling around her neck.

I cough a laugh out. "That's a riot. Thank God one of you had their mind in the gutter."

Mom lifts Opal's spoon then dips it into her tapioca. "I'm not following." She scrunches her nose.

"Do you know what a pearl necklace is?"

"Ought to. I have three in my jewelry box besides this one." After sliding a spoonful of tapioca into her mouth, she taps her pearls with her index finger. "You don't mind sharing, do you, Opal?"

"Ma, he meant when a guy blows his wad all over your tits. That's a pearl necklace."

"You're disgusting, Lenny." She frowns and tilts her head toward the ceiling. "Fine. I'll tell her you said that."

"What?" I take a swig of beer, eager to hear what Dad told her. Jesus, I'm losing it right along with her.

"Can't repeat it." She purses her lips and shakes a finger.

"You told him you'd tell me. Come on. Spill it!" I lightly elbow her in the side.

She laughs, licks her spoon, then hangs it on the end of her nose. I breathe on my spoon then do the same. Some things never change with family no matter how much time has passed or how weird people become.

"The deads don't care about lies," she says.

The thing about Mom is that she says this stuff like it's the gospel truth. I'm starting to believe that her conversations with Dad and Opal are the real deal.

My spoon falls onto my lap.

She cheers. "I won!"

I shrug and continue eating my tapioca. Mom loves winning. Everything is some form of competition, and she likes keeping score if she's the one winning.

She nods at my wrist, a quirky smile forming on her mouth. "How's your wrist?"

"It's not my wrist that hurts." And that's the truth.

I want to say those words to Rebel, but he'll come out with something nasty and his big wall will close me out again. Hate is such an ugly thing. I know because I hated the Kline boys for ruining my life. Then I realized I wasn't going to give those fucks power over my emotions. I needed every ounce of power to put myself together again. And, piece by piece, it's happening.

I may never be done building myself up, but I sure as shit won't let what someone else did break me. What a great life lesson pain and healing provide. You sure do learn what you're made of when the shit stick is shaken on you.

"He's got every right to be angry," Mom says. "It might take him some time to invite you back into his heart. He loved you. Needed you." She stares into my eyes with the most intense vibe. It's part motherly, like she really feels for us as we figure this thing out.

But her stare is also somewhat disapproving. What began as warm-fuzzies quickly nosedives into Mom's arctic dip. And I know what's coming next. The sock in the gut, her one hit.

"I didn't miss you. That's what happens when you leave. Some people forget about you."

"Thanks, Mom," I say. "That's a feel-good thing to hear."

Crazy as it sounds, I know there's truth in what she's said. *"Some people forget about you."* Yeah, I've tried that. It's a way to deal with who you really miss. You tell yourself to forget about them, you don't need them. I'll protect what matters most: my heart.

Mom fidgets with her necklace, twisting it around on her fingers the way she does with her rosary. "You needed to leave."

Maybe I'm reading into things. Or maybe she's hiding something. If only I could get all the pieces onto the table at once and see how they fit together.

"And why's that?" I ask.

"Things."

I dip my spoon into my bowl, scoop another bite up, and ponder what "things" means as sweet tapioca pearls roll across my tongue. "Are you going to elaborate?"

Mom saunters to a lone dust-covered photo of our family. It's been hanging on the wall in the same spot since I was a kid. And, with her pinkie finger, she dusts Opal's face off.

"Ask me a stupid question." She takes the photo off the wall, a bright patch of sky-blue paint left behind in a perfect rectangle.

"Why did I leave, Mom?"

"That was a stupid question." She sits next to me and hugs the photo like it's all that matters in the world. And, to her, the memories from that photo might hold more than I know.

"Everything isn't about you." There she is again. Mom could clear a forest with her tongue.

I wish she could distinguish between a pleasant mother-daughter exchange and judgment. I know there's a tender part of her buried deep inside. But I haven't had the honor of seeing it all that often.

I thought age might soften her. But, in truth, at sixty-five, she's more of who she was. Bitter with a side of snob-caked insecurity. But she's my mom and I love her. I've just always wanted something deeper that I'll never get from her. She's always wanted more too. Of other things. Namely, stuff. She was always a have-not who wanted more and wanted to be more.

Mom presses a finger to my lips. "Echo takes a scrapbooking class at the center. Rocket's his teacher. The gays are very crafty." She waggles her eyebrows.

"Etta, and she's not gay, Ma. She's as much a woman as you are."

"No." She clears her throat three times and dusts off all the faces on the photo except mine. "No…he's not."

We glare at each other for a few seconds. I want to push harder on this, but I can't change her. Can't make her softer or more understanding. Some people are stuck in one gear all their lives. They will never see the other side, and they will war with you to convince you *they* are right. All I can do is learn from her and hope I don't become who she is. At least not the parts I find offensive.

"He's not a woman, and just because you think you're something special—" She pauses, putting a hand to her ear. "Lenny doesn't want to talk about it, either. Says it's time for *Jeopardy* and his beer. It's after six ya know."

"Mom, listen."

Her lips form a thin line, her eyes filling. I have no idea what set her off. But the last thing I want is to be a reason for tears.

"Don't call her gay, okay?" I twist my body to face Mom, crossing my legs in my lap. "She's a nice person and Rebel cares very much about her. Maybe try to appreciate your differences."

"I don't mind different. But it's a very unusual situation to understand."

"I know. Put yourself in her shoes."

Mom licks one finger and drags it under my eye then examines the black smudge on her fingertip. "I do put myself in his shoes, and I put him in my dresses. At least he looks proper once in a while. Most gays tend to have nicer taste. He's an off one."

"She's not off. She's cool as fuck."

"That sounds violent. Most gays aren't violent from what I've read. Do you think he's safe around Echo?"

I twist a loose thread dangling from my shorts around my finger. How do I tell her she's horribly offensive without losing our relationship? I don't think she understands that there are always two sides; that everyone has a story that matters. How do I tell her about the pain Etta went through to get where she is? Maybe she and Etta are more similar than not?

It's as if her insecurities blind her. Maybe something happened to her along the way. Something she's never shared with anyone. Is her wall covering her pain too?

"Ma, listen to me. I know you have a good heart, and you mean well. But please… Just…um, think before you judge her and let things fall out of your mouth. Imagine what she went through all those years living as a man when all she wanted was to feel like her true self."

"Fall out of my mouth? Hardly. God's voice comes through me."

"What the hell does that mean?" I cover my face with one of the flimsy pillows separating us and release a silent scream. "You can't take responsibility for what you say? That's crap."

"Ruby. Let's not get physical."

"What?"

"You know… Apademics."

"You mean academics?"

"As in philosophical?"

God help me. No, better yet…God help her. *Now, please.*

Mom stands, her hands perched on her hips, the scowl on her face about to rain acid on me. "Traveling around the world did not make you better than us. I haven't lived a fancy life like you. But I know enough. Philosophical, yes. That's what I meant."

I nod and smile as she rubs her temples.

She yanks a rosary out of her apron pocket and works the beads like she's polishing silver. "I know plenty about philosophers. I took a class on them in college. Picasso and that other one with the sunflowers."

"Those are artists, Mom. Not philosophers."

Mom scowls. Then she yanks her wig off, tosses it on the couch, and scratches her head like it's infected with lice. "Stop trying to confuse me. At least I have a college degree."

She's derailing when she goes down the path of her *special* armor. The college degree. The last bastion of true intelligence, and her big one-up on me. She claims she hates that I ditched my full ride to Northwestern for world travel and a brainless career. Zero fucks right here.

"I wasn't trying to confuse you," I tell her.

"Don't worry, Ruby. You don't matter so much that something you say could hurt me."

Mom storms out of the room after saying goodnight to the deads. But not to me.

I kick my shoes off and finish my beer and the rest of the tapioca—lovely combo that it is. Then I bury my head in a pillow. Maybe I should have told her I understand, but really…I don't. I don't understand so much about so many things. Maybe I ought to ask some stupid questions of my own.

Chapter 11

Smoke Into Fire

Rebel

She's tough as nails, but that crack of hers is getting wider. She needs to fess up and clue me in on a whole shit-ton of things. The ring, the crosses… Hell, even the baseball I was questioned about. Especially considering I still have mine. Did she do it? Could my girl be a killer?

After grabbing the mail, I drive up to the house, eager to check on Gilbert, my about-to-give-birth mutt I had fixed six years ago. The vet couldn't explain it when he told me that she wasn't overweight but rather pregnant.

A whinny comes from the barn. I assume the pony that belongs to Bubble Valentine, Rifle's girlfriend and the daughter of my friends Tully and Wolfgang.

Etta strolls out the screen door as I head up the porch steps. A long, colorful tail of something she's crocheting hangs down from her hands as she arrives at my side. "Kids are in the barn." She gestures to her left. "Been out there a while."

"I heard the pony," I say, kneeling to scratch Gilbert's belly, marveling at its fullness.

"That Bubble sure is a pretty girl. Looks a little like Ruby did in high school."

"She is pretty. And sweet. Rifle might be in deep with that girl."

"Balls-deep," Etta says. We chuckle as she continues to crochet.

"She does kind of have that special flair about her like Ruby."

My Ruby was something else in high school. She's even more now. How long will I be able to wait before I tell her that my hands want to hold her. That my lips want to kiss, devour, and drown in her taste. I want to shine light on her darkness. I want her back. Free and whole the way she was before she left. She told me not to follow. Told me not to wait. But she sent me vibes I couldn't sidestep. That's what united souls do. And every last one of them is locked inside me. That smoke turned into fire, and it's been burning all these years. For Ruby—only for her.

"Saw Ruby at the five-n-dime." Etta sits on the top step, removes her heels, then rubs her bright-red-painted toes. "Nice work on the welcome home, slugger."

A stab of regret swims in my stomach. "It was an accident; a small break is all."

"Didn't mean her wrist." She looks up from her crocheting and smirks.

I stand and flip through mail. "You going to give me relationship advice?"

Etta grabs my wrist and pulls herself up. "Somebody needs to jump-start you."

I sling an arm over her shoulder and chuckle. "Sounds serious. Let me get a beer first. You want a sherry?"

"Yes! We should celebrate your girl coming home. I always liked Ruby. Never seemed to mind what others thought of her." She elbows me in the ribs then kisses my cheek. "My kind of woman!"

"You and Ruby marching to your own bands."

People can judge Etta all they want. But, inside, they probably know she did what she had to do. There was no choice in her heart. Most people don't have those kinds of guts. The average person cares too much what others think and makes their life choices around it. Living in safe bubbles where nothing changes. Making choices that don't let them stand out.

Being yourself is too much for most. Too much probable judgment. And, though Etta went for it and is living her truth, even she sometimes struggles with the snickers and the judgers.

After I pop a beer open and pour Etta a sherry, we head to the porch and park ourselves in the old wicker rockers like we do most nights. Etta adjusts the collar on her top.

"I haven't seen you wear that before," I say. "Did Mrs. Rose give it to you?"

"Yes. It's from France. Must be something Ruby bought for her. Nice that we wear almost the same size." She grins. "Echo brought it today. You know Monday still calls me Rocket."

I place my hand on hers. "Does it bother you?"

Etta shrugs then takes a slow sip of sherry. "I look the other way. Sometimes you should. Forgiveness is good for the heart."

"That sounds like it's punching more meaning than surface talk."

"You could forgive her for leaving," she says after a quiet minute.

She's right. I could drop everything and forgive Ruby, but the fire in my belly tells me I need answers first. But I also need to be cautious not to push so hard that she runs. "She has something to fess up to."

"Everything's not black and white," Etta says.

"You got something more to say? Spit it out." I tip my beer back for a long pull.

"I think you're punishing a woman who loves you. A woman you've missed. You deep down love her. Let it go, Rebel. Let her in."

I stand and stretch. Then I lean on the porch rail. "It's not that simple."

"It is that simple. Let bygones be bygones and move on from your pain. She doesn't deserve more punishment."

My gut twists into a knot as I turn to face Etta. "You think I punished her and made her leave? The fuck?"

"What I meant was…" Her eyes fill, and her lips tremble. "She loves you. Needs you."

"How do you know all this, and why are you getting emotional over me and Ruby?"

"Because I love you and I want to see you happy and in love with a good woman who also deserves happiness. You want her to stay?"

"Fuck yeah. I want to marry her. But she lives in Paris, has a whole life there. Why the fuck would she want to live here?"

"She's getting older, maybe she wants to settle down. I'm sure she's made plenty of money, could likely retire. She always did like the cherry farm as I recall. You ought to get on with the courting before another man snags her."

"You know damn well no man in this town will touch her. It would be a bloodbath."

Etta covers her mouth and gasps. "Rebel."

"What?" Sometimes I swear Etta knows something no one else does. She gets all fidgety over shit like this then clams up. "Christ. You think I could've killed 'em then taken Dick Kline's millions? What the fuck would my motivation have been? Sure, they were idiots and always messing with Ruby, but she handled 'em."

"She?"

"You know what I meant."

Etta stands, wringing her hands. "I hear the word bloodbath and I see that scene. Some scenes never leave your mind."

"I still don't get why you were never questioned, since you're the one who found them."

Her ghost-white skin sends a prickle across my scalp. She looks away and opens the screen door snail slow. The creaking metal sound of the spring camouflages her soft, low voice so much that I almost miss her words.

"I have an alibi." The door slams behind her.

"What?" I yank the door open and follow her in. "Why have you never mentioned this?"

"Doesn't matter now." With a trembling hand, she fills her sherry glass, lifts it to her mouth, and then empties it. "I will never speak of it again."

We don't often talk about that summer. There was so much crazy wrapped into it. The kind of moments that, in time, you erase from your mind for fear they'll haunt you. Looking back isn't always the best route to the future. Hell, I'm not sure it's a route to anywhere but grief. I say that and yet here I am, asking Ruby for a piece of the past. I have to know, because everything that happened that week was so out of character for her.

"Hey." I scoop Etta's arm in mine.

When our gazes meet, hers holds a terror-filled warning. One I've never seen.

"I won't bring it up again," I tell her. "Promise."

She nods. "I'm going to read. Goodnight, son."

"Turning in kind of early. What about dinner?"

Etta says nothing as she saunters down the hall, enters her room, and closes the door behind her.

What the hell was all that? Ruby Mae comes to town and shit gets weird. And damn, the can of worms hasn't even begun to open. Maybe I ought to tell her what I did. Or maybe I'll be patient and see if she's still got the balls she once had to fess up. My guess is her balls are bigger than mine.

I grab a second beer and walk to the barn in search of Rifle. Bubble's pony spooks when I enter, her prance kicking up dust that dances in a stream of sunlight. Walking down the aisle, following a trail of clothes, I pick up a pink bra, lacy underwear, a tank top, and a skirt.

"Rifle Field," I say. It's loud, certain to make the two of them jump as I knock on the tack room door. "Bubble Valentine. Get your naked asses dressed and out here. Clothes are outside the door. I'll be on the porch."

After a few minutes, Rifle and Bubble stride toward the porch, both teens red-faced and hickey-kissed.

"Sorry, Dad."

"I know you're sixteen and horny as rabbits. I've been there. Just promise me you're using protection."

"I'm um…on the pill," Bubble says.

"That's good. Rifle, tell me you know better than to have sex without a condom regardless of how much you trust a woman? There are all kinds of diseases and shit that'll make your dick fall off."

Rifle takes a giant step toward me, Bubble's hand twined with his. "Dad, Jesus… Apologize to her."

I nod at Bubble, whose eyes are deer-in-headlights petrified and wide. "I meant no offense, Bubble. Do you understand the same goes for you? What if Rifle had some skank growing on his dick and now it's in you?"

Rifle clenches his teeth and scowls at me. "Dad? What the fuck?"

I chuckle as I look them over. Fuck if it doesn't take me back to high school. Me and Ruby messing around every quiet corner we could find.

"Oh, you offended now too? Listen, son. If you're man enough to have sex, you ought to be man enough to be honest with yourself and the woman you're with."

"Please don't tell my dad you caught us," Bubble says.

I chuckle a little at her state of panic. "Sweetheart, I won't say a word. That's not my business."

"Thank you." She rushes to me and wraps her arms around my shoulders.

"Rifle, time to make dinner. You're on deck with pot pie. Bubble, you're more than welcome to stay for dinner."

"You know how to make pot pie?" Bubble asks, throwing her hands in the air.

She shoots Rifle a look so drunk with awe and curiosity that I burst out laughing. Teenage love is cute as fuck to witness firsthand.

"I know how to make everything." Rifle threads his fingers through hers and waggles his brow.

"That includes babies," I say, cuffing Rifle on the head. "But don't. I'm not ready to be a grandpa yet."

Rifle and Bubble leave me on the porch as they proceed to the kitchen. I eavesdrop on their giggling and flirting, remembering the way Ruby and I used to do the same when I made dinner and dessert for her on occasion. Maybe that's it? She wants a date. I'll give her a damn fine one once she fesses up. More than a friend date though. I'll play up this bullshit girlfriend act. Then, after that house of cards falls, I'll take her back to our beginning and we'll build a new house and life together.

Open the door, Ruby. Tell me you got the box I sent. Tell me why those things in the box were tangled up together. What else is tangled up? Tell me I'm not making up stories in my head that'll put you in a different house. *The big house.*

Chapter 12

To The Core

Ruby

Between the painkiller, the beer, and the meandering thoughts of Rebel and me, I finally fell asleep on the couch. At dawn, I wake up to Echo driving matchbox cars up and down my arms, his hot breath smelling of odiferous cheese gone one month too far.

"Echo, sweetie. Go brush your teeth." I kiss his forehead then nudge him.

"Brushed last week." He smiles, his teeth coated with miniscule butter-colored sweaters I can't look at for a second longer.

"Now." I peel the cars from his massive hands and point to the bathroom.

He stands, pouting. "Going," he says, stomping away, his head hanging.

"I'll give the cars back when your teeth are white and shiny!"

Echo arrives at my side a minute later, greedy palms open as he grunts at me. I place the cars on his palms and marvel at what a man he's become. It makes me laugh because he's six-two with a full beard that's four inches long. My little twenty-nine-year-old brother.

A pit forms in my stomach as I imagine what Opal would be like now and how different my life would be had she not died that disturbing night. I would have gone to Northwestern University with my full ride instead of opting for that modeling contract, and I would have kept dating Rebel, who never planned on going to college in the first place. He was going to start his own business. He was an idea a minute but hadn't a dime to his name. Though I never doubted him.

He worked two jobs all through high school, saving every penny to put toward his dream of becoming an entrepreneur. Crazy how things turned out. My demise allowed for his windfall of cash—or so I want to believe.

Echo kneels in front of me and drives his cars up and down my arms again.

"Hey," I say to him. "I hear you're taking classes at the center from Etta."

"Mama told me the gays go to Hell."

"Honey, Etta's not gay. She's…" I stop and think for a long sec. "She's like Mom and me. She's a woman."

"Not a man like me?" He pounds his chest and grins.

God, he melts everything inside me.

"No, not like you. She has female parts. Does that make sense?" I assume all he knows about anatomy is from Mom, which is something like, "If you touch your wee-wee, it will turn black and fall off."

"Like Opal?" His bottom lip thrusts out.

"Yes, Opal was a woman like Etta."

"Is." He scowls. "Opal is." Echo looks away, wiping the edge of his eyes with the back of his hand, crushing me.

I cup his cheek, bringing his face to mine. "Do you feel like Opal is still here?"

"Mama talks to her, but I can't find her." He bends and peeks under the couch. Then he straightens. "She's hiding." He grins.

"Where do you think she's hiding?"

"Away." He points at various spots in the room and giggles.

"But you remember she died? She's gone."

Echo whines and shakes his head. "They took her."

"Yes. But she's in our hearts." I take his hands in mine and kiss them.

Echo licks my kisses from his hands like a puppy might. His voice darkens, and his eyelids grow heavy. "She was my Opal."

"I know, honey. We miss her, don't we?"

He races cars across my shoulders, making sounds that fit his movements. "She told me bye."

"What?" I gasp, my insides frozen in fear. What did she say to him?

"She gave me a goodbye picture."

Echo and Opal had talked mostly through cartoon drawings. It was their special way of communicating.

"She said you hurt for her and she was going to hurt for you."

Covering my mouth, I wheeze in an unstable breath. My whole body jolts. "Echo…um…listen." What do I tell him? I should have guessed she would confide in him. My mind zips around like a bumblebee.

"Echo!" Mom screams. Then she whistles. "We're waiting."

"Going on triples ride with Ma."

I stand and follow Echo outside. Mom busies herself with strapping Lake into the basket on the tandem bike.

I cup Echo's cheeks as we stare at each other. "Are you okay?"

"I'm a man." He hauls me into his arms and squeezes me like I'm his teddy bear. Squeezes me so hard that I fart. Then we both laugh.

"Yes, you're a man. I love you, E."

"You're my Ruby. Don't hide like Opal."

I nod because any words I want to say stick in my throat. Guilt floods my senses. Again.

I urge him toward the bike. "I'll see you guys later."

With Mom and Echo out on a bike ride, I go for a clear-my-head run. Curiosity gets the best of me, taking me down the road Rebel's farm is on. I pick up speed as I near his driveway, my pulse racing in accord. Heartache thrives on torture.

One second, I'm taking pleasure in the view of his manicured storybook farm nestled in rolling hills. The next, I'm flat on my back, no air coming or going, a pain in my ribs so severe, I roll my head to the side, looking for the punk with a steel bat who hit me.

Air begins flowing into my lungs little bits at a time. I cannot have a broken rib, a broken wrist, and a broken heart.

"Ruby?"

I open my eyes and see a gorgeous, sweaty man over me. I hallucinate that it's Rebel. Wait. It *is* Rebel. Great. I'm at the end of his driveway. That's not obvious or mortifying. His beautiful, naked, drenched chest is dripping on me. His neck bulges with engorged veins as he stares into my eyes.

"I know you don't want me around," I tell him. "But killing me is not the way to go."

"You trying to steal my mailbox?" He chuckles.

I groan, trying to draw air into my achy lungs. Okay, maybe I didn't break a rib. *Please, God, for once…do something for me. Heal me fast. Then let Rebel lay his sweaty body on mine.* I've had the weight of the world on me for years, when the only weight I want is his body pressed to mine. Naked. Sweaty. Rebel.

"It attacked me."

"It won." He smirks.

"Will you see if my ribs are in it? I'll take those and be on my way." I lift my head, the pain in it and my chest so severe that I groan again.

"Man, you're just looking for attention left and right, aren't you?"

"That's me." I grunt and smile. "Little miss swim with the sharks when she's bleeding out."

"I don't want to move you until I take a look." Rebel pushes my sweaty tank up my stomach. Then he shocks me to the core.

Chapter 13

Flipside

Rebel

She was racing so fast, like she knew I was behind her. Did she think she'd get a glimpse of my "girlfriend"? She slammed hard into my mailbox then flipped over the steel monster like a sozzled gymnast gut-checking a vault. She didn't move for twenty seconds as I sprinted the last leg of my run toward her dead-still form lying half on the road, half on the gravel. Then she moaned.

Ruby Mae Rose might have had the wind knocked out of her, but when she moaned, it didn't matter. That moan got me. Hard. And, as I knelt over her sweaty body, I wanted more than to help her. I wanted to help myself. And claim her as mine.

Peeling her top inch by glorious inch over her hard, sweat-covered abs, I suck a breath in through my nose. I'm unable to stop my fingers from shoving the drenched fabric higher. Then higher yet. I glide it over her perfect tits saddled tight in her running bra, waiting for eminent release. Ruby's gaze meets mine, her lips parting, her tongue lining the slit until she pulls her bottom lip between her pearl-white teeth.

"Rebel."

"I just want to make sure you're okay," I lie. *I just want to see you naked.*

"I think my tits are fine."

"Yes, they are. Always been fine."

I travel my hands across the wet flesh of her waist, applying gentle pressure as I trace each rib. My dick isn't the only part of me that wants her. My fingertips do too. My mouth wants in as well. Every cell in my body pulses to merge with hers. And fuck yes…I take my sweet-ass time meandering.

Starting at one rib, I glide along with light pressure and promises of midnight fucks to come. At the next rib, I slow things down and appreciate her lips and the way her tongue cannot seem to get enough licking in. She must be hungry like I am. Poor girl is in agony, and I'm ready to come in my shorts like a seventeen-year-old.

Pathetic as it is, I can't stop. Jaws of Life couldn't pry my hands off her. At the next rib, my fingertips take an exit route along her sweaty midriff. Her stomach undulates, which causes my dick to jolt. More than my next ten meals, I want to slide my fingers into her shorts. I tug them down; it's nothing really. Harmless. Just a peek at her hip bones—that's all I want. Just need to make sure she's…okay.

"Does this hurt?" I rub my thumb along a plum-colored bruise. "Can you take a deeper breath?"

"I don't think so." She inhales a half breath. It hitches like she loves my touch. Hitches like she wants more right here on this country road.

"Because it hurts too much right here?" I move my fingertips up along another bruise, scooting the bottom of her bra up until half her areola is exposed.

Her throat bobs as she works small breaths in and out. Her chest blooms with color as her knees open wider, and her fingertips dig into the gravel at her sides.

"Where does it hurt, baby?" I swallow hard and press my hips to hers. And I thrust once. Then once again.

"Rebel." She moans out my name. It's so damn quiet. And sweet. And needy. I press harder and watch for more signs of need. Her face lights up like a Las Vegas billboard.

Jesus, fuck me already. I'm dry-humping her. Roadside.

"Here." She moves my hand over her breast, exposing all of it until our joined hands rest on her heart.

The beat of it is so strong I can hear it. I lower my head to her taut nipple and suckle her tit like it's going to feed me for life.

"Ruby. Fuck…" Lifting my chest, I press my forehead to hers, my face hovering over her lips, her sweet breath feathering my mouth. I need to kiss her. No. I need answers first. "Ruby. Dammit, woman."

"Rebel. I need it to stop hurting."

Fuck…so do I. And, if I keep this roadside exploration going, we might end up worse off than we were before I found her.

"I think you're going to be fine," I tell her. And, though it kills me, I tug her bra over her breast, my heart aching as I do. Then, gently, I pull her drenched top down. "Got the wind knocked out of you." Same as me. Almost got some common sense knocked out of me too. "You'll be fine."

I help her up, embarrassment sitting on her face in streaks of pink.

We stare at each other, both waiting for the other to say something, neither of us crossing the center line.

"Talk to me, Ruby."

"I… Thanks for showing up." That's all she says.

It would be wrong to shake the answers I want out of her, but it's what I want to do. She's not gonna budge an inch. So I nod. Then I cross the road and jog up my driveway. It was either that or I was going to shake her then fuck her in the ditch.

"Say hey to your girlfriend," she says.

I know she thinks I might not have heard that snarky bullshit she's tossing out. She's forgotten; I survived.

I turn, hands on my hips, dry patch in my throat. God fucking damn her.

"I will, baby—when she wakes up. It was a long night. Then round three this morning."

"Just three?" She laughs then rubs her side and winces.

Ruby Mae is still that same ballsy girl I fell in love with way back.

"Well, yeah." I chuckle. "Haven't flipped her over yet."

Ruby smirks. "Well, enjoy that, Wishbone. Oh, and no need to help with the move. Rowdy stopped by earlier with donuts and coffee. He's going to help me with the move. I don't need you."

Well, fuck that shit. "Rowdy, huh?"

"Yeah. We'll be getting a late start since he's taking me out dancing tonight at Tincat."

"Well, I guess I'll see you there. 'Cause my girl and I have tickets for the band."

"Then you might want to make rounds four through eight on the flipside gentle."

"Don't worry 'bout us, baby. We've perfected the art of fucking." I walk toward her, talking shit all the while. I got game. All-fucking-day-and-night game. Super Bowl game. "I start her out real slow, my lips meandering every inch of her so she'll come a few times before I fuck her hard. Then we make love like we're one. You know how that is? Skin melting onto each other…hearts pounding…mouths parting only for air…"

"You have to part for air?" Ruby glides a finger along my collarbone then up my throat. She stops on my Adam's apple when it bobs. "That's a shame, Rebel. If you were soul mates, all your air would come from her, because she'd take your breath away. Every last bit of it. Maybe you haven't found *the one* yet. Now, that's interesting."

Chapter 14

Too Much Hurt

Ruby

Haven't flipped her over yet, my ass. The only thing he hasn't flipped over is his hard-on. For me. More like tripped over because it might be permanent considering I've seen it multiple times since I've come home. Felt it too.

Maybe he thinks I didn't notice it when he pressed his hips to mine while feeling up my ribs, my hip bones, and elsewhere. I should have feigned more pain. *My other side… Check there too, Rebel. I think it hurts lower… Yeah…right where you're pressing yourself against me. Don't stop now.*

I need to get to the feed mill. Fast. If he beats me there, I'm toast. I'm up for playing this cat- and-mouse game if it's what he needs to realize *I'm* his girl. What am I saying? *His girl?* Is this truly what I want? I'm so fucked if I fall hard again and then decide I can't live in this damn town. Because the truth is, I don't know if I can. But he'll never leave it. He's a Midwestern boy to the marrow of his bones. What if we fell in love again and neither of us was willing to move? Then what? That's a hell of a commute. I want to call it impossible, though I'm willing to be hopeful. But first we need to be friends again and get beyond all his hate.

Two miles to run. In high school, I ran a five-minute mile. Six is about all I can pull these days. And, now, I have this aching rib cage and the broken wrist I'm lugging. Maybe I can do eight. Yeah, right.

Knowing Rebel, he's already in his truck, racing the other way, while I'm lazing down the road like a hobbling turtle. Yeah, he's dashing there now because he wants to see my freaked-out expression when Rowdy asks what the hell I'm talking about.

When I round the corner to the mill, nearly dead, I see him. There's more pain in my chest than I thought could exist, and for numerous reasons. When I approach him, I don't know who he's talking to, but holy man beasts.

"Hey." I bend and place my hands on my knees, huffing and puffing like I've topped Mount Everest while toting a small village on my back.

"Clocked in pretty quick, baby," Rebel says, confident as the king of a lion pride. "Not quite your record, though." He slaps my ass, and I jump.

Straightening my stance, I glare at him. Mr. Flipside. "Aren't you supposed to be flipping your pancake…buttering her backside? Li'l Missus Go Missing?"

"She was a little sore. Said I split her too hard last night."

I burst out laughing. It's big and fake, and goddamn, it hurts my chest, but I'm not backing down from his shit. "Wouldn't have been the case if she were wet."

That scores me a dirty look.

I turn my attention to the gents. "Ruby Mae Rose." I shake the sexy beasts' hands, holding on extra-long to ignite a spark in Rebel's inner jealous jackass.

When they introduce themselves, I all but lick their heavy British accents off the pavement.

"Balthazar Cox."

The treble sinks lower.

"Wolfgang Valentine."

Oh, Jesus. "Well, the pleasure is all mine." I twist more toward them, my back facing Rebel, my chest jutted out even though it's killing me.

He clears his throat, dragging my attention to him. Oh, and there it is. Jealousy. That same jealous look he wore when any boy in high school talked to me. Especially the Kline boys.

Rowdy swaggers down the stairs, two bags of feed slung over his shoulder, a girl in overalls following him.

"Rowdy." I grab his elbow and trot beside him. "I'm so excited about the Tincat tonight. I was thinking we should do a picnic at the lake before." I waggle my eyebrows so Rebel will take note. I talk fast as I follow him to a truck. "Please pretend you're with me like we did in high school. Pretend we're going on a date."

Rowdy grins. "I was going to take you out for a homecoming dinner," he says in a put-on act that's so pathetic I want to disappear through a sinkhole. He always did suck in drama class. "A picnic at the lake, girl? Shit, I'll bring beer and—"

"Pick me up at six." I paste my fingers to his lips.

God help me. Don't quit your day job, Rowdy.

"Don't forget the whipping cream," Rebel says, chuckling. "She used to like that as I recall."

"Funny?" I glare at Rebel. "I don't remember us doing anything with whipping cream."

Rebel strolls toward me, his eyes at half-mast and drenched with arrogance. His sweat-covered chest is begging for a lick all the way from the low-slung band of his shorts to his hair-dusted, bulked-up pecs. I shouldn't be ogling him like I'm in heat, but he makes it impossible not to.

"Shit. You know…you're right," he says. His gaze reeks of smug pride. "Must have been something I did with some other girl while you were fucking your way through the European Union."

Balthazar and Wolfgang eye me up, smirks on their faces as I turn ten shades of raspberry in five seconds flat. Screaming on the inside, I approach Rebel. Damn him. I edge up onto my toes, getting so close I can smell the stink of his sweat. I wish it didn't turn me on. It does. Oh, shit, it does.

But I'm so pissed that I push that wild emotion down. "I asked you nicely not to be a dick. But you can't seem to get your head on straight. Maybe that's because it's stuck so far up your ass that you didn't hear me the first time."

Rebel cocks his head and licks his top lip. Then he drags his thumb along his bottom lip.

"I'll say this one more time," I tell him, my eyes stinging with impending tears. "You bring up me fucking other people and I will…" I spin and start jogging. Then I break into a sprint. Tears fall as I struggle for air.

If he follows me, I will punch him in the throat. Why is he punishing me? He thinks I deserve pain—more pain. If he knew what kind of pain his not showing up graduation night caused me, he'd never forgive himself.

I love him too much to hurt him. But does he love me enough to stop hurting me?

Chapter 15

Fishing

Rebel

I knew she didn't have a date with Rowdy. That look of surprise on his face when she whispered something at his neck while trotting after him like a lost puppy confirmed it.

She wants me so badly she's gulping the air I'm breathing out. Now, I have to manufacture a girlfriend to keep up my end of the charade. Which I will do until Ruby produces that ring or a solid story. All bets are off once I see it dangling from her neck. And when I do, I'll yank that chain in a snap, slide the ring on her finger, then slide my cock inside her, where it should've been nestled all those fucking years ago.

"Don't worry, Rebel. I won't touch her," Rowdy says.

"I know you won't, but thanks for going along with her bullshit."

"Dude, not sure why you're resisting that girl. But fuck, you might want to forgive her for whatever wrong she did," Balthazar says, gently backhanding my jaw. "She all but fucked you with her eyes, and you were doing it right back. Hell, we're in a parking lot and I felt dirty watching you go at it. What kind of heat do you two kick off when you're alone? Might want to warn the fire department."

"She knows what she needs to do," I say. "And, when she does, I will split her with my cock, because it's been hard for her most of my adult life."

Rowdy whistles and nods. "Okay, then. But, if she climbs all over me while play-acting on this date thing, don't kill me."

"Just keep your dick in your pants and I'll play along," I answer.

"Poker, my house this week," Balthazar says. "Bring the ladies."

"I need to find one." I shove a hand through my hair. "Someone smokin'. Any ideas?"

"I have a friend in from England who's staying with us," Wolfgang says. "She's single, sexy, and a circus acrobat." He waggles his eyebrows.

I fist-bump him. "Christ, perfect! Think she'll be up for being my fake girlfriend?"

"No question. She's a gamer."

"Rowdy, you bring Ruby to poker night," I say. "That work for you?"

"Happy to collude." Rowdy chuckles. "Though I'm going for Hazel if she shows up at any of these get-togethers. Word is she's an ass doc now. Can you fucking imagine Hazel fingering your ass?" He wipes his brow.

"I gotta go apologize," I say, regretting what a dick I was. "She's pissed."

I'm in my truck, flying through town, searching everywhere for my girl. After swinging through the Stop-N-Go for an I'm-sorry donut, I drive out to her mom's place.

When I pull in the drive, Monday, who's wearing a hat and sunglasses so oversized that she could shade an island, is sitting in a kiddie pool with her swan, pink flamingoes stabbed in the ground all around them.

"Rebel, Rebel." She lowers her sunglasses and fans her face.

"How's Mrs. Rose doing today?"

"Happy as a dead pig in the sunshine."

"Atta girl."

"Just missed Ruby Mae, hon. Madder than a wet hen about something." Monday reaches into a cooler next to the kiddie pool and snatches a bottle of beer. Then she pops the top and hands it to me.

I reach for the beer. "That would be me."

"I don't think so. She said she's not talking to you. Said you broke her wrist, then her ribs, and her heart. You want to win her back? You might want to stop breaking things."

"Yes, ma'am. I plan on it." I take a swig of beer. Then I realize it can't be eleven a.m.

"I have some more dresses for your daddy. I'll have Ruby bring them over."

"Thank you. Etta admires your style."

"Everyone does," she purrs out, nestling her head against Lake's.

"Any idea where the pistol took off to?" I have a few ideas, but those'll have me driving this whole town.

"Likely the same place she's been going since junior high when she needed to blow off steam."

"Guess I'm going fishing."

Now, to tell Ruby I'm sorry for pissing her off without giving in too much.

Post renting a row boat from the marina, I head out into the bay. Immediately, I spot Ruby floating around and singing. If she hadn't become a model, she sure as shit could have become a singer. The voice of an angel is nestled inside her lungs.

I bump my boat into the back of hers, causing her to jump. "Brought you something."

She turns and stares; the torn look on her face pains me. Shit, I went too far.

"Sorry 'bout that back there." I hand her the pink donut.

She grabs it, looks it over, then chucks it into the lake. "My ass you're sorry. It's one thing to disrespect me when it's just us, and that's crap too, but to do it in front of Rowdy and those other guys? You aren't hardened. You're a bigger..." She mops tears off her cheeks then looks away.

Dick. She was going to call me a big dick again.

"Ruby, look at me."

Maybe I am being too hard on her. Maybe this isn't the way to get her back. I'm sure honey isn't going to get her to tell me anything though, either. What will?

"Hey." I tap her shoulder then rub that spot.

Nothing. I work the tickle angle, and all she gifts me with is a pissy growl.

"Come on. We need to talk."

She picks her book up and thumbs through pages. "I came out here to be alone. Why don't you go to work or play 'hide the wishbone' with that girlfriend I can't wait to meet tonight?"

"It was a joke. I'm sorry. I should have shut my mouth."

"Yeah? Feels more like I'm the joke around you. You won't have to worry about me being your joke for much longer. I'm out of here after the move."

My heart sinks. "You were going to stay?" I drag her chin toward me with a gentle tug. "Tell me, Ruby. Were you going to stay? And then tell me why."

"Yes, I was considering sticking around for more than two weeks. But then…" She looks past me, a dreamy air in her eyes. Something filled with promise. Or is it lost promise?

"Never mind," she says softly. A boat pulling two water skiers catches her attention as it hauls past us faster than it should be going, causing our boats to rock against each other.

"Ruby Mae Rose, look at me. Why would you stay?"

"A reason," she says, brushing my hand away, dropping her chin to her chest. "I need a reason. And I don't have any."

Ouch. Deep down, ugly ouch.

"There is a reason," I tell her. "You know damn well."

She lifts her head, her sad, drooped eyelids and quivering lips weakening me. "I know what you want. But I can't put that ring around my neck or on my finger. You don't understand."

"I want to." I cup her cheek with my palm. "More than you know. Just talk to me. I know you, baby. I know you can do this."

Do I tell her now that I'm the one who anonymously sent her the box? Do I ask her why my ring was on the necklace with the Kline boys' crosses? And then I should ask another stupid question. Why was it in Etta's possession in the first place?

Chapter 16

Thread By Thread

Ruby

"You don't know a thing about me anymore."

"The hell I don't. You think you've changed?" Rebel grips my arm and squeezes.

When I squirm away, he eases up.

"A little," I reply.

"So you went from broke to rich. Cute to sexy. Girl to woman." He searches my face. Then his gaze meanders down my neck and onto my chest, which is rising and falling faster than I'd like. Every bit of emotion is right there under his raw stare. "So you've seen the world. Graced magazine covers and TVs. Big fucking deal. You haven't changed."

"I've changed inside."

Maybe changed isn't the right word, though. Been knifed. If I were turned inside out, he'd see my scars. They'd make him cry. *You weren't there to stop them. And I may never tell you that you could have changed my world if all you had done was show up like we agreed. I can't because it would hurt you too much.*

I twist out of his hand. I can't have this conversation while he's touching me. I can scarcely look at him without climbing into his boat and onto his lap.

"You can't see inside me," I say.

"That's because you won't give me what I want. I'm not asking for much, just a fucking reason. You still look at me like you want me. Like you want me to kiss you. You need me. I know you need me."

"I don't." That sounded as believable as telling a fifteen-year-old the Easter bunny is real.

"You do." He stares at my lips as I lick them. His gaze bumps up to mine then back to my mouth. "And you want me. You miss me." He fingers the hollow between my collarbone. Then he stills his hand on my pulse and smiles. "You miss me undressing you thread by thread." He traces a line down to the top of my blouse and unfastens one button, then another.

My breathing falters. "No. I don't."

I wrap my hand around his and shake my head. This makes him smile the smallest bit, and that smile dissolves me.

"Yes, baby. Yes, you do," he insists. "You miss me unfastening your bra." He slips his hand inside my shirt and glides it to the clasp on my back, which is open a second later.

"No, I don't." *Please don't stop.*

He closes his eyes and sighs. Then he drags his plump bottom lip through his teeth. "And you miss me pulling your titties out for a good licking."

Oh, those words and his dripping-with-need deep voice. I wilt.

My shoulders sag, and my pulse snowballs. "Rebel."

"God, I fucking loved playing with your hard, ruby-red nipples." He edges my bra off my chest and peeks down my shirt. Why am I letting him do this? I should stop him, but I can't. "Ruby.

Such gorgeous tits." He cups his jaw, one thumb between his teeth, where I want my nipples. Yesterday.

"Don't talk to me like that unless you plan on doing something about it." Here we go, I might have jumped off the cliff. Will he catch me? Shit.

"Doing what?" He slips one hand to the back of my neck then wraps an arm around my waist, scooting me closer to him. "Sucking and pinching you till you come?" His bottomless voice sends a throb through my groin. An ache I need him to take care of. "Yeah. You need it bad." He closes his eyes and drags a hand down his face, then rubs his jaw. "Fess up."

Now he's torturing me. It's working. I knew better. What an idiot I am.

"Stop it."

"Stop what?" Rebel's breathing deepens, matching mine.

He's too close, too sexy, too under my skin to mess with me like this.

"You don't want me tracing my tongue down your belly?" he asks. "Unfastening your jeans with my teeth to find you commando just for me the way you used to do? You little sassy tease."

"Just quit it."

"Ruby baby, you loved to tease me. That was your foreplay...all that teasing and taunting." He opens his legs and grips his filled-out groin.

I push away from him. "I'm serious. Knock it the fuck off."

"Knock what off? Your jean shorts?" He hooks his hands under my bare legs and jerks me toward him as he climbs half into my boat. He leans against my neck. "Yeah, I thought so, Ruby. Knock 'em off so I can see your ruby-red pussy lips, part them, and taste you." He groans out something sexy and dark.

But this is going nowhere. He's teasing the tease.

"Fuck you!"

"Oh, baby." He chuckles and winks. "I would have, wanted it bad. You never let me. Instead, I tongued you, pinning you down till you came again and again. Sometimes three…four times. Five on occasion. I know you remember."

"Why are you doing this to me?" I ask. "What are you getting from it? Can't you have faith in me, believe when I say I cannot put on that necklace or ring? Don't you trust I have a good reason?"

"No, I don't. There is not one reason I can think of besides…that you don't want a future with me."

He has no idea how his words shred me. Maybe his pain was so great that this is his redemption. Why do that to someone you love? He doesn't love me anymore; that's all this can mean. How can it be? I waited too long, stewing in my pain. Have I lost the only man I ever loved? Is this it…the end of us? Again. I never should have come here. Paris was safe. Teddy was safe even if I don't love him like a woman should to get married. Rebel is trouble, and pain and memories I need to forget.

He scoots back onto his boat and stretches his arms over his head. Then he glances at his watch. "Anyway, my acrobat girlfriend is waiting for me."

God, I want to slap him.

"Well, no wonder you love fucking her."

"Oh, I do. Girl can bend and contort…do all kinds of things with her body." He pushes his boat off mine, his chest puffed.

"Well, it's good to know you believe in someone." The words nearly die on my tongue.

Why doesn't he like me anymore? Maybe that girl is truly gone in his eyes. Well, she's partly gone in mine too. Thank God I became someone else—the pretty cover girl millionaire no one knew was dying on the inside. It's amazing how much a smile can cover.

"Give it up, Ruby. And you'll get everything you want."

"Not even you can give me everything I want, Rebel. That was stolen a long time ago."

Chapter 17

Crosses And Lies

Rebel

I shouldn't have sent that box to her, but the second I heard that Monday and Echo were moving into a house on the lake, I knew Ruby would come home. I'm assuming she got it. I would have done anything to see her face when she opened it. I'll bet her guts twisted into a lethal knot—just like mine did when I found those things.

But what if she didn't get the box? Is that why she can't wear the ring? I never did think of that, and it's a real possibility.

The day I found those things was a shocker. And it was also when the story first got sticky. When I asked Etta why she had those items in her possession, she claimed she was going to give the crosses to the twins for graduation. But she's lying; they wore them at graduation.

I remember thinking how funny it was that those dickwads who were the biggest sinners and bullies in our school were wearing crosses. What the hell for? And I remember too. They weren't wearing them at the graduation party Ruby never showed up to. I was so fucking pissed she never showed that I couldn't even call her.

Why would Etta lie to me and tell me the guys had died before she could give them the crosses?

When I asked Etta for some explanation about the ring and necklace, she said that she found them at Opal's gravesite after Ruby had left for Paris. And, when I asked why she never gave them to me, she serenely replied that I was married to Paris by then and she didn't want to stir anything up between us.

Someone is lying; maybe more than someone. How many layers of lies are there between me and Ruby and the truth?

"How long you going to do this for?" I ask.

"What is it you think I'm doing?" she responds.

I collect myself for a quiet few seconds, afraid I'll explode. When I look up, her lips are quivering.

"You're lying about something, or protecting someone. Who?"

She faces away and snivels. I delay more questions as patiently as I can. How much longer must I wait? Years have gone by.

"Time's up."

She peeks over her shoulder and whispers, "Me and you...and others too."

"That right?"

"Yeah," she whispers.

"You're protecting me and others? A martyr, huh? Ruby Mae is a martyr!" I laugh.

Her face crumbles, her hand reaching up to get to her quivering lips. "Don't call me that again." She rows away like I'm going to gut her with my bare hands. Rows with every ounce of her being. Rowing and bawling.

What has gotten into her? I'm almost afraid to know.

"Ruby! Christ almighty." I go after her, catching up in seconds. Then I haul ass to her side. Latching on to her boat, I grip her arm. "Look at me!" I yell.

"Stop it!" she says through clenched teeth. She's as pissed as a devil getting soused in arctic water. "Stop picking and poking and trying to..." she screams. Then she covers her face with her book and howls.

"To figure you out?" I touch her arm. "Hey?"

"Please stop," she says, her voice soaked in sorrow.

"Okay, baby, but isn't that part of why you came home?" I peel the book from her face. I need to see those eyes, need to understand what she's hiding behind. Or from.

"I just wanted you to love me, or at the very least be my friend," she admits. "I didn't think it would be so hard."

"You didn't, huh? What'd you think would happen?" I thumb away her tears—so many falling tears. Each one of them expectant with stories. "You left without telling me why, I married, had a kid, and then buried my wife. And, now, you're back. No answers still."

"I know," she whispers. "Lots of time has passed."

"Been lonely, been brokenhearted, been wondering why... So many things—why?"

When I move strands of her hair from her wet cheeks, she nods.

"Life is hard," I say. "Love is hard, especially when everything is muddy and has been for a long time. Time does not clear things up, baby. It makes things harder, adds more layers. Complicates." I cross my arms over my chest, and again, I wait.

What's it going to take for her to bare her truths? When will she strip the layers away and come clean with me?

"You don't seem to like me anymore." Her face scrunches. "Maybe I made a mistake by coming home. I should never have left Paris."

"I don't like you." I grab her boat and yank it toward mine. Then I crawl half onto it, my lips at her ear, my hand steadying her shaking body and I steady myself. "I am in fucking love with you. In love. I always have been. I need you. You fucked us up. You did this to us. Not me."

"I didn't fuck anything up." She sobs as she hugs herself and rocks. "That's what you don't get. I got fucked! And, now, I'm getting fucked again. I just never thought you'd be the guy doing that."

Chapter 18

Privilege Of Damage

Ruby

"You see, Ruby, here's where our communicating is failing us. I want to be fucking you."

"I don't believe you. Don't follow me. Don't anything me." With every ounce of strength I have, I row away like a hog-tied duckling.

"No problem. Let's do things your way. Yet again!" Rebel shouts. "If I recall, when you left last time, you said the same thing: Don't follow me. So I let you go. Tried to forget you. Tried to move on. So tell me. Why the hell are you in front of me, telling me not to follow you, when I'm the reason you came back? And don't lie and say you came to move your mother and brother. You fucking came home for me!"

He rows to me. When he reaches my boat, he yanks both oars from my hands with little effort. Then he pushes out of my reach.

"Give those back!" I reach out for them.

He laughs. The motherfucker laughs at me. Then he slaps one oar against the water, dousing me. After he does it again he laughs harder.

"Nope," he says.

How is this conversation funny to him? I'm out-of-my-mind pissed and he's laughing, and now, he's tucking my oars out of sight.

"What is wrong with you? You're crazy!" I paddle with one hand, trying to reach him. Then I use my book as an oar. Oh, and that goes well. Fucking dandy! I whip the soggy mess at him and scream, "Crazy!"

"Yep. For you. Funny how you don't want me to follow you and you're trying to get to me. You gonna follow me? Better start paddling harder." He rows farther away as he smiles.

This is fun for him?

"Are you going to leave me stranded?" I shout.

"You don't like that feeling, do you? I know what that feels like. Shitty, isn't it?"

We glare at each other. Enemy stares fueled with lust.

"Seriously, you should go to the ER and get your head examined."

"Nah. I know how crazy I am for you. Certifiable. I'd be willing to dump my sexy girlfriend who can fuck me while doing the splits. Now, that is one crazy man. I'll bet you can't fuck like that, can you, Ruby?"

"No, I can't fuck while doing the splits, asshole. Now, give me the oars or I will come after them." My boat wobbles as I stand, which causes me to almost fall into the water. Panicked, I slump onto the seat and shoot Rebel a death glare.

"How do you fuck, baby?" Rebel spreads his legs and rubs his groin. "You like it slow and deep…a nice grind?"

"Shut up."

"Oh, got it. You like it hard. Rag doll Ruby." He waggles his brow then licks his top lip. "Rag doll style is fine by me, baby."

"Rag doll Ruby."

I push that night out of my head. They no longer have the privilege of damaging me. *Get out of my head, you bullies. I am not your victim.* I squeeze my eyes shut and growl to drive them away.

"Shut up, Rebel."

"That got you, didn't it? You like being rag-dolled? Good to know." He clucks his tongue.

The force of evil takes over inside me. His words blur as I fly at him, prepared to sink his boat with my one-hundred-twenty-five-pound frame. My cast arm crashes against his face. Then I plunge headfirst into the freezing lake.

With one hand gripping the edge of his boat, I come up gasping for air. Blood trickles down Rebel's face, a will-need-stitches gash slicing his eyebrow.

"I'm not sure how to read you right now." He shakes his head, his brow creased. "Did that turn you on or piss you off?"

I clench my jaw, angry words sticking in my throat then firing at him. "Pissed me off."

"Got it." He presses his fingertips to the gash on his forehead, glances at the blood coating them, then licks it.

As pissed as I am, I still find it sexy. Everything about him is sexy.

"I like it both ways," I say while dangling on the side of his boat like a Christmas ornament hung on the tip of the weakest branch.

"Just…don't ever use that rag doll phrase again or I swear I will take you out. And I will win."

Rebel reaches over the side of the boat and hauls me up in a swift motion. Talk about breathless.

"Goddammit, Ruby." He places me on his lap in a straddle. His gaze roams every inch of my face, his tongue and teeth working his bottom lip in a mind-bending proposition.

Breaths shake out of me and my heart races while my nerves unravel. Rebel Field owns every fiber of my soul. I was born to love him, and though fate worked her fierce magic to kill our union, she lost.

His hands grip my waist, pressing into my skin like a hot knife on butter.

"Rebel, what are you doing?"

"Trying to get my girl back. Trying to get back to her."

Oh, Rebel. He nips my top lip, a tiny tug. I moan and wilt. Slow and steady, his fingers travel up my body and onto my face.

"I want to kiss you," he says. "Want to kiss you for hours. Every inch of you. I want to burn the feel of my lips onto your body."

His words thread tentacles around and through my heart.

"Rebel Field, I never stopped loving you."

"Ruby, you can't say that and not give me more. I want to kiss you now, but I need more, baby." He peppers kisses across my cheeks. Wet, wild kisses, each one easing another stitch into my soul.

"It's all I have. I gave you every ounce of me in those words. And I mean them with all my heart. Don't let anything else matter.

Please trust me. It's all I'm asking for. Your trust. If I give you more, it'll ruin us."

Rebel presses his forehead to mine. His hot, sweet breath is an invitation tickling my lips. I wait for his kiss to land. Closing my eyes, I part my lips and inch closer.

"It's not enough, baby." He presses his fingers to my pout. "Not enough."

"Then I'm not enough. If my all isn't enough…nothing else will be. I can't give more than all of me."

"You're better than this. Dig deeper." Rebel threads his fingers through my hair and drags my head back, exposing my throat. He licks a line from my collarbone up to my ear, where he bites my lobe hard.

I squeal, but I love his ferocity.

"Give me more. Find it. I don't care how. I don't care what it does to you. Find it in your heart to give me more. Tell me what I need to know. Tell me why you ended us."

"Don't care what it does to me?" God, does that sting like a bitch. "It's just a stupid ring. It's a piece of metal and doesn't mean shit."

"Is it? Or is it something else? A symbol of something you aren't telling me? If it doesn't mean shit, then fess up and tell me why you aren't wearing it. Tell me where the fuck the ring is."

"If I had something to tell you, wouldn't I have done that already?"

"That's what I thought too." His arms drop to his sides. Is he giving up? "This ain't gonna end well, is it?"

"End? That's up to you," I answer. I stare into the depths of his eyes. And, in them, I see myself along with pain and questions that will never be answered.

"No, baby, it really isn't. The ball is in your court. Been there a long time."

"I lost them." My fingers zip to my earlobe for a reassuring squeeze. Choking on my spit, I fight to say it again. "Lost the necklace and ring. I'm sorry."

"Did you now? Lost them? You couldn't tell me that all the times I asked? Couldn't say it the day you left? Couldn't say it yesterday or five minutes ago? Sounds like you just manufactured that crap to shut me up."

"I thought you'd be mad." I place my hands on his shoulders, but he shrugs them off.

"What a crock of shit!"

"This is why I didn't tell you. I knew you'd act like this."

"I wouldn't have cared if you lost the ring and necklace. What I care about is your lies. You are not telling me something."

"What's this, Ruby Mae?" Kent fingers the ring on my necklace. "The dickwad boyfriend give you a promise ring? What sort of promise? He bone you yet?" He and Kyle snicker. "Tell me the truth. Tell me if this perfect little does-everything-right ass got dicked."

I spit on his face. "That's none of your fucking business."

He wipes the wet gob off, adds a layer of spit into his hand, and pries my mouth open. Then he wipes the inside of it with the slimy mix of us. I gag, bile rising in my throat.

"Gimme this crap." Kent yanks my necklace off. Then he adds the cross from his necklace to it and holds his hand out for Kyle's cross. "Our pansy godfather gave us these. You're going to wear them along with that ring while we give you a special graduation present. Gonna give the word 'promise' a whole new meaning."

Chapter 19

This Could Be Us

Rebel

We sit across from each other in the ER. I require stitches, and Ruby needs a new cast. Stewing in anger and want, I stare at her as she flips through fashion magazines. Occasionally, she glances up, our eyes locking for a wicked second. I want to have faith that, one of these times, she's going to fess up and tell me why she first said she couldn't wear the ring then changed it to *I lost it*.

This whole thing is about more than the ring. It's about what's true between us, and at this point, I don't know that anything is. Except this: I still love her and she says she loves me. But where will love take us without trust? You can love someone only so much without trust.

When my name is called, I rise, nod to the nurse, and then walk to Ruby.

"Meet me back here. I'll give you a ride home."

"I'll find my own way," she says to the magazine.

"Perfect."

"Great."

After a doctor whips seven stitches into my incision, I stalk out to the waiting room, more pissed than before. But then I'm stopped cold.

"Still here?" I ask. My insides slush when I see Ruby belly-down, propped on her elbows, playing with toddler boys on the floor.

"Tommy came in. It was an emergency."

"Did you know he and India got married?"

"Nope," she says. Her fingers skip across the boys' faces as they giggle.

I can't peel my eyes from her as she plays on the floor with the children. I want to make babies with this woman. I want to slow-dance around my kitchen with her in my arms while we cook dinner together. I want to wrap her wet body in a warm towel when she steps out of the shower, take her to my bed, and then make love to her all night. I want to grow old with her.

"They adopted these boys 'cause she couldn't get pregnant," I say. I kneel beside her, a moment of weakness swamping me.

Maybe I'm making too much of everything. *This could be us.* We could be together like I've always wanted. Ruby could be my wife, my kids' mother. There's nothing Rifle wants more than a brother or a sister, which I've been telling him for years isn't likely. But it could be. *We* could happen. Could the ball be in my court after all? Maybe I do hold the key. Damn that long-standing, rusty lock. Damn my pride.

One of the boys craps himself as I'm fantasizing.

"Barn burner," I say.

We chuckle, and Ruby claps her hands.

"Smells like one." She snickers and reaches for a diaper bag. "I hope Tommy left me some diapers."

"You ever changed a baby?" I smirk.

"Nope." She yanks a diaper and a container of wipes from the bag. "But I'm sure it's not *that* hard."

"Well, good. Have at it, girl."

A wet cast on one arm, and her trigger fingers on the other hand. If only I had chopsticks to hand her.

"See if there's a changing pad in there," I tell her. "It can get messy." *And I am going to take pleasure in watching you navigate.*

"Right."

She dives in like a pro. Lays the kid on his back, hands him a toy from the diaper bag, and strips his pants off. *I wish it were me.* Then comes the diaper. I cross my fingers, hopeful it's a shit-up-the-back crap. Oh, and it is. It's beautiful, and right now, I am loving my life.

"Is this normal? Oh my God."

"There's no normal with shit." I wink. "Just happens. You know, sort of like between us. Sometimes crap flies and stinks and is messy as fuck to clean up."

Ruby glares at me. "I love how you're comparing a poopie diaper to us."

"It's a metaphor." I stand, glancing at my watch. "Gotta get going."

"You're leaving me with this?" The shocked, slack-jawed expression on her face makes me laugh damn hard.

"Told my girl I'd get her early," I lie.

"Your stripper friend?"

"Acrobat. Lady on the street, whore in the bedroom—every man's fantasy." I grin and lick my lips.

"Great. Yes, go get your girl and leave me with the crap."

"You'll be fine. You've been slinging shit for a while now. 'Bout time you clean it up."

She looks at the kid, then her shit-covered hands, then me. How a woman can look gorgeous while doing what she's doing is fucked up. But Ruby Mae wins.

"You're relentless," she says.

"Just calling it like I see it."

After opening the wipes, she starts mopping the kid's belly and legs. There might be more crap on her cast than on the kid at this point.

I kneel beside her. "Move over. All you're doing is dragging crap around this poor kid's body."

"Good idea. Show me how a real man cleans up shit." Ruby shifts away from me.

"I've been trying to do that."

"Be careful, Rebel."

"I'm just sayin', some shit is more slippery than others."

When I arrive home, I find my sister, Storm's, truck parked in the driveway. Tied to the front porch is Bubble's pink-maned pony.

We're starting to see Bubble about every day now. Good damn thing I grabbed a box of condoms for these kids.

Around the kitchen table sits my crew, a mean game of Scrabble in the middle. Gilbert's flopped on the floor next to Storm, looking as uncomfortable as a stuck pig.

"Who's winning?" I ask, tossing the box of condoms to Rifle.

He catches them in midair and grins. "Thanks, Dad. I'm winning."

"Are those? Wait… He's…" Storm's eyes widen when the realization of what I threw him hits her.

"You didn't tell your only aunt?" I ask.

"Rifle!" Storm slugs Rifle in the arm.

"Dad." Rifle shrugs, rolling his eyes. "Give it a rest."

"Relax. You can take a little ribbing, can't you? Speaking of, I didn't buy the ribbed ones and I guessed on size. Bought large… That about right?"

Storm snorts out a laugh and grabs the box from Rifle's grip to examine it.

"Probably nailed it," Etta says. She lifts her glass of sherry and winks at Rifle. "Don was large before I flipped him inside out to make Donatella."

"Don was Rocket's dick before he became Etta. Welcome to my family," Rifle says, slinging an arm over Bubble's shoulder when she cracks up.

"I live in a circus. Not much fazes me," Bubble says. "I mean, come on. An elephant lives in my home."

"An elephant?" Storm pushes the condoms toward Rifle.

"Yes, Queenie. She's pretty much my sister."

"Hot damn. My nephew made his manly debut with a girl who lives in a circus. Well, that's cool. Mine wasn't quite so illustrious."

"Hate to break it to you, Storm, but uh, it's been a while now since my debut," Rifle says.

I clear my throat, press my knuckles onto the kitchen table, then lean toward my cocky son. "This I didn't know. A while?"

"Hey, if we're all okay with the informality, then yeah. Last year." Rifle waggles his eyebrows. Little shit.

"The fuck am I buying condoms for? You drive. Get some next time you're in town."

"I have some." He shoots me a cocky smirk.

"But you weren't using one yesterday?"

"It's better bare."

"Are we really doing this?" Storm asks, pushing back from the table. "I mean, if we are, I agree bare is better, but wow. This is pretty out there as far as family sharing goes. Rebel, are you going to put your two cents in now that Ruby's home?"

Silence hangs in the air as I look around at my family. "I have no fucking idea what sex is like with Ruby. Never had it."

I stomp up the stairs with Gilbert following. How have I never had sex with Ruby? Christ, I'm a grown man in love with his high school girlfriend. In fucking love. How can a man marry another woman, have a child with her, bury her, and still be in love with his *old* flame, who he never slept with? What is it with us? Something massive, complicated, and boundless. Love?

I remember the day I fell hard and never recovered. She was it from that day forward.

The second she walked into shop class, my dick twitched and my heart jumped. Lanky with smallish curves and strong, wide shoulders like a swimmer, the girl moved like a petal floating through a breeze. Her emerald eyes pierced mine when she sat at the only vacant desk in front of the room. Not one boy was looking at anything but her high tight ass in those painted-on jeans.

"Brave," I said as she slinked into her chair.

"You going to give me shit because I'm the only girl in here?"

"Shit is the last thing I'd like to give you."

"Funny." She reached into her leather backpack and produced a box of Red Hots seconds later. After shaking a few into her palm, she dumped a few onto my open palm.

"I meant impressive. Girls don't take shop. I know 'cause my dad is the teacher."

Her eyebrows rose as she licked one of the Red Hots pinched between her fingers. And I licked mine like I wanted to lick her pert nipples, which were pressing against her see-through baby-blue top.

"Your dad is Mr. Field?"

"Yeah. You from Saint Teresa?"

"Yeah." She popped the Red Hot in her mouth, licked her fingers, then thrust her hand toward me. "Ruby Mae Rose."

"Rebel Field." I held her hand a little longer than seemed right.

"I know who you are."

"That bad, eh?"

She cleared her throat three times. Then once more. "Bad can be good."

Christ, did we have our fun in high school, but damn, that girl held out. I was sure her "bad could be good" comment was going to get me somewhere with her.

Well, it did. Heartbroken.

Yet here I sit, almost two decades later, wondering what bare would be like with Ruby Mae Rose.

Chapter 20

Tincat

Ruby

Rowdy picks me up at seven on the dot. Freshly cast wrist, sundress and heels on, my hair down my back—like Rebel loves it. I'm jumping into a pickup with my first boyfriend. Pre-Rebel.

Rowdy and I dated as freshmen when I transferred from Saint Teresa. Rowdy was a good starter. Rebel though—he was a smorgasbord. He made my butterflies hump butterflies. He wore cool and daring like most boys wear insecurity and ambiguity. With Rebel, it was never what or why or when. It was now, it was his way, it was…perfect.

"I won't touch you, Ruby Mae," Rowdy says as we stroll into the Tincat. We bagged out on the picnic because I didn't get home until six.

"Just play along." I swat him on the ass. "You can flirt with me. And you can dance with me. Let's just make him jealous."

I don't want to be mean; I just want Rebel to wake up.

I wish I weren't searching the noisy, jam-packed bar for Rebel like my life depended on it, but I am. And I'm already envious of this acrobat who'll be flirting with him all night. He's going to put on a prize performance and I'm dreading it. Even if it is fake.

What was I thinking, telling him I lost the ring? Even though, technically, I did. I went back for it later that night. I don't know how in my state of distress. I had to find the ring. But it was nowhere. The ring, the crosses, and the necklace were all gone.

I scope the scene out while Rowdy orders beer for us. One of the hunky British guys waves me over to their table.

"Tully?" I say.

Theophile Charlotte was a sophomore when I was a senior. We ran track together, so I knew her a little from that—until she was sent to juvie for pushing her mother down a staircase. I had no idea she was out of jail. God, I've missed a lifetime.

"I heard you came home!" Tully says. "Wow, you look as pretty in person as you do on those magazine covers. You really made it big!"

I stare at the hunk of beast next to her. "Is he your…"

"My husband." She grins. "Wolfgang Valentine."

"Yes, we met at the feed mill this morning." I gaze at her belly when she comes around the table. "And you're pregnant? Wow! Congrats, you guys!"

Tully and I embrace in a long hug. Her full stomach presses to my flat one. What would it be like to carry Rebel's baby? I'll never know.

"Where's Rebel?" Tully asks, looking around the bar.

"He'll be here." A shot of nervous energy shoots through my stomach. "Long story. I won't bore you with the details. Rowdy's just playing along as my date."

"You don't have to tell me. I get it." She waves her hand. Do you remember Matilda Pearl? She summered here." She gestures across the table.

"Hey, yeah. Of course, I do." I lean over the width of the table when Matilda does and kiss her cheek. "How are you?"

"I'm great!" Matilda answers.

The other massive Brit throws an arm over her shoulder when she sits. I ogle him for longer than I should, but shit. He's hot as hell.

"He's yours?" I nod to Balthazar.

She smiles and nestles into the crook of his arm.

"Wow. You girls scored some hunks."

"You guys are joining us. Sit," Balthazar commands.

I obey like I'm his dog, slumping into a chair across from Matilda. No woman would tell this man no.

"I'm going to warn you guys," I tell the group. "I told Rowdy to really lay on the flirting, so don't mind us tonight. It might get a little silly. I need Rebel to pay attention."

"Don't worry. I already live in a circus," Tully says, giggling as she waddles to the other side of the table and plunks into her chair.

Rowdy saunters to the table with our beer and sits to my right. Perfect—Rebel can sit to my left.

"You do know Rebel is coming with Verushka?" he whispers at my ear. "Don't shoot the messenger."

"Verushka? The circus acrobat who can do the splits while they fuck? Yeah, he's filled me in. And, apparently, her."

Beer shoots out of Matilda's mouth when she laughs. "He hasn't fucked her. They just met today. What a shitbag. Did he tell you that?"

I draw a long guzzle of beer from my bottle. Liquid courage. "Oh, he's been laying it on thick. And I've been playing along. It's like we're high school kids, but less mature."

"This might be better entertainment than the band," Tully says, winking at me.

"I'm just hoping for progress," I say, raising my beer. "I'd be happy if drama didn't join us."

I don't have to turn to know Rebel is walking toward our table. I could feel Rebel in a room if I lost every sense. Because the day we began dating in high school, something happened to my heart. He caused a fissure in it that will not ever heal. My heart and his have a cosmic connection I can't comprehend.

Every smirk on every face around the table says game on. I swallow hard, my pulse racing as I swig the second half of my beer. One down. One Rebel to go.

"Hey," he says at my neck, hot breath making my hair stand on end when he sits next to me.

Great. I'm nervous and turned on and we've yet to make eye contact.

"Hey." My voice shakes.

He looks good. That scar adds the right amount of wrong to his rough, handsome face. *You're welcome.*

He eyes my empty beer then draws a sip from his bottle. My gaze stays glued to his sexy lips. He winks at me, catching me midstare. My gaze drifts to his taut, black T-shirt, which is riding the hard edges of his beautiful veined arms. *Look away.*

Then in comes the bait. A goddess. He threads his fingers with hers like it's a habit, and my stomach sinks along with my heart. My tongue, suddenly coated in cotton, sticks to the roof of my mouth. I don't care if this is fake; it feels real to me.

"Verushka, this is a pal of mine, Ruby."

A pal? A fucking pal? Like a pail of shit is how that label makes me feel.

Verusssshhhhka straddles him after shaking my hand. Now, I need a pail to barf in. Of course she's a doll and gorgeous and all fucking over him. This was my stupid idea to come here in the first place and I'm the one suffering. He doesn't look tormented. No, and why would he be? Verushka is riding his lap like he's stuffing her bra with fifty-dollar bills.

And shit, it's doing a job on me. My inner sassy girl fails me just when I need her most, and a little troublesome pain wrestles its way through my chest, settling in my tear ducts. God, no. The sting. *Don't cry.* But I can't help it when a few tears roll down my cheeks. Because, as Mom would say, Rebel looks happier than a tornado in a trailer park.

Chapter 21

Sweet Thing

Rebel

I gave Verushka the lowdown on me and Ruby and how I need to get her good tonight. So good that she'll open up to me so we can move the fuck on from this child's play. I'm going to be blue-balled soon if things don't move forward between us, because there is nothing I want more than Ruby in my arms. In my bed. Bare naked.

Ruby's irrefutably agitated by Verushka's devotion. Part of me feels bad that Ruby seems troubled. Part of me is thrilled because this might do the trick. Something is gonna give soon.

When a new song plays, I want to high-five the DJ who's operating the pre-band music. It's not just any song; it's one of our songs. Mine and Ruby's. Chaka Khan's "Sweet Thing." I forever called Ruby my sweet thing. I haven't once since she's been home. Haven't been able to look into the depths of her emerald eyes and say those words. Maybe I will later tonight if the trail of crumbs I'm laying is tempting enough.

It takes every ounce of my vigor to invite Verushka to the dance floor instead of Ruby. I can't even look at her when I stand. Ruby and I can dance. Did way back, anyway. We always loved dancing. It was one of our things. Even the day we said goodbye in a pool of tears and grief, I hugged her and we slow-danced to my humming.

This might hurt her or convince her. It's a risk I'm willing to take, and I'm hopeful it's the latter.

Verushka slides up and down my body, her limber, cat-like frame undulating with mine. "How are we doing?" she asks. "You think she believes us?"

"I can't look at her. It'll kill me." I press my forehead to hers like we're lovers. "Just keep going. You're doing great."

We continue to dance, the area around us populating. Every second feels like an hour. Any other night, I'd be thrilled. But tonight, the only girl my heart pounds for is my sweet thing.

Halfway through the song, Rowdy strolls toward us, Ruby in tow. I bury my face in my date's hair, wishing it were Ruby's golden locks.

Ruby and I exchange glances when she wraps her arms around Rowdy's neck. There's a spark in her eyes that says war, and fuck if I'm not up for it. But, when she rises to her toes and starts kissing Rowdy like she means it, war becomes child's play and goes in for the kill.

"Excuse me, Verushka." I wrap my hand around Ruby's bicep and drag her off Rowdy's mouth like he's the deadliest sin. "Ruby fucking Mae, I swear to God."

We snake our way through the crowd, as I tug her to the back of the bar then out the screen door. She says nothing the whole time, but she's not fighting me, either.

Outside, my face one inch from hers, I back her against the wall. "You're mine. Enough already. You're fucking mine. If you don't produce that ring in the next ten seconds or something more than a lie about where it went, I will strip you bare naked and find it myself."

A whack of her hand lands on my face.

She has the nerve to slap me? Not just a slap: a slug-slap. Then she does it again. I pin her arms beside her head, growling at her like the furious bear in me has wanted to all day. The other thing I've wanted all day happens next, and it's not gentle. It's a force so intense wrapped in the kiss I've been holding out on that it makes kissing seem juvenile.

Everything I am travels into our kiss, every tingling nerve stirred. And, by her finger-grabbing, hip-thrusting response, I think she's having the same sensations. Our moans collide, creating a composition so sexy that I haul her onto my body, her legs wrapping around me in answer. I can't get deep enough into her mouth, can't get close enough to her core. I need more. I need all of her.

God, I'm spinning. I lay her on the picnic table. Her long, blond locks fan like a halo around her head. Her arms go around me, her fingers digging for purchase. I close my eyes in appreciation.

When she gasps as my hands explore her curves, I open my eyes and see tears flowing down her temples.

"Baby?" I thread my fingers through her hair and thumb her tears away. "Don't cry, sweet thing."

"I can't give you what you want." Ruby wheezes for air, her sad eyes causing mine to water. "And all I want is you."

I press my cheek to hers. "You don't understand. You're all I want too. We lost a few years, but here we are. We have everything in front of us. Just talk to me."

Ruby presses her hands against my chest and pushes me back. Her eyes dart with worry when she softly says, "I'm about to tell you something you're not going to want to hear."

My pulse jumps. She's finally going to do it. Either we've arrived or, based on her petrified gaze, we are about to unravel.

She drops back, and I place my hands on either side of her head and lean over her body, dropping a gentle kiss on her furrowed brow.

"I want to hear everything," I tell her. "I'm trying so hard to get back to you. Tell me how to do that? I want in, Ruby… I want inside every pore. I want every nighttime whisper to begin or end with my name. I need you, sweet thing. Tell me what you need from me to get us moving forward as one. I want to know what you're keeping from me."

Ruby pins her eyes shut then bursts out crying, but still, she manages to spit out a string of words that knock me on my ass. "I lost more than the ring graduation night. I lost my virginity."

Chapter 22

What You Wanted

Ruby

What would happen if I told him the truth about graduation night? I've toyed with it, talked myself through it more than once. But the obstacles are too much for me to navigate.

Rebel came to my house later that night after Opal had died. He was the only person I called. He held me in his arms when Opal was zipped into a black bag and rolled out our front door. Echo tried to climb onto the gurney, not understanding where his twin was going.

Do I tell Rebel I was the reason she died? I would have died had they touched her. It was bad enough they slit the flap of skin under her tongue, which made her already-difficult-to-understand speaking style nearly impossible to decipher. Then they slit her tongue down the middle when she spat blood in their faces.

Do I tell him everything was stolen that night? My sanity. Virginity. Sister. Faith. Confidence. Boyfriend. Promise ring. And future.

I can't. I simply cannot. Because, if I tell him what happened to me, it'll ruin his life in more ways than one. How will he walk into his hardware store knowing the money that bought it came from the boys who raped me? How will he continue to live on his farm knowing that those trusts funded it too? How will he look at Etta knowing that her operation was feasible because of those sick fucks?

Rebel shoves backward and stands. His mouth twists into a polluted scowl, an angry hand shoved through his hair disturbing his already messy locks. One fist at his mouth, a feral groan forcing its way up his throat, he spins in a circle.

Veins bulge on his forehead and his neck, his jaw sewn shut. Ice-glazed eyes pierce mine.

"Who?"

"No." My shaky voice matches my hands.

What have I done? I let my emotions go, and now, this? Rebel might skin me alive by the way he's baring his teeth. I'm done talking.

"That's all I'm giving you," I tell him. "Nothing else. This is what you wanted."

I've given him something and it's not enough. It's a fraction of the truth, which he's going to twist into an ugly fate that will end us. What's worse? The end of us...or the end of him? I'll take the fall. The guilt would kill him. Will I ever stop being a martyr?

"Who the fuck was it? Who, Ruby?" Rebel punches through a plastic soda sign leaning against the wall.

"Rebel, I'm putting my heart on the line by giving you that piece. If I say another thing, it'll destroy your life. Please stop. I'm begging you. I can't take anything else away from you. I love you that much."

"Love me? You were going to let me take your virginity. We were going to do it that night. And, like some fucking whore, you gave it to someone else while you were wearing my promise ring around your neck? Did it rest over your heart when he popped your cherry, sweet thing? Did he yank it off your neck when he spilled his seed in you? Is that how you lost my ring?" He gently pins me to the picnic bench, pressing me backward, then leans over my body. "Tell me."

I wish it weren't a growl coming from him, but it is.

"I was with you most of high school. We were not just *some* couple." Rebel covers his face with one hand, and I'm certain I hear the rip of his heart shredding. "We were everything," he says softly.

His pained, water-filled eyes and furled brow panic me. Where do I go with this now? How do I undo what I've done?

Rebel quiets for long minutes as he paces in circles, while I schlep through the hell in my mind to come up with something to pacify him. But nothing, not one idea, feels right. How do you mend a hole with edges that are so frayed you can't find the threads to snug them together? How do you put a love that's missed years of knowing looks and trust and layers of lost time back together? A love that was meant to blossom but instead was plucked apart one delicate petal at a time. A love that feels like a held breath you're finally releasing as you ready for the next beautiful taste of life and all of its unpolluted air.

"I waited years for you to come to me," he says. "You should have told me this…told me back then. Why would you punish me? What did I ever do to deserve this?" He stifles what might have been a tormented cry. "How did I not know this is who you were? I knew you… I thought I fucking knew you."

My sadness flips inside out, anger flooding me. "You've been asking me for something and I've given you a piece you don't like.

Don't ask for more. It only gets worse. You can't even handle this. You think I want to hurt you more?"

Rebel stomps away, swinging his muscular limbs, punching the air. I hug my legs, deciding if I should stay and watch him implode or leave him be to calm down.

"What happened to Opal?" he shouts, his red face and his brutish tone another attack on my delicate self-worth. After slogging toward me he plants his fists on either side of me and positions his sweat-beaded face inches from mine. "I can see it on your face. Guilt. She knew I loved you, and I'll bet she walked in on you fucking that guy. Is that why you won't tell me who? Because you destroyed her too?" He groans out a pained sound as he stares at the sky. The veins in his neck fill with blood and hate as they bulge. "Is it Rowdy? Tell me!"

What is it that makes us want the ugliest truths? Why do we stop and gawk at accidents? What is the irrational thing inside us that craves the sins of others laid bare? Every promise I made to myself about finding him again evaporates with every second as time stands still.

I made it through all these years by telling myself I'd find him someday. I lied to myself that he'd be single. Convinced myself, no matter what life he was living, that he'd take me back. What a selfish thing to do to one's own heart. Feed it with things it will never be able to live on. Was it preservation or greed? Maybe they're borne of the same need.

I shouldn't have come. Shouldn't have dreamt about us. Because the nightmare unfolding in broad daylight between me and the love of my life is a toxic punch I may never recover from.

"No, wait. Oh my fucking God." He slams a hand on his forehead. "It was one of the Kline boys, wasn't it? You finally let 'em have it. Which one?" He laughs out a sinister sound. It's a train wreck colliding with hope. It's a future of two lovers that will never fulfill their fates. "Kent?" he asks.

My insides burn with shame.

Goodbye, soul.

"Yeah, I'll bet it was Kent." Rebel glares at me with something I've never seen in a man's gaze besides the Kline boys.

It's disgust. And it sinks me to my core. Sinks me and returns me to that night. But the martyr in me knew that it would come to this if he pushed too far for answers. I wonder if he feels anything for me beyond hate. Is he already missing the morning kisses he'll never give me? Or the whispers in the dark I'll never hear?

He sneers when I choke out a sob. Because he thinks he's uncovered the *real* me. We think we know people. We don't. You don't. You never will because everyone buries parts of themselves. No one wants to be as raw as the first flesh they're born with.

And, once again, I play the martyr. I'm good at this. I'm willing to take a blow for him. For love. I'm willing to let him think he knows who I am—though it chips away at my hard-built exterior—so he can keep his farm, his hardware store, and his humility. Why?

Because, once you've lost as much as I have and you're still thriving, you find your strength and take on more for those you love so they don't have to suffer.

But, still, I'm numb. Not everywhere, just where it hurts the most: my heart.

Rebel traces my hairline with his fingertips then rubs them across my trembling lips. "His mouth never stopped watering over you. The one time I wasn't there to stand between you and him…you opened your legs like the little slut he'd been praying you were all along."

I don't want to hate him. I only want to love him. But his words—Jesus, they cut me. Almost more than the physical pain I'm on the other side of.

He claps his hands when I bow my head in repulsion and loss. Honesty wants to surface, but if it does, we'll both drown in its stink.

"Congratulations, Ruby. You now hold a few records in our town. Track star. Supermodel. Bitch extraordinaire."

Chapter 23

You & Me

Rebel

Her eyes might say she's livid, but her soul is filled with sin. Of all the shit I thought she might have stored away, this was not a possibility I considered.

"Don't ever come near me or my family again. Don't come into my hardware store or on my road or on my end of the lake. You hear me?"

"Rebel, please, don't do this." Ruby reaches out to my hand as I back away. "Don't bulldoze what we have."

"What we have?" I laugh and laugh. She's lost her shit now. Certifiable. "The fuck are you saying? We have nothing. Sounds like we never had anything. Did you consider that for one second when you let him bone you?"

I should stop talking and go home. I have nothing left here to dissect. She's laid out something so vile and confusing that I'm not sure what to make of her or the fantasy I foolishly turned us into.

"You need to stop," Ruby says between sobbing pants.

I shouldn't feel pangs of worry. I shouldn't feel anything but numb.

"You're talking out of your ass," she says, "saying things you can't take back. Calling me names no one should be called. Especially not your girl."

I take two steps toward her, closing the empty space between us. A space I called sacred minutes ago. "Let me tell you something 'bout my girl. She's buried at the cemetery. Her name was Paris Louise Long. She had more respect for me in her sparkling eyes and loving heart than you could in ten lives of your corrupt soul."

Ruby storms past me and into the bar. The screen door screeches then slams shut with a howl. I follow, not giving two fucks that she's crying over her boo-hoo lost virginity. No wonder she couldn't tell me about the ring. Of course she couldn't wear it if he fucked her while she had it on. Lost it, my ass. The only thing she lost was her virginity. And me.

"You feeling like getting out of here, baby?" I ask Verushka so loud that I know Ruby hears it while whispering to Rowdy.

"Anytime you're ready," Verushka says, winking.

"I was ready for you hours ago, gorgeous." I loop her arm in mine, giving a nod to the fellas as I turn to leave.

Ruby spins to face me then grabs a fistful of my T-shirt in the fingertips of her cast hand as she gets up in my face. "You're going to regret this," she says.

Her sneer is so sincere that I nearly believe her. But I can't trust a fucking thread of her shit now.

"I'll give you one chance to tell me you're sorry," she says, "but that's it. I put myself out there and you turned me into the devil. I didn't have to tell you shit. But you pushed and pushed, so I gave in, knowing it was a risk for my heart and yours."

But what she gave me was my new hell. Why would she do that to someone she loves? Why didn't she lie to me? I pushed—that's why. We want the truth, or so we think… Then we scorn it once it's delivered and has ruined what we have because of our selfish needs. All of us beg for the truth, thinking it'll save us…

We're idiots. The truth can answer, yes, but it can also destroy. It can ruin years of love. But is the truth worth it?

"The only regret I have is all those wasted years I could have been fucking the cheerleading squad in high school while I blue-balled it waiting for you."

She slugs me across the face with her cast. "Fuck you, Rebel!"

"No, that would be the guy who popped your cherry." Blood rivering down the side of my face tickles. "The only thing you get to call me is ex."

I scoop my date's arm in mine and take three steps from the table. Ruby screams so loud that the entire bar goes pin-drop silent save the song playing. "You and Me" by Lifehouse. The first song I learned to play on my guitar because it was Ruby's favorite.

"You're right, Rebel." She saunters toward me, light streaking down her face like moonbeams along with glistening tears. "It was a Kline boy. Not just one. Both. And, yes, Opal was there—saw the whole thing. Feel better now that you know all my dirty secrets? You fucking fuck!"

Yeah. I feel good. Good and ready to vomit. But why does she look forlorn? Why is her face saying she lost when, in truth, I did?

Why does it feel like she just delivered part of a nightmare versus a victory? What the hell am I missing in this mess?

I don't know, but my anger still owns my tongue and speaks on its own volition. "I will when your slutty ass leaves my town."

It's immoral enough that she gave it away. But, of all the guys to give it to, the motherfucking Kline twins? Fuck them and her. I'd strangle 'em if they were alive. My bare hands would squeeze the life out of their smart-mouthed, rich, preppy, piece-of-shit-football-playing asses.

Their deaths were ruled a murder-suicide. Their guns were the same ones they used when they went deer hunting. The boys were hotheads who fought plenty over girls, sports, cars, titles. But murder? Now, though, thanks to Ruby, it makes some sense. One of them must have had Ruby and the other must have found out, gotten jealous, and gone after her for the same. Then some kind of fight over her ensued and boom, two shots.

I storm out of the bar, not another look back at Ruby or my past. After dropping Verushka off at the Valentine castle, and thanking her for playing along with my senseless charade, I head home.

Etta and I sit at the kitchen table while she plays Solitaire and I read the *New Yorker*, stewing over Ruby, a beer in my hand, a thimble-sized glass of sherry in hers.

I would have been there to stop her from making the biggest mistake of her life had I not been with Dad the night of graduation.

He'd told me earlier in the day that he was getting extra gussied up for the graduation party at the Klines', where Mom was already helping set up.

I figured I'd do the same for once—dress up—even though going to the Klines' was the last thing I wanted to do. Unable to find my tie, I went to borrow one from Dad. After a knock, and with an innocent turn of the knob, I opened his bedroom door and discovered the other life my father was living and hiding behind.

If only I had known what running away from him, would end up meaning for my future.

Chapter 24

Martyr

Ruby

"Ruby?" Hazel clutches my arm as I track toward the back door to escape the bar. "What the hell was that?" she asks, her eyes wild and filled with wonder.

"I've got to get out of here. Want to join me for a drink?" I steady myself on a nearby table, the throttle on my nerves wrecked.

"I was meeting some of the hospital staff. Let me text one of the girls and we'll go somewhere. You look like hell."

After Hazel shoots off a text, she dabs my eyes with her sleeve and motions me down the alley. We walk two doors down and arrive at a little hole-in-the-wall bar.

"I think I walked in on the tail end of something," Hazel says.

What have I done? It's like I fell through a hole and guilt went on autopilot, steering my tongue while blocking my brain. This is how people ruin relationships. They say things with no thought or consequence. Spitting out half-truths, a trail of mystery with scattered clues.

"Let's hope it's not the end," I say, my hands shaking so vigorously that I tuck them under my armpits to still them.

"You hated the Kline boys," she says.

"Still do."

We order beer then settle in a dark corner.

"Why did you sleep with them? You guys could barely have a civil conversation."

I draw a long swallow from my bottle. "It wasn't intentional."

She pats my hand, her forehead creasing with worry. "Sex doesn't happen any other way, honey."

"Aww, Hazel. No one knows what I'm going to tell you. And no one has ever been a better secret keeper than you." I start crying. A few small tears at first. Then I really let it go. "How do I tell you what they did?" The lump in my throat thickens.

"Oh, Jesus." Hazel's eyes fill with tears. "No."

I cover my face, humiliation creeping up my skin like a poisonous rash. "It was me or Opal."

"Why didn't you tell anyone?"

"It was such a shitstorm. My family could have lost everything if I outed the boys. Mr. Kline had just given my folks a new mortgage even though they were dead broke and Dad wasn't working. Opal had killed herself. I was a wreck…almost took my own life. Everything felt like my fault. I needed to run away. From…life."

Hazel threads her fingers with mine and squeezes. "How… I mean, when did it happen?"

"Graduation night. Rebel was supposed to come and join us behind the bleachers where Opal and I ran the stairs… He never showed."

"But they did?" she whispers. "Oh, honey."

Hazel hugs me, and the realization of what I've shared hits me with a tidal wave force. She's the first and only person. It's freeing and terrifying. What if she slips up and tells Rebel?

"Haz...Rebel cannot know. For lots of reasons, please not a whisper to anyone."

"Of course. I am so sorry and in shock and...I can't believe I'm asking this..." Hazel's eyes widen, and she shakes her head.

"What?" I ask.

"Never mind. I'm an idiot." Her face reddens.

"Did I have anything to do with their deaths? No. But I wish I had. If I could go back, I would." A few people from Tincat saunter into the bar and I slouch in my chair to hide.

"Do you think it was a murder-suicide? Everyone in town questioned it."

"I have no idea. But there are weird things I don't have answers for. Rebel gave me a promise ring on a necklace the morning of graduation." I toy with the salt shaker on the table, twisting the top off and on.

"I promised him my virginity." I choke the words out. "They put their crosses on that chain along with my ring, tied it around my neck...and then they..."

Hazel nods, her hands cupping my face, both of us wet-cheeked. "Holy fuck. I was out of town when all that crazy went down, and then you'd disappeared by the time I came home."

"The necklace and the ring and crosses... I yanked them off afterward. Then went back later to find them and they were gone."

"Anyone who walked back there could have grabbed them."

"Sure. And then sent them to my modeling agency seventeen years later?" I gulp a swallow of beer, tears falling again. My thoughts scatter in accord. Where is Rebel now? What's going through his head? Will he ever forgive me? Would I forgive him if it were the other way around? He'd have to have a damn good excuse. One as massive as mine.

"Is that who you think murdered them? The person who sent them to you?"

"I have no idea. But it gets worse. You know Dick Kline is Rebel's godfather. He assigned the boys' fat trusts to Rebel, who then opened his hardware store, bought a massive farm on the lake, and paid for Rocket to become Etta. Can you imagine what he would do if he knew the truth about that night?"

"What a twisted mess." Hazel dabs my eyes with a balled-up Kleenex she dug out of her purse.

"So, do I tell him?" I ask.

Hazel dips her face onto her palms and groans. "I honestly don't know."

"Now, he just thinks I'm a slut." I swallow hard. "Nice feeling."

"That's disgusting." She smacks the table with both hands, startling me to a jump. "He needs to know. What's the worst thing that could happen if you tell him?"

"He'll feel more guilt and pain than I do. He never showed up for our run, never told me why. He knows what all that money bought and provided. I'll be a symbol of guilt to him, and not only will he lose faith in himself and carry the guilt I've been burdened with all these years…he may walk away. From everything. Me included. He may run like I did. He doesn't do guilt very well."

Rebel would blame himself for not showing up. I decided that it was my burden to carry. Mostly because of the fear of God they put in me when they slit Opal's tongue so she wouldn't talk and I wouldn't, either. They said that, if I reported them, they'd come for her. And, after what they had done to me, I believed them.

That night, when Opal and I arrived home after the incident, our house was empty. She ran to the bathroom, crying, and I went to my bedroom and locked my door. I should have been there more for her, but I was in a cyclone of hell. Shock. A whirling shitstorm of confusion, anger, and pain.

On my bed was an envelope containing a modeling contract. Another one. It was the third I'd received. And, for the first time, I considered the idea. Maybe going to Northwestern, where the Kline boys were set to go, was a bad idea. Maybe I'd be better off leaving this country. I could live abroad, forget everything, and then eventually come back to Rebel.

But, in my distress, something greater than I could control took me over. I needed to leave my body, not just leave the country.

I was that close. Desperate…like a junkie on her last fix to freedom. I was freaked on adrenaline and shock. A drunken mix of temporary insanity. I wanted to die. It was the only route I could come up with to stop the pain. The one way I was going to get the Klines out of me. Death. I went to the bathroom for blades, itching to scrape those creeps out of my soul, but what I found drained more from me than a million gutted souls combined.

Opal had beaten me to it.

My sweet, innocent baby girl. Opal. Her pale skin and her white hair danced in the tub, forming an anemone circle around her blue-gone-gray eyes. The toaster was in there too, a deadly fixture, its gleaming surface presenting a reflection of her small, porcelain breasts.

She must have seen it on TV, the idea of killing oneself this way, then copied it. She did that with everything; it was how she learned. It wouldn't have worked in any other house per Mom's brother, who's an electrician two towns over. Our house was dust old, wind weeping through cracks, cheaply built, and as far as electrical went, well, let's just say it went with the flow right through Opal's veins.

She's gone. But is Rebel? Have I lost him for good?

Chapter 25

Lie Worth Living

Rebel

Etta pats my hand. "You haven't said much tonight. You okay?"

"Just working through stuff." I huff out a frustrated breath.

I don't really know what to do now. How can you hate and love someone? How can you want to push someone away as much as you want to pull them in?

"Ruby stuff?" she asks.

I fold the magazine into thirds and swat a fly. Then I flick it off the table. "Yeah."

"Did you see her tonight?"

"I saw her, all right. Saw and heard things I wish I hadn't."

Etta gathers her playing cards, shuffles them, and then lays another hand. "You saw that with me once too, and you found a way to forgive me and love me for the other person I was."

"You're a good person. It wasn't that hard."

"So is Ruby."

"That is going to take a lot of convincing."

Etta reaches for her sherry. "And why's that?"

"She told me she fucked the Kline boys on graduation night. I never told you this, but she was going to be mine that night. Then I found you in the bedroom in your lingerie and I freaked out and ran."

Etta shifts in her chair, crossing her legs. A few seconds later, she reaches her hand out to mine and we lock eyes. Hers are filled with layers of fear.

"Because the idea of who I was terrified you?"

"Well…yeah. But it was temporary." I squeeze her hand. I don't ever want her to think anything other than how proud I am of her and how much I love her.

"Of course," she says, her gaze dropping from mine.

"Were you going somewhere?" I'm not sure why I never asked this question before. Maybe it felt too intrusive.

She pulls her hand away, tapping her red nails on the edge of the table. She quietly offers, "I was meeting someone."

"Who?"

She pours another splash of sherry into her crystal glass then takes a few sips, her hand shaking.

"You don't need to answer that," I say when she rests her elbows on the table and buries her face in her palms.

"Dick Kline."

"What?" I work to close my mouth, though it's a struggle. "Jesus Christ. You were meeting him and she was fucking them? What the hell?" I thrust my hands through my hair. "Can you shed more light on…you and Dick?"

"We're complicated."

"No shit. That why he and his wife split?"

"Dick and Shirley had an arrangement, though she doesn't know the whole truth. It wasn't exactly a typical affair." Etta motions her hands in the air.

"Got it. You know what's fucked up? I was supposed to meet Ruby and Opal behind the school to run the stairs that night. I never made it because I was running the other way. I'm guessing that's why she decided to give it up to them. I'm late one fucking time and I get punished. The fuck does that say about what we had?"

"Rebel…it's easy to assume things about people. Try not to." Etta fidgets with her necklace as I gather my irrational thoughts.

I want to ask more, but the distressed look on her face stops me. Damn the fucking Klines.

"You've always said that, and I try not to assume, but come on."

"Maybe you don't know the whole story…about anyone."

"Maybe I don't give a shit."

"But you do. You always have. That's why you're okay with who I am. And that's why she's come back." She places her hands on the table, palms up, and I place my hands on hers. "You love her?"

"Hate her right now."

"You hated me for a long time too. You hated who I needed to be. But, inside, you knew better."

Lifting my hands from hers, I grab the bottle and guzzle half of my beer, remembering the hell our family went through when Rocket decided to become Etta. Why? Mostly our inability to accept who she was. We were idiots, me and my mom. We thought her change would make everyone think odd of us. What was it our business to judge her truths? And why the fuck am I judging Ruby? It's like I can't put this thing together in my brain. I know what forgiveness is. So why can't I give it to the woman I love the most?

"I did," I finally say. "It was a tough thing to accept."

"I know you know this, but I was going to take my life if I couldn't be me. Because it wasn't worth living a lie like that."

I nod, and we lock eyes. My heart sinks at her words and the idea that her need was that intense.

"What stopped you?" I ask.

"After you took off, I did too. Dick and I were together...and a series of events occurred that stopped me. Things I can't share."

Gilbert scratches the door. I saunter to the screen and push it open for her. When the door slams, I brace myself on the jamb, watching moths circle the porch light. Dick and my father—who was dressed as a woman—were together? This is a new twist.

I glance over my shoulder. "I respect that." I'm such a hypocrite. I respect Etta for her silence, but not Ruby? Why?

Etta scoots her chair back and comes to my side. Worry marks her forehead when she encloses my jaw in her hands. "Try to see her and consider that you don't have all the answers. Maybe Ruby doesn't, either. Maybe she can't tell you more than she has. There is always a reason the whole truth isn't shared. You forgave me. Give her the same respect. That's what you do when you truly love someone."

"You are really into your feminine side these days." Laughter rumbles in my chest. "But you're right, and I'll consider your advice. It might take me a little while like it did with you."

"That's okay, just don't block her out of your life like you almost did me. You've got a good heart." A satisfied smile settles on her face.

"How come you never told me 'bout you and Dick?"

"He's your godfather and…" She blushes.

"It's cool. I get it." I don't think I want to know more than my imagination is producing. Christ, just when I thought this town couldn't get any more bizarre.

"You see how you let that slide? Try it with Ruby."

"I'll try harder."

Etta cuts a piece of pie for herself then one for me. I take the plate and the fork she pushed toward me and dig in as I lean against the counter and watch her busy herself.

"Rebel, thank you for being so human." Her eyes tear up. And deep under my skin and along my arms, everything prickles when my hair stands. "What would I have done had you not come around?"

"It took me a bit, but yeah, I knew it was gonna happen. And I wanted you to be happy. And looks like Dick stood up too. He basically funded your entire surgery. Though maybe it was couched in the whole godson thing to hide the fact?"

"There are many moving parts. Some aren't mine to tell."

We eat our pie in silence for a minute, my brain jumping everywhere. The murder-suicide. The trusts. Me running away from

Etta. Ruby running away from what? Why did she do what she did? *Forgive her.*

"You still see him?" I ask.

Etta clears her throat, one hand covering her mouth. She hesitates then stares at the floor and softly says, "I do."

How have I not known this all these years? "You love him?"

Etta shakes her head, a coy smile forming when she looks up. "Since high school."

"But you both married and had kids." I drag my fork along the edge of the pie, needing another few bites.

"Sometimes you do what you think you're supposed to do. What society expects. Then you grow up and look inside and do what you need to. What you have no choice about if you're willing to be truthful. Not everyone is. I've spent my adult life soul-searching. For a long time, I soaked in a bathtub of guilt and worry. Loving without uncertainty seems impossible for me. So, I've learned, to be happy, I simply love."

"Do you feel guilty because you're happy?"

"Sometimes." She rubs one temple and shrugs. "Yes, often."

When we lock in a stare, I know she's telling me not only her truths, but some of mine too. Can I forgive Ruby? It was so long ago. She was young, and maybe I don't know what was behind her and the Kline boys getting together. Maybe it's not my place to know, though it hurts like hell that I feel betrayed. It's different than how I felt about Etta, it's more painful.

"I need to give that a try. Simply loving. I need her."

"I know you do, son." Etta's lips form a thin line that curls into a smile of encouragement. "And she needs you, especially now that she's opening up and sharing things. That's the hardest part. You abandon her now and you might not get the whole truth. There is always more. And maybe you won't like it, or maybe it'll make your union stronger. Try to find a way to love instead of working so hard to dig up the past. You might not like what you find once it's exposed. The past can be ugly, and it can't be changed. Are you willing to give up a future with her because you can't neglect what's done and over with? That's most people's problem. And you, Rebel, are not most people."

"Nor are you." I chuckle, amazed by the depths of our relationship and how it continues to grow. "I admire you, Etta."

"Don't put me on a pedestal. There are things in my past I'm not proud of. But I'm not going to dwell. I'm going to live."

Now, I feel like an ass that I left Ruby the way I did. And the things I called her. Fuck, they were vile. I reacted like a seventeen-year-old punk. I'm not where I need to be yet, right in the mind and okay about hearing this stuff. And I'm not ready to consider that Ruby didn't fuck them to spite me. Crazy thing is, Ruby isn't a spiteful person. She wouldn't have done something that far out to get back at me for not showing up for her and Opal's run. And that's the piece of the past I can't let go. Why the hell would she have done what she did if she didn't have a decent reason for it?

Chapter 26

Make Some Men

Ruby

Hazel drops me off at midnight. I stroll in to find Mom donning a colorful caftan as she grooms her wigs in the kitchen while dancing around to old Fleetwood Mac tunes. After kissing her on the cheek as I pass her, I snag an orange cream soda from the refrigerator.

"I didn't expect to see you tonight." She clinks her grape soda to my bottle.

"No?"

"I thought you'd stay at Rebel's."

"I wasn't invited." I huff out a sigh. "I don't think Rebel wants me any longer. I singlehandedly sealed the deal tonight."

"That's nonsense. Lenny says you had a fight."

"What?" I'm starting to believe in ghosts. I lean against the counter as she positions bobby pins on a wig in a tidy row.

"Your father tells me you and Rebel had a scribble."

I chuckle. "A scuffle? Yeah, you could say that."

Mom scoops up a handful of popcorn then proceeds to eat one piece at a time, her tongue poking out to stick to each one like an insect. "Stop correcting me all the time. You know what I meant. Now, ask me a stupid question."

"What makes you think Rebel and I fought?"

"That is a stupid question, Ruby Mae. I already told you your father clued me in."

"Yes, we got into it. And it was uglier than... It was ugly."

"You know what Lenny would say?" Mom shakes salt across the popcorn. "You look like you been 'et by a wolf and shit over a cliff."

We laugh so hard that Mom ends up in a wheezing fit. Dad was raised in the South, so everything he said came out coated in Southern charm, and Mom continues to use all his sayings.

"That's how I feel." I reach into the bowl of popcorn and scoop a handful. "Have you ever told somebody something then regretted it?"

"Of course I have. Everyone does, and then you make some men." Mom purses her lips as I smirk.

"Make some men? Are you going to make some men with anyone soon? I might be able to offer a suggestion." I toss a piece of popcorn in the air then catch it in my mouth.

Mom does the same, telling me she's won after she scores six catches to my two. "I have someone in mind I need to make some men with."

"Amends, Mom. Make amends."

"Maybe you should make some men too and stop correcting my linkage."

Linkage? I think fast. Language? Good God. What has happened to her brain since I've been gone?

"What do you suggest I do?"

"Go fuck his brains out. Show him what he needs." She doesn't even crack a smile.

But I do. Then soda sprays out of my mouth when she fist-bumps her open palm.

"What did you say, and where did you put my mother?"

"Lenny told me to say that," she whispers and winks. "I don't tell Lenny no. Deads always get the green light."

"I think you're on to something, Mom. Thank you."

"I think you're going to be onto something too, or maybe under something. And you're welcome."

The rattle of glass mirrors my trembling hands when I knock on Rebel's front door. It's pitch-black in there. No lights. No sound. What if he's with the pretend girlfriend and they're making it not so pretend?

Like a thief seeking the fattest rock in a diamond mine, I turn the whiney, brass knob on his front door then quietly open the screen.

One slow breath in, two steps across the threshold, and a screech slashes through the darkness. A fur ball slaps my leg with a clawed paw, bouncing off me then scrambling toward a wall. Well, this is a good start.

Having no idea where I'm going, I tiptoe up creaky wooden steps. My cringes and nerves meet in a tango, shooting daggers into my threadbare heart.

Please, Rebel, don't push me away when I climb into your bed bare naked, bare souled, my heart on the chopping block, your massive, muscled grip on the axe handle once again. Please believe in us and try to hear the quiet truths my heart is whispering to yours. You've always been mine, you'll always be mine. Rebel Field, turn your hate inside out and see me. See the girl you love, see that she wasn't a whore, but rather…yes…a martyr.

Chapter 27

Unless

Rebel

My dream is the same as it's been for years. Ruby naked in my bed. My match and the missing piece to my internal puzzle. It's always real, but never more than tonight. Her velvet breasts pressing against my back, her hips nestled against my ass.

"Ruby, baby."

"Come to me," she says.

Crickets sound and hot night winds breathe through the window, playing alongside her command.

"I didn't mean to hurt you. I was answering you," she says.

Am I still dreaming? While shifting across my wet pillow, I groan. God, this feels real. Feels like she's next to me. Her scent invades my senses, her touch wrapping me in ropes, knots, and impossible-to-undo entanglements.

"I love you, Ruby Mae. Love you more than all the lovers in the world could love their one true love. Why did you hurt me? You're all I ever wanted. Every star to each constellation… All beats to all hearts."

"Why didn't you come to me that night?" she asks. "I waited and waited for you."

Hot, naked skin presses to mine. Skin so embedded in my memory that it couldn't be bleached. Skin I crave, hate, love, loathe, need, want.

"Ruby." My heart races.

"Rebel."

"What are you doing in my bed?"

"Saving us," she whispers.

"Baby, I can't…" *Unless.*

"I said I'd ask once…for sorry. And you left me. I'm asking once for a make love to me even though you still owe me an I'm sorry. This is it for us. We can start here or say goodbye here. I've pushed every worry and fear aside to do this. I'm giving you my last drops of belief. And I'm scared shitless. If you refuse me now, while my soul and body are bared, you will, I promise, never see me again. Think hard before you say no."

I turn and pull her to me, my chin resting on her head, my hands on the ass I've wanted to own for long years. Ruby Mae Rose is naked, in my arms, tempting my heart and my soul. My character and my resolve. I dig my heels in deep for long, agonizing seconds. Then I edge to the clearing, free-falling into the one woman who owns my soul regardless of her sins.

"Ruby." I tip her chin up, nip her top lip, and then part them with my tongue.

Our kiss sweeps through me, force-of-nature strong. Nothing I know, nothing I've felt in my life, comes close to the intense surge of carnal lust coursing through my veins. Wet, soft, discovering lips meet ache, desire, and pent-up hunger. I love her for finding me, for breaking into my house and my heart. For forgiving...and remembering. For seeing a future I overlooked. My hand still hurts from the hole I dug to bury our love.

"If I make love to you right now," I say, "like I've wanted to forever, what will happen tomorrow? And the next day?"

"I don't know, but I'm willing to set aside everything in my past to find out, because a future with you has to trump all my pain." Her voice cracks and her fingertips dig into my hips.

"Pain, baby?"

She hugs me harder and wraps her legs around my thighs and her arms around my back as her heart fuses to mine. Tears river down her face, soaking her golden locks and the depths of my heart.

"Kiss me." She breathes. "Make love to me. Please, Rebel."

"I've only ever wanted you. No other man was supposed to have you… You were mine. You took that from me." I wish I hadn't said that, but it hurts. How something that happened so many years ago can cause an ache in my heart still seems impossible.

"I've never been anyone else's. I promise you on your ring, my heart, Opal's grave. It's only ever been you. Please believe me."

Is it possible? I honestly don't know, because lies carry weight no matter when they're revealed or how long they've lived.

Chapter 28

Another Face

Ruby

Rebel's warm skin meets mine. His sweaty, hair-dusted, rock-hard torso presses against my breasts. All these years of trying to heal, one man—now in my arms—and mission in mind.

"Tell me, Ruby. Eyes on mine. You love me? I can leap, but I need to hear it. No more bullshit. Honest-to-fucking-God, bare-our-souls love. You got that, woman?"

"I got it, and yes, I love you." My lips tremble, mirroring my nerves.

The movie of my life is coming to fruition. My crazy leap into faith is taking hold like a winning lottery ticket. He wants me. After all I've said…he wants me. And here I am, crying.

"Hey, what are these tears for?" Rebel kisses the corners of my eyes. Then pulls back and stills in a deep gaze.

"I've never, in all my life, wanted anything more than you," I whisper as I hold his face in my hands and revel in our closeness. Can we do this? Move forward?

"Tell me you're on the pill or planning on marrying me when my seed makes our kid."

"We have nothing to worry about." I can't say more than that. Can't ruin this moment with more of my truths.

"Thank fuck." Rebel nestles between my legs and time dissolves. Nothing in the world matters but us and our togetherness.

"Ruby Mae, I love you. For all we've gone through, I will love you through anything no matter what words escape me."

"No matter," I answer.

The love of my life enters me, and worlds fall away. Faded thoughts of pain, healing, and angst hurtle time to forget, forgive, and claim my future. My soul is his to take and anchor. My heart is ripped from my chest and in safe keeping, nestled with his. My future is now wound in puzzling knots, needing-to-be-discovered stories, and ready-to-be-exposed first chapters. And I'm good with all of it.

I knew he'd be lovely, fierce, and commanding. All consuming. And my God, it's all want with us. Fingers meeting in union, teeth clashing between wet aggressive kisses, hips and slippery abs crashing onto each other in waves of claim. Rebel owning me. Body and soul.

If this isn't forgiveness, I don't know what is. But what if forgiveness has another face I've not yet seen?

Chapter 29

Promise

Rebel

"Look at you." I kiss Ruby's tear-stained cheeks and trembling lips. "Do you know how many times I've jerked off to this vision?"

"Yeah?" She giggles. "That cracks me up. You've been jerking off to me?"

"Fuck yeah." Inch by perfect inch, I slide into Ruby.

"Rebel, Jesus." She gasps, her eyes squeezing shut then opening in a slow appreciative gaze that makes my cock impossibly hard.

"Baby, you're so gorgeous." And wet. Christ, is she ready for me. Wet, tight, and exactly what I thought she'd be.

We grind in slow motion, Ruby's moans, my growls, and our sliding skin the soundtrack I've waited most of my life to hear. I claim her mouth, entering her deep, every thrust backed with emotion.

I suck her taut nipples, my tongue flicking her the way I remember she liked it, and based on her arched back and yesss and don't stops, she still apparently does.

"Your beautiful tits are bigger, and shit, they taste like you've always tasted. Sweet and sexy. You're still my Ruby, only better." Pushing her soft full breasts together, I drag my mouth from peak to peak, nipping each one when they tickle my lips. "I can't believe I'm fucking this pussy."

"Rebel." My name is an achy whisper wrapped with desire. "Don't stop doing that."

"This?" I shove her legs wider, anchor my hands on her shoulders, and drive hard. "You like that, baby? Hard and deep?"

"Yeah." Her sex voice makes me crazy. It's soft as powder and greedy as spring is for rain.

I've forever wondered what she'd sound like when I fucked her. It's the most gorgeous noise my ears have heard. My name and the yeahs coming out of Ruby's lusty throat crank up my desire. Her hips curl and she tightens on me, the arch of her neck and her begging for more almost pushing me over the top with her. Fuck. I am not coming yet. I'm taking my sweet-ass time with her.

"Not yet, baby." I pull out, though it almost kills me. There's so much I want to do with her. Years of tasting and touching need to happen. I nip her neck then suck her there. "I want you spread on my mouth, want your pussy on my tongue."

She smiles, and my already flipped world somersaults.

"I love the shit out of you."

"I love you too, Rebel."

Like a hungry hunter, I travel down her curves, following the moonlit path to my target. "Baby, why is your pussy hair blue?" I pull back then dive in, nipping at her gorgeous hip bones and sweet lines waiting for my tongue. Blue pussy hair? My silly girl is all I can think.

"It's just something I do." She bites her lips then sucks one finger and giggles. "I'm colorful like that."

"You're still silly. Always been a silly girl. Ruby Mae, bring those fingers down here and open your pussy lips for me. Show me what you want me to eat. I want your whole soaked cunt on display for my eyes."

"Jesus, you haven't changed." She laughs. "You are filthy. No, you're worse! You're the man version of filthy!"

"Damn right I am. And there are things...so many things, ways I can make you feel, that I promise no one else ever has. Come on, baby. Open your lips and show me. I want you to touch yourself for me. Show me what you want."

Ruby was never very shy with me, save one thing: She would not let me fuck her. Christ, I wanted to. More than anything, I wanted to be with her like that. To lie with her and love her with my whole body, not just my heart. Right now, though, I see shy. A curl on her mouth, her eyes darting, that bottom lip sucked between her teeth. It's provoking. Sexy. And it's a mystery I want to crack. She is.

"Don't you want me to?" I slide my hands between her thighs and press them apart, more ready than ever to taste my girl again.

She shakes her head and squeezes her knees on my shoulders. "I just ended my period. Remember?"

"Jesus, you think I give a fuck?"

"Well, yeah."

"Not a chance." I lift her knees over my shoulders and kiss her inner thighs. I could live in the sweet, soft crease of her thigh, my face nestled here for all of eternity. "I could dip your pussy in pig shit and eat it out."

"Rebel...that's gross." Ruby laughs and covers her face with her hands.

"This tongue is not missing an inch of you tonight. Not one fucking inch, Ruby Mae. It will lick every spot on your body, and by that, I mean every fucking one."

She tucks her chin and rolls her eyes, doing that shy thing again.

"I'm done waiting." I drag my thumbs in a line across her skin, her soft curls and her lips parting. "This fucking pussy, I swear." Her hips lift off the bed, her hands threading my hair. Her moans chasing one another. "My sweet thing."

"Rebel, oh God."

I thrust my tongue deep inside her then drag it up for another suck, my mouth bearing down when she gyrates and moans out my name time and again.

"You taste like a promise."

With her ass in the air, resting on my open palms, I open her wider. My tongue delights in her taste and texture. All of my senses come alive as I inhale her beautiful scent.

"You like that, don't you? I told you I'd lick you everywhere. Now, I'm gonna make you come in my mouth, gonna make you squirm." And I do. Jesus. "Beautiful, baby." My greed-filled climb up her body makes my dick ache for her. "Time for me to fuck some ruby-red pussy again."

Ruby's mouth forms an oval when I slam balls-deep inside her. At first, I see pleasure. Then her eyes mist and tears fall again. For the life of me, I don't know why. But I guess all the years we've waited are crashing down hard on her emotions.

"Rebel...don't say that again."

"That I'm going to fuck your ruby-red pussy? Or what? Tell me you love how it feels." I thrust deeper, so close to coming. Then again, so deep. So fucking deep and close. "Tell me you love it."

"Rebel...I..." Ruby bursts into a full-on ugly cry.

What now? There can't possibly be worse news than what she's already dumped on me.

Chapter 30

A Sliver Of Moonshine

Ruby

Those fucking Kline boys. I wish they weren't here, but they are. They said something so similar the night they stole everything from me. And that's why I dye my hair blue. We all cope differently. We all find a way to camouflage our pain.

"Baby, what's wrong?" Rebel flips to my side, my face crushed to his chest.

I've healed; mostly, I have. But being with Rebel brings so much of that night back to me. Part of me feels silly for having these feelings, but I know what they're attached to. And there's not an ounce of silly in them.

"There's more to tell, isn't there?" A sliver of moonshine highlights Rebel's stare. In it I see fear.

"No, there isn't," I say quietly, hopeful he believes me.

"You're naked in my arms, we just made love for the first time, and you're lying to me?"

Ouch. There's hurt in his words, but I'm sure he can't imagine what he's doing to me by spilling his feelings.

"There is nothing else to tell," I say.

"Why does it look like you're reliving something?"

"I'm not. Now, leave it." I twist my body and bury my face in the crook of my arm.

Rebel's hands surround my biceps, and he turns me to him in a swift motion. "Then why did you tell me not to say that about your pussy?"

"I just don't—"

"And why is your hair blue? Do women really do shit like this? Is it some European trend?"

I scramble for an answer. Anything. "Because I wanted to give you my virginity."

"And you're blue because you didn't? You've been dying your hair blue for seventeen fucking years over me? Not sure I'm buying it."

I nod, grateful he came up with something better than I could have. Like the truth. But then he keeps going.

"Why didn't you give it to me? Just spit it out once and for all." He presses his forehead to mine then lifts his head and kisses that spot. "Why, baby? Just tell me."

"I couldn't." Shit. Shit. This cannot go further than it already has.

"We talked about it. Planned on it. Knew where it was going to happen. I had champagne. I had those fucking cookies you like. And what, you had a weak moment? None of it makes sense. It's not like you. Not the girl I knew, anyway."

"Can't you leave the past alone?"

"It's not that simple," he says.

"Something about us has to be."

Rebel wraps his arms around me and whispers in my ear. "You're shaking, crying, and I'm loving you, holding you. I'm trying to give you everything right now. Can't you do the same for me?"

"I'm giving you everything I am. I came to your house and into your bed after you called me awful things. I forgave you because…"

"Because you have no choice? You feel guilty about something. What woman would climb into a man's bed after he called her the things I called you?"

I pull away and sit up. This is going nowhere. "Rebel, please don't. I'm trying here."

His warm hands land on my back. What do I say to soothe him but not turn his life upside down?

"Tell me now or get out of my bed." It's a command, and it hurts like vinegar in an open wound.

I feel bad for us. Because the truth will hurt him too much to share.

"I don't know what I did," I say quietly. And God, there is so much truth in those words.

I don't know what I did to deserve what happened. Or why being a martyr made things worse. And here I am, doing it again. Are their deaths enough redemption? I wish they were, but mysteries don't get answered with redemption. Mysteries get answered with explanations, and there are too many coincidences that happened that week. Too many I know about.

The question I've pondered for months now feels like a never-ending bleeding wound: Who else in this town knows what I went through?

Chapter 31

Good Reason

Rebel

Ruby scoots off the edge of the bed, scoops her clothes off the floor, and tiptoes toward the door.

"You're really doing this? Leaving? Because you can't tell me what you did?"

"You told me to leave."

I grip handfuls of sheets, wishing it were handfuls of her. "Fucking tell me already! This is insane."

"I told you I don't know what I did." She slips into her sundress. With her back to me, she sniffles, glancing over her shoulder before walking out of my bedroom barefoot, her shoes dangling from her fingertips.

Rolling off the bed, I land hard and stomp to the door.

"Goodnight, Rebel," she says as she descends the staircase.

That's it?

"Goodbye, sweet thing." I slam the door, undoubtedly waking Rifle and Etta with the muscle I put behind it.

Gripping the windowsill, about to rip it off the wall, I watch Ruby climb into her car and drive away. What isn't she telling me? Flipping onto the bed, I rewind my mind while sprawled out, annoyed, crushed, and confused. Whatever she's holding on to must be massive. Dots connecting to dots, intersections meeting in riddles and retorts.

I shoot off the bed and pace in circles. Holy Christ. No. Don't go there. Jesus…could she be? Ruby Mae Rose, a murderer? How am I even entertaining this? A chill zings up my spine, my heart heavy. Why would she get it on with them one day then kill 'em days later? None of it makes sense.

Ruby did borrow Rocket's gun that week, though. I delivered it to her house so she could shoot a pesky possum that was getting in their garbage. Or so she claimed. The next day, the twins' murder-suicide occurred and the gun was back in our locked case that night. But I swear the article in the paper claimed it was *their* hunting guns that were used. And then something went down between Etta and Dick Kline. What? There were no autopsies, though everyone questioned the entire situation. So, did someone besides me get a shit-ton of cash? Who?

Ruby left for Paris the day of their funerals. Hell, maybe she was running from everything. Murder, her sister's death, and me. Why me? Why would someone run from the person they love unless they have a damn good reason? Unspeakable guilt? I'd say that's a good reason.

The woman I love…a murderer? Fucking great. Of course, she can't tell me. What would I do if she confessed? I have no idea. I couldn't turn Ruby in. She'd spend her life in jail. Not turning her in, though, would make me a criminal too.

Is this why Etta had the crosses, the necklace, and the ring in her jewelry box? Ruby killed the twins and Etta knows? Impossible. How the hell would Etta know? She would have turned Ruby in if she knew. But she did lay some thick shit out about letting go of the past earlier. Are Etta and Ruby in cahoots?

Well, this is one fucking dandy crossroad. I don't want to know if Ruby killed the Kline boys. Don't want to know if Etta was involved.

I don't want to know a damn thing now.

I rise at the crack of dawn. My mind's whirling when I show up at the Rose house at eight to help with the move. Rowdy's beat me here, and by the haggard look on Ruby's face combined with no hello, I deduce she never slept.

"We're good here," she says, making zero eye contact as she muscles a box around. "You can go."

"I'm helping, and you shouldn't be using your arm that way. You aren't doing yourself any favors." I jail the box she's struggling with between us, easing it out of her arms.

"The only favor I'm doing today is staying clear of you. Since that's what you want from your slutty ex."

"Ruby." My voice cracks through the thickness in my throat.

"Or wait—skank whore. Which is it?"

"Don't act like this." I place the box on the ground and square up with her, my hands gripping her shoulders to still her squirming agitation.

"How would you like me to act? More like I was last night?" She squints, her impatient gaze pinned on me as her chin rises.

"We should talk."

"I already told you there is nothing else to say." She pulls an imaginary zipper across her lips then drops her gaze.

I grunt out a long sigh and lift her chin. Her eyes—her soft, sad, and angry emerald eyes—are so gorgeous, so captivating. But are they the eyes of a murderer?

"You don't have to tell me anything," I say.

"Really?" She belly laughs, her eyes lit with mischief. It's a sinister laugh. I don't blame her. "I don't believe you. You want more game out of me than this. You're going to corner me and force me to tell you things I can't for reasons, I will not, reasons that'll put you in a very—"

I press a finger on her lips. "Not another word," I scold.

Ruby smacks my hand away. "What's changed?" She searches my face as my jaw grinds. "You know something, don't you? You know something and you aren't going to admit it?" She cringes and clutches her arms to her chest.

"I know nothing." I wipe the sweat off the back of my neck as my chest tightens. "No more questions."

She narrows her eyes and cocks her head. Is that how she looked at them before she shot them? Did they think she was really going to kill them? And what did they do beyond have sex that made her livid enough to take their lives? I look away, spinning my baseball cap around and knuckle my forehead.

"Something's bothering you. You only knuckle your forehead when you're worried."

Now, I have something I'm lying about. I can't tell her I know a thing, or she might confess. I'd be the only person who knew she did it. Unless Etta does. I can't bear to think about it. But what if her guilt gets the best of her? What if she panics and opens up? Decides to trust me?

Worse yet—what if she doesn't?

Chapter 32

Overnight

Ruby

Rebel has this look on his face like he's suddenly solved all the world's mysteries. And maybe the one I'm pondering.

Who sent that box to me, and why?

And this mystery: How did Rebel go from "tell me what you're lying about" to "don't tell me anything" overnight?

"That's mine," my mom says, yanking a box out of Rebel's arms. "I'll carry it on my lap. It's the one."

By that, she means the reminder. She's had it since I can remember. Sometimes she'll go through it and bless everything in it, as if each thing holds a particular sin or consecration. Mom comes by religion honestly. Her dad was a Baptist preacher who married a Catholic nun who left the order when she fell in love with him. Dad was Jewish. Growing up in our home was…interesting. Invented holidays included.

"Where's Lake going?" Rebel asks. "'Cause we're almost out of room. You want me to take you and the bird to the house first, Mrs. Rose?" He's sweet with Mom considering what an ass she is about Etta. Rebel has the patience of a saint.

At least for some things. And some people. Certainly, not everything.

"No, Opal and Lenny want to ride with me too."

"They're welcome to ride in the Jeep," I say. There's plenty of room in there for ghosts and lies and secrets.

"Lenny doesn't think that's a good idea, do you, honey?" She waltzes a few steps away and cups her hand to her ear. "He says it's fine that we go with Rebel."

"Wonderful. You get the deads and Mom." I ram Rebel's shoulder as I pass him.

"Rebel." Mom clucks her tongue, capturing his attention. "Next week, we're celebrating deads day with a potluck." She wanders around his truck twice, like she can't figure out how to get in.

I want to suggest the doors, but she seems so oversensitive in regards to anything I suggest lately.

"Be sure you bring your daddy and Rifle," she tells him. "And at least one of the deads with each of you."

I swear to God we are the weirdest family on the planet. And Rebel, God bless him, is going along with all of it like we're as normal as hot dogs at a baseball game.

"Wouldn't miss it. Etta'll be happy you've invited her." A slow smile builds on Rebel's face as he nods. Then he opens the passenger door and herds Mom to it.

She mutters something about Lenny and Opal beating her into the car and the unfairness of their *special abilities*. Even the deads are in a contest she wants to win. She seems to be getting dafter by the day. All kinds of oddities pop up, from the word mix-ups to the wandering in circles.

"Hang on," Rebel says. "Let me move this." He hauls a squatty glass terrarium out of the truck and proudly holds it up. "Etta made this for you, a housewarming gift."

Oh, and the peculiar grin on Mom's face? Priceless.

"The gays are certainly creative, aren't they? He really is touched."

Rebel leans toward Mom and speaks slowly, as if she's foreign. "Etta isn't gay, Mrs. Rose." He sets the gift on the sidewalk amongst a pile of boxes.

"It's all the same," Mom squawks. "No need to put a bow on it. Please tell him thank you. I'm going to make some men with him when he visits for the deads potluck."

"Amends?" Rebel asks, his brow rising. "Make amends. That's very kind of you."

"You and Ruby... Honestly." Mom waves a hand at Rebel in dismissal. "I have a college degree, you know. Neither one of you do."

"I'm well aware." Rebel's voice rises as he forges a hard smile.

He's good with her. Better than I am. He settles Lake on Mom's lap and double buckles them. Then he climbs in on the driver's side.

"I'll swing back for you in a few, sweet thing. Rowdy can drive the moving van."

I edge toward him, breathing through my nose as I bite the inside of my cheek. "Are you taking something for your current state of delusion? Now, I'm suddenly sweet thing? I'll drive the Jeep." I spin and march away, chuckling. What has gotten into him?

"You've always been my sweet thing, and I'll drive you. Rowdy and I'll deal with the Jeep. This isn't an argument. It's what we're doing." He doesn't wait for my answer.

I wasn't going to argue anyway.

I'm so confused. Rebel's a different man today. Maybe he's hearing ghosts too. Great, the deads are speaking to everyone but me. Maybe the deads sent me that box.

Speaking of… Shit, the box. I jog inside and fling the coat closet open. But my purse is gone. Maybe Mom grabbed it. My stuff will be strewn everywhere if Echo found my purse. I keep it in the coat closet because he won't open that door.

All I need now is for Rebel to find the box.

Chapter 33

Meaningful Things

Rebel

"I see you're ditching all your hunting gear, Mrs. Rose. Why's that?" I back out of the driveway, passing a heap of stuff.

"Haven't gone hunting since my rifle was stolen. I know who it was, but I won't point fingers at the deads, God bless them all."

She rattles off her list of deads as I fiddle with the air conditioning.

"Bet you're glad Ruby's back in town."

She straightens her wig then pulls a compact out of her purse, her lips forming a unique shape when she refreshes her coral-colored lipstick. "Opal says she's thrilled."

"But not you?"

"I'm not sure this town is right for Ruby Mae." She carefully tucks her lipstick into her purse as she hums.

"Why's that?"

"Just things. This town can be trouble for some. I'd hate for Ruby to find more trouble."

More trouble? This is insane. Does she know that Ruby's a murderer? Fuck. I can't keep calling the woman I love a murderer. Every time the thought crosses my mind, another knot forms in my stomach.

"Trouble how?"

She sighs long and low. "Lenny says you ask too many questions. God bless the deads."

The names of dozens of deads fill the rest of our drive time. She even tosses a few dead presidents into the mix. And she doesn't tell me to ask a stupid question when she's done. Though I think I have plenty of them that someone knows the answers to. But who?

After Lake, Monday, and—I assume—the deads are settled, Rowdy pulls up with the moving van and Echo. When they begin to unload, Rowdy shoos me off to get Ruby.

As I turn in the driveway to pick her up, she approaches my window, breathless. "Did you happen to see my purse? It's red and funky…a boho leather thing."

"Nope. But I wasn't looking for it, either. You look a little panicked."

"It's just…I can't lose it."

I climb out of the truck and follow Ruby to a pile of giveaways. "I'm sure it'll show up."

"Fuck," she mutters as she covers her mouth with a fist. "Where is it?" She rummages through the pile of discarded items on the lawn.

"You think your mom would have put it in here?" I squat next to her and help her rifle through what looks like garbage.

"I have no idea. I keep it in the coat closet so Echo doesn't take it. He likes purses. Likes to dig through them."

"I'm sure you have more than one purse. Stuff always get lost during moves."

"That purse cannot for anything get lost… I can't…" Her breath hitches and she punches her fists against her thighs.

"Baby, what's up? You're getting pretty emotional over a purse."

"It has some important things in it."

"What kinds of things?" The second I ask, I want to take the words back, fearing she might tell me something about her crime that I've all but incarcerated her for.

"Meaningful things. Leave it at that." Ruby climbs into the truck.

I fasten her seat belt without a second thought. "You got it, boss."

On the drive to the house, once she seems calmed, I close my hand around hers. "I want to take you out tonight. Would you like that? Just you and me."

"A date?" She fans herself and smiles wide. "A real date?"

"Yes, a date." I pinch her waist to receive a giggle.

"You're confusing."

"You're beautiful, Ruby. More beautiful than you were in high school, baby, but you're a little confusing too."

And hopefully not a murderer.

Chapter 34

Rock, Paper, Scissors

Ruby

I'm confused and confusing. But we're going on a date. Which is a major leap for us after last night. Everything since I've come home has been nonstop push-pull. Hopefully, tonight, we can make some progress.

Rebel picks me up in his truck just as the sun is setting, and it's all rainbows and unicorns, my version anyway. I can't help but feel suspicious of all the feels and happiness. Could we be this? A normal couple who's reinvigorated their long-lost love? Maybe? But then what? I can't stop picturing a future without him; problem is, I'm not sure where that future puts us. Paris or Wisconsin? How will we ever work? What will I give up for love?

We park in front of Storm Field Bakery, Rebel's younger sister's business.

"I'm so impressed with my Stormy girl!" I say.

"Works her ass off but loves it." Rebel's proud smile turns my insides to pudding.

I love how he walks the line of rough-and-tumble one minute and sweet protector the next. He's such a family man. Maybe he'll be my family man at some point. A girl can dream.

"She was terrified to start her own thing," he says, "so she made those filled donut holes I taught her to make when she was in junior high. We sold out of 'em at the hardware store in two hours one weekend. That was all she needed."

My throat grows thick as my nerves tingle. I cup his whiskered jaw in my palm. "Rebel Field, you're still the same boy, aren't you? Encouraging everybody around you to go for it."

"Do I seem like a boy to you? When I push your skirt up later, the only boy you're going to be talking about is the boy-oh-boy orgasm you'll be getting. With my tongue."

We share a look, and he winks.

"And then I'll give you some man-oh-man."

"You think you're getting some later?" I laugh.

"*Some* later, baby? You're giving me all. This pussy…" He leans over and strokes the front of my skirt. Then he slides his hand under the fabric and up along my thigh. Oh God. "She's not going to purr, naw. She's gonna drown in cream. First yours. Then mine."

Oh, Lord. Yes, please. "You've always been sure of yourself, Rebel."

"I want what I want. Right now, I want to take you into the bakery for our date."

I glance at the hand-painted sign on the door. "It's closed."

"Baby, really?" He shakes his head, his smirk adorable, as he opens my door, taking me back to high school and our first date.

My guess is I'm about to relive it. Only dirtier.

"First date do-over?" I ask as Rebel unlocks the front door of the bakery.

"You've always been a smart girl." He holds the door open, his warm hand on my lower back urging me in.

"Dirty do-over?"

He hums low. "Mmm-hmmm."

That says everything—along with the way he licks his lips.

Rebel takes my hand and leads me through the antique-filled space. A chandelier-dotted ceiling, every tiny table, overstuffed chair, and mismatched piece of furniture drool worthy. Storm was always a girl with a point of view. Funky and offbeat. This place has her touch all over it.

"Did you make donut holes?"

"Had Storm make 'em this time."

"Yay! Are we going to fill them tonight?" I bounce up onto my toes and kiss his cheek.

"We're gonna fill everything, baby. Every little hole."

"Such a naughty boy." I nestle under his arm, happy as a girl could possibly be, crossing my fingers nothing comes up to ruin the sexy mood he seems intent on setting.

On our first date, when we were sophomores, Rebel invited me to his house. In their tiny kitchen was a cloth-covered table with a vase of flowers and two place settings including printed linen napkins.

He made omelets, the eggs having been collected from the coop he'd built and the chickens he'd raised. My crush soared while I watched him whisk the eggs like a pro then cook the omelets in a bubbly pool of butter. God, he was cute. His tousled, black hair, his sparkling eat-me-alive eyes, and his bring-me-to-my-knees smile. We rock-paper-scissored which dessert we'd have. He had two options premade. But I only wanted him. A sweet, sexy, rough-and-tumble bad boy who liked to bake, cook, and build? He could have told me we were having dirt for dessert and I'd have taken the first bite.

He won two out of three games. Then he decided we were having filled holes. Donut holes, that is. Cream and cherry, the two fillings he'd made. I nearly died with desire when he shared the plan and slid a cream-covered finger into my mouth for a taste.

"Rebel, this is…" My pulse zips, my eyes welling, when he pulls the curtain of the bakery's kitchen back. "God, I missed you." And yes, it's a redo. A beautiful redo of our first date, right down to the cloth-covered table and flowers.

He presses himself to my back, his arms around me in a hug. "I wondered."

"I wish you hadn't." I lie my head back and feel his heart thunder.

"Hard not to considering the circumstances."

I pivot in his arms and look up at his weather-worn brow. My palms sweat, and I tearfully ask, "What do I have to do to win you back for good?"

Chapter 35

I Lost You

Rebel

Her gaze darts around as she blushes. She still has me. Am I worried that someone else may know what she might have done? Hell, yeah. The last thing I want is to lose her that way. Any way.

She must feel me giving off something that says she's lost me, judging by her watery eyes and her unsure smile. I'm working overtime to hide my concern, which is not an easy thing to do when you wear love on your sleeve.

I skim my fingers along her jawline, her chin, and then her trembling lips. Her gaze settles and lands on mine.

"You never lost me, Ruby. I lost you."

"Only in geographical proximity. And we'll have to talk about that again if we can make something out of this thing between us."

I pull a chair out for her, light candles, and uncork the wine. Then I pour it. "Yes, we do. Because I know you've got your career over there. Not to mention your life. So, tell me something…you really had me in your heart all those years?"

"Not just in my heart, in my everything. In my thoughts, in my dreams, in my wake-up-sipping-coffees."

I slump onto a chair directly in front of her and slide my hand around the back of her neck, drawing her close to whisper at her ear, "You still consider me your man?"

She inches back. "I never didn't. I'm glad I didn't know you were married. That might have killed me. I knew you were probably dating, but married... How did it all come about? Marriage is big."

"It is big. It was a major change in my life when Paris told me she was pregnant."

Ruby grimaces, her gaze shifting to the candle, one finger playing up and down the dripping wax.

"So you waited a few months for me?" she asks just before tipping her glass for a long sip. "Then you fell in love?" A fake smile forms on her lips at the same time knots bundle in my stomach.

I inch my fingers to hers then twine them. She wants answers, but the defeated slump in her shoulders and the cheerless pucker of her lips say something else. It must pain her to hear this, though I'm not sure why, because *she* left me.

"We had a one-nighter."

"You married a woman you had a one-nighter with?" Her voice rises. "In this day? Rebel...I mean, my God."

"I felt responsible, and really, she was a nice girl. Sweet. She couldn't have done it alone. Hell, not even the pregnancy. Was sick as hell. I felt guilty every time she puked, which was nonstop."

Ruby stares at her fingertip as she traces a line down her cast. "You loved her?"

"Once we got to know each other, I did love her."

She glances up, breaking away from our gaze the second our eyes meet. It crushes me to see her pain. I wish we weren't talking about me and Paris, but it was bound to come up at some point. We have years of things to talk about, wade through, and explore. Hopefully not many more landmines to navigate— though, somehow, I doubt it.

I tip her chin up, scoot closer to her, then lean in. "You ever fall in love with anyone?" *Please say no.*

She cocks her head and closes her eyes. When they open, there's a dreamlike serenity in them. "Else?" she asks.

"Yeah." I kiss her forehead, confident I know the answer, though the confirmation will be nice.

"I loved, yeah. But fall in love forever? No. Only with you," she whispers. But it sounds like a marching band in my heart. *Only with you.*

I look up, letting my head fall back as I close my eyes and utter a soft, "Thank God." Then I look intently at Ruby. "Though I find it hard to believe my sweet thing never found another true love, I'm relieved."

"Had a few proposals." She shrugs and smiles. "But I wasn't in love enough."

"In love enough?" I chuckle. "That's a funny saying."

"In love enough…like…" Ruby fills our wine glasses. "You get a little nervous excited when your eyes meet."

"Like this?" I ask.

We're motionless in a perfect time-standing-still stare. One of those turn-you-inside-out stares. A prelude-to-a-first kiss, first-handhold, first-take-your-clothes-off stare. Wonder and curiosity, the unknown as beautiful as anything you've ever felt.

"Mmmm-hmm." She wets her lips, parting them with her tongue. "Or your heart beats go crazy when—"

"When I touch you like this?" I open her knees with my palms then, one inch at a time, skim her skirt higher, my thumbs floating on the soft peach fuzz of her inner thighs.

"Rebel."

"What else says…you're in love enough? Something like this?" I ask and graze a wet line of kisses down her throat—until I meet her cleavage and pepper it with kisses too.

"Definitely that." She inhales a shaky breath.

"This too?" I ease a hand inside the front of her underwear, slick coating my fingertips when I slip them lower.

"Rebel, oh God."

"Tell me you love me enough that you'll stay…that you'll be mine like I've wanted for too long."

"I will consider staying—if you tell me why you didn't come for me on graduation night. Why…when I asked…could you not tell me where you were?"

Chapter 36

Dessert

Ruby

"How 'bout we not talk about that night right now. How 'bout we talk about this down here," he says, glancing at his busy fingers. "And about what's going to happen any second." His upper lip rises in the sexiest, my-hand-is-loving-what-it's-feeling way. Like he's so focused on my pleasure he doesn't have control over his mouth. He grips a fist full of my hair, my head falling back in slow motion.

"Rebel, I…"

With his tongue on my throat, one hand stilling my head, and the other working me to imminent orgasm, I moan out a sound, a claim, then his name. My noises are most definitely turning him on as much as he's turning me on.

"Not gonna lie, baby. When you moan like that…then say my name while my fingers are deep in your wet pussy, coated in your slick…fuck…makes me so hard… I'm gonna fuck you, Ruby. Fuck you hard after you come on my hand then face."

I don't know what he's doing with his fingers, but I'm suddenly full of them—everywhere. And, when he bites my nipple through my dress, I wilt onto him, my fingers thrusting into then gripping his hair, my hips finding a rhythm with his hands, and God, I come so hard that I bite the meat of his shoulder just to brace myself.

"Time for dessert." Rebel's half-mast eyes when he lifts me off the chair and positions me on the white marble pastry counter say one thing. He's starved.

But he still hasn't told me why he didn't come that night. And, while the timing stinks, it matters that he fesses up. Later.

"What are you smiling about?" I ask when he walks backward to the cooler while waggling his brow.

"You know what I'm smiling about." He rummages through the cooler then emerges, his arms loaded.

I tuck my legs to the side when he saunters toward me with a few small bowls on a tray. Fillings. I dip a finger into the cream then wipe it across his lips, hoping he'll come closer so I can lick it off.

"Get your ass over here." He yanks me to the edge and spreads my knees, all the while circling his lips with his tongue.

"What are you planning on doing?" I ask. "That look on your face is pretty sinful, Wishbone."

"Gonna strip you the fuck down—that's what."

My underwear is off, falling-star fast.

"Then I'm going eat some cream-filled holes," he says. "You know my motto." He grins.

"Dessert first," we say in unison, and he winks at me.

"Not just any dessert," he says at my ear between sucks of my lobe. "Put out your tongue, sweet thing." Rebel dips his pinkie into the chocolate, licks it, then sucks my tongue into his mouth.

"This is a little more advanced than our first date." I'm lightheaded over my newfound crush with the man Rebel has become.

"That's because I'm a little more advanced than I was as a teenage boy."

We fall into a kiss so intense and deep, so sexy and arousing, that I'm sure I'll slip off the counter. Rebel does things with his lips and his tongue that seem unimaginable. His gift for making me fall into his kisses and dragging me with him has always been magic, but those were high-school-boy kisses wrapped in innocence and yet-to-be-discovered pleasures we never had the chance to share. Now, though, Rebel as a man, with his roughness and aggressive nature, his ownership of me and the way he combines his intense side with his take-care-of-me side… It's that first bite of a sundae when the hot fudge and the cold cream mingle on your tongue and you moan because the balance of it hits you like it was made by Mother Nature for your taste buds alone.

Rebel's hands travel down my curves. Tingles skate over my skin at his engaging touch. He undresses me with skill as he continues to make love to my mouth.

"I've always had a dirty fantasy about your tits." He unfastens my bra, his rough hands cupping both breasts while he sucks my nipples with vigor. "Something I've never told you." He glances up, one nipple rolling around the tip of his tongue. "Had it since we were sixteen."

"Dirty, huh?"

"Filthy. Wrong." He chuckles. "Perfect."

I close my eyes and arch into him. Cold hits my already hard tips seconds later as he coats my nipples with cream then sucks them off.

"Think you'll tell me now?"

"I'll knock you up someday. Then I'll show you. Knock you up and watch your gorgeous tits grow and fill with milk for the baby and then for me."

All these things were bound to come out at some point. The this-can't-happen-because-that-did. The don't-ask-me-to-do-that-because-they-did-it. The don't-say-those-words-to-me-because-they-said-them. Even dead, the Kline boys won't stop badgering me.

"Rebel." Ah, fuck. How do I tell him? And why do I feel shame over what happened?

After I knock you up. I wish. How do I tell him one more thing they took from me, from us, without telling him exactly *how* they did it?

"Hey," he says. "What's up? Seems like I just lost you."

I don't realize I've sunk into my safe-inside-me place until he says my name repeatedly. Until he's kissing my face. Until I look into his eyes and see a man I love, a man who I wish had saved me. *He couldn't have known.*

"Ruby, talk to me."

"You'll—" I stop on that one word, knowing how much is attached to it. *Say the words.* "You'll never be able to knock me up. I had a situation… I can't."

He knows before I say more, his eyes tender with concern. The actual words never form, but they don't need to.

Chapter 37

Forgiveness

Rebel

Jesus, what else? Ruby's eyes fill with disappointment, which matches my own.

"Hey, it's okay. Ruby, look at me. I need you to know it's okay."

"It's not okay," she says. "But thanks for not getting mad. It's heartbreaking. No woman…" She buries her face in my neck.

"Why would I be mad? No woman what?"

"No woman wants that choice to be made for her."

"Of course not, baby. I'm so sorry it makes you sad. I hate seeing you cry, especially about something like this."

"Something we could have had." She pauses then whispers, "Together."

"We can have all kinds of things together. A lifetime." I press my forehead to hers and wrap my arms around her shivering frame.

"This though… It was something I always wanted. You know, since I was a little girl." She swallows hard then looks at me like she's stolen my future. "To someday be a mother. To carry, um…*your* child."

The reality of her words overrides my nerves when my pulse races. But her cheerless, vacant eyes and her clammy, limp hands bring me back to her. My girl.

"How did you find out you can't carry a child?"

Ruby stares off into the distance, a deep crease on her forehead, her scarlet cheeks looking like memories she wants to stop thinking about. "I had a botched abortion. I hope that doesn't freak you out. I never would have, but there was no choice. It was a medical thing. The baby had no spine."

I reinforce my hold and snug her body closer when she wiggles away. "Why would that freak me out? All it does is make me feel bad that you went through that." I peel her fingers off her face and kiss them.

After a stretch of silence, she stares at me. In her gaze is a request for forgiveness and sorrow.

"Was he there for you?"

"No, they weren't."

"They? It was one of theirs? The Kline boys?" Like a shot of adrenaline, I'm jolted out of a tender moment and into my reoccurring nightmare. "Jesus fucking Christ." I turn, shoving my hands through my hair, warring with myself to gain composure. I want to scrub her down with a wire fucking brush.

"I wasn't planning on telling you yet," Ruby says, soft as cotton. "It's just…I'm being honest. Please don't be angry."

I pace in small circles, swearing and tightening my fists. Growls like from a beaten animal scrape my throat, though my heartbeats are louder. "I'm hurt, and yes a little angry, and tell me… Why the fuck didn't you use something? And then why did you tell me last night you were on the pill or—"

"I never said I was on the pill. I said we didn't have to worry. I didn't want to ruin the mood."

"Well, the mood is ruined now."

"Rebel, why are you mad?" Ruby's eyebrows pinch together as her eyes redden.

"Well, let's see here." I place my hands on the counter, one on either side of her. "You had sex with Kent and Kyle on graduation night, got knocked up, left for Paris, had a botched abortion and…"

"And what? Just say it. You're revolted by me because of it. You don't have to say the words. I can read you."

"I don't want to fight anymore… That's all," I say.

"I don't, either. I just want to be honest. I guess you don't want that."

"I can't tell you what to do. You're a grown woman, been making interesting choices for a while now."

"That sounds judgmental." Ruby cocks her head as color bleaches from her face.

"I was put on this earth to love you. I know that is the truest thing in my heart. But you've made all kinds of choices that have and will affect us. I just hope, as they continue to show themselves, they don't blow us off course entirely."

"If we can't talk without it destroying us, what good are we?"

"What's good mean to you? I feel like, every time I get you naked, something else falls out of your mouth that has you crying or confessing. Shit, maybe we ought to just keep our clothes on from now on. I'm almost afraid to touch you."

"Do you resent me?"

"You want the truth?" I say, ready to fire out something I shouldn't.

Ruby's gaze drops from mine as her shoulders slump and she whispers, "I just got it."

Chapter 38

Surrender

Ruby

I hop off the counter and scramble into my clothes. The hollow in my chest and the knots in my belly collide in a painful reunion I know too well to ignore. Rebel's hand clamps around my bicep before I make it to the door. He spins me, hurt hanging heavily on his brow, disappointment clenched on his jaw. What's in his heart? Can we get past things we may never discuss?

"How the hell did I fail you?" His voice cracks along with my forged composure.

"You ready for this, Rebel?" We could lose everything if I tell him. We still might if I don't. Either way, we're on the line. "You want the truth?"

He rams his palms onto his forehead. "Fuck, Ruby. What are we doing?"

"We're dancing around." I turn, ready to leave. "This is what most couples who keep secrets do. They dance around topics until they lose each other for good."

"We're not most couples."

"What are we, then?"

Rebel hauls me onto his waist, my legs wrapping his hips as he walks us back to the kitchen. In one level sweep, the tablecloth and its toppings crash to the ground. Candle flames die on the floor as heat inside me burns.

"Don't say anything else," Rebel whispers as he places me on the table's edge. "Just touch me."

I work his jeans open, my fingers somehow maneuvering in tugs and greedy jerks. He kisses my neck, licking and sucking…making me insane the way his tongue finds tiny orgasmic spots I never knew existed. I slip my hands inside his briefs, his long thick cock, hot to the touch, heavily veined and ready for me, the tip already wet.

In seconds, he strips me down, continuing his ravenous consumption of every inch of my body. I fist handfuls of his hair when he buries his face between my legs, then mouths and nibbles a path across my stomach and up to my breasts. Squeezing my rib cage, then each breast with wide spread hands, he sucks and devotes himself to me in a way I've never experienced with anyone else. Then he demolishes me with his kiss. And Jesus…in it is an intensity and ownership that I meet with a fervor I've never known myself to fall into. His mouth open and wet, his tongue jutting past my lips with force and passion. He groans, one hand sliding behind my neck as he pulls me into him, making me wonder if my lips will be bruised tomorrow. But I don't care, all I want is more of him. I shove his jeans and briefs past his hips, my nails scraping his skin as I hurry to get him bare. My need for him to be inside me makes me wild, an uncontrollable eagerness for his skin to be on mine, his body to be in mine, his heart to wrap itself around my own so tightly that we're locked for life.

He shoves my thighs back, grabs my hands, kisses my fingertips, then places them on the insides of my knees. "Hold them there, open and wide. Can you do that?" I nod, mesmerized by him. I would do anything he'd ask of me right now, anything at all. "Good, I want you spread." His voice is hoarse and dark, like he might detonate into the core of the earth. I fall backward, relaxing in my spread eagle-like pose, waiting for whatever he wants to do to me…with me. The heat between us ratchets up when he rubs his length along my wet slit and says, "Look at us. Look at us there." I awkwardly lift onto my elbows while still holding myself wide for him. "You see that, Ruby? You see your wet pussy all over me and how hard my cock is for you?"

I nod, so turned on by his words I can't find any of my own.

"Watch it, baby…watch me impale you." He curves a hand around my waist, then stares into my eyes with a hunger that sends a bolt of energy through me so strong I might call it whiplash if it didn't feel so euphoric.

"Look there, watch me fuck you, baby." I drop my gaze to where we meet. He thrusts fast, once. Deep. His balls snugged against my ass. His chest rising and falling rapidly, sweat beading and rivering between his pecs. He seats himself for long seconds, his grip on my waist a lifeline. "Rebel." I lean onto him, my forehead against his chest, then my ear to hear and feel his heartbeat, and the truth in it. Wrapping my legs around him, I lean back on the table. He grins while perusing my naked body. Slowly, he pulls out to his tip, then presses my thighs back hard and thrusts into me again so deep that I cry out, his hunger startling and exciting me as our hips fuse when he impales me with need time and again. He yanks my ass past the edge of the table and grunts when he looks to where we meet and thrusts hard again. Each penetration an electrical current that rides up my middle, connecting to every nerve in my body.

"I want you to love me," I say.

"I never stopped."

"Love me now, no matter what happens…no matter…"

"Shhh, baby." He leans over my body, his lips capturing mine, crushing me with a worship-filled kiss. His fingers dig into my hips and tow me onto his rigid shaft again.

Messy kisses, tangled hair, and whispers of need and want swallow me. His strain, sweat, and fervor marry my whimpers and abandon. The friction… Fuck, it's…good. No, it's insane. We're a fever that's burning, rivers that are meeting and becoming one. We're lost in our togetherness, so lost that we're found.

"Ruby."

I have nothing but elation and freedom as I writhe under him. Sweat from his chest drips onto my breasts, a look of surrender on his mouth as I tighten and release in a full-bodied, delirious orgasm.

"You're merciless," I utter as he falls onto me.

"You're a goddess."

"You sound drugged."

"I am. I'm fucking high. I've wanted to fuck you like that since we were teenagers." Rebel cradles me onto his lap, his clothes under us as we slump onto the floor amidst the rubble.

"I remember so much about us," I say.

"Me too." He drags his nose along mine.

This is all I want: tender moments and the comfort of being in his arms again.

"What do you remember the most?" I ask.

"How much I missed you… There was so much to miss about you. Your laugh when I'd make you a cake from scratch. Your whimpers when you came on my tongue under the oak trees where we rode horses. Your eyes when they glittered with love… I always felt loved by you, Ruby."

A lump thickens in my throat. "That's because you were. Are."

"We were so good together, baby. We had fun… We had crazy… We had…"

"Each other," I say.

Rebel kisses a line down my throat as I play with the wet hair on his chest and marvel at the span of his shoulders and the muscles wrapping them.

"Yes, we did."

"Do you remember when we got busted for jumping off the bridge?" He shifts his weight then lifts me onto his legs to straddle him. His hard abs lead down to the juncture where our bodies meet, and it's so sexy that I curl my hips to feel the friction of us.

"Yeah. Everything about it," I say. "Especially what we did to get so hot that we stripped down and jumped naked." I nip at his lips, his tongue meeting mine for a slow, drawn-out kiss tasting of the past and present and sounding like budding, new love.

Funny how something you once had can still feel like something you need to rediscover.

"At least we didn't get caught doing that." He chuckles and smooths his hand down my spine, grabbing my cheeks upon arrival.

"Those stupid cops. They only busted us so they could see me get out of the water naked." I run my fingers through Rebel's messy locks then trace the tattoos across his chest.

"Can you blame 'em? Hell, I'd have busted you too. Your dad was so pissed at me. Pissed as hell when they brought us home."

"Dad loved you. He knew we were good together. Didn't you, Dad?" I look up to the heavens and laugh. *Ghost whisperer. My mother myself, I chide.*

"We'll be good together again." His voice cracks, his eyes wet. "I promise." He swipes the back of his hand across his eyes and bites his bottom lip as it curves into a smile.

I cup his face in my hands, rubbing my thumbs over his full lips. "Rebel, it wasn't my fault."

He grabs my ass and scoots me closer, plants a kiss on my neck, then several more. "What?"

"That I got pregnant. Just please know…I never wanted that. Not any of it. But you never came for me and…it happened."

"I'm not going to ask what any of that means. If you need to talk to me, you can. If you can't, that's okay. I couldn't come to you that night. But I feel like you're putting something on me. Something like blame…maybe more."

We say nothing for noiseless minutes, but behind our eyes are all the words. Anyway, behind his eyes. And in mine? A question and an answer. How many minutes does it take to alter the course of a life? In my case…less than ten.

"I'm sorry. I've owned that night for so long, felt guilty for many things," Rebel says, threading his fingers with mine. "My dad and you and… Honestly, I wish I had come to you. It's not your fault things happened… It's mine. That night was full-moon crazy." He searches my face, his fingertips tracing paths over the landscape of my body.

"Just tell me you had a good reason," I say.

The past is something I may never figure out. Just when I thought I'd buried the bitch, she scratches her way to the surface of my heart. She's the devil in disguise with endless reach.

"I was running away," he says. "Guess I was running the wrong way."

Chapter 39

Then I Ran

Rebel

In truth, perhaps that whole night is my fault. But it's so puzzling. She slept with them because I never came to her? What we had was massive love. I thought. Maybe she always had a crush on them that I took for something else. Maybe all those times I interrupted the spats they had, the poking fun of her, and the going out of their way to yell nasty shit at her in the halls were I-hate-you-but-I'm-crushin'-on-you things. High school is weird like that.

"Did something happen?" Ruby asks.

Yeah, everything. "I walked in on my dad, and my world tilted then crashed. He was staring at himself in a full-length mirror. The only clothing he had on was a red lacy bra and matching ladies underwear. He had no idea I was in the cracked-open doorway, my jaw on the ground. My father, the man I looked up to, my hero… Who was he?"

"Jesus." Ruby's eyes widen when her mouth drops open. "That's how you found out?"

"Yeah. I caught him ogling himself. His bra was stuffed, and he had on neon-red lipstick. And the cat was on the bed, playing with other lingerie, and…me and Dad… We met in this weird-as-fuck stare. Time stopped, and I remember the rain, the sounds of it like a clock ticking. Then I smelled an oriental perfume I vaguely recalled floating down the hall a few other times. Everything was stuck in that moment.

My pulse, caught between boy and man…fantasy and reality. Time was... It was motionless and dense and impenetrable. And all I wanted to do was become one of those damn raindrops that melted into the earth. Then I ran."

Tears river down Ruby's face as a bitter tonic seeps into my gut. I've persecuted her when I might be the one who messed up.

"I forgot about you…and look what happened," I say. "Everything changed that night because I walked in on my father and couldn't deal with what I saw. I wasn't man enough to understand who he needed to be."

"I'm sorry you went through that. You lost things too. You lost your innocence just like I did," she says.

"Yeah, I lost so much that night. We did."

Had I known my running away would destroy us, what would I have done? Regret doesn't show her face until it's too late. There was no crystal ball. All of my truths vanished in that moment, my future wants and needs trailing along shortly after.

"We were both lost in something powerful and mind-blowing, and we forgot about each other," Ruby says.

Ruby slouches onto me. I follow a path down her arms then travel up her waist and onto her shoulders.

"Tell me?" I ask. "How did you think I was deserting you since it was just one night? One night, Ruby. I loved you, and you chose them."

"I begged you to come. I begged the universe to send you to me. I prayed to the God I grew up loving with all my heart. And He never sent you."

"Well, that was your first problem. That crap doesn't work. And it's not the answer I'm looking for. Don't hide behind God like most people do. Like your mom does."

Hell, with her parents being as whacked as they were on religion, I was sure Ruby had her head screwed on straight and could see through the fluff and BS of her faith. Guess I was wrong.

"I know," she whispers so softly that not even an angel on her lips would hear it.

"I can't forgive you for so many things, but I will love you despite them. You deserve love even if what you did still feels wrong to me."

"What I did?" Her top lip curls as she scoots off my lap and sits next to me. Curls as if she smells something rancid.

Do lies smell the same as truths? Bitter and sweet depending on whose tongue they're dancing from?

"I wish you understood I didn't do anything wrong," she says.

How the fuck is she so resolute?

"Whatever you want to tell yourself," I say.

"Or I could tell you the truth." Ruby slides her hand toward mine, the tips of our fingers meeting.

"No, you can't. Because I don't know how I'll be able to handle the truth, and I need to be able to love you. I can love around this thing."

"Love around?" She laughs. Then her smile flips and turns criminally sad.

"Yes."

"Is that like half love?"

"No, I can't half love you. You are too everything to me. I half loved once. Who the hell is that fair to? When I say love around, I mean there is something between us we can't discuss because it has the potential to end us. Anyway, I'm guessing. So I'll turn a blind eye because not having you in my life is no longer an option. Not ever again, no matter what happened that night."

"Rebel, most people only ever get half love or none at all."

"I guess I'm too bullheaded." I shake my head and stare off at nothing. "What were you expecting when you came home, Ruby?"

"It wasn't so much an expectation as it was a hope." She throws off a halfhearted shrug.

"Same thing, but…what were you hoping?"

"You first. You were so pissed when I came into your hardware store. But were you excited? I mean…to see me. It didn't seem like it."

"I was confused, excited, scared, heartbroken. I have never in my life wanted anything more than your love. And I know that makes me sound like a chump. But it's true."

"You're my chump." She rubs her hand over her heart as her eyes mist with tears.

"I'll be honest. I was also fucking starstruck by everything about you."

"Me? That's a riot!" She snorts. "I mean, shit, I'm a complete goof. Hardly a girl to be starstruck by."

"Now you're blowing smoke up my ass. You know exactly what I mean." I peck a kiss on her lips and tickle her ribs to receive a giggle. She's so fucking gorgeous. "Your turn. What were you hoping for?"

She chews her thumbnail for long seconds and grunts out a few ums and I's. Then, after her gaze dances between my eyes and my chin, she utters, "Forgiveness."

Fuck. I can give her brazen kisses in public and moonlit dancing in firefly meadows at midnight. I can promise her a future of unbroken bonds and making love on cold blanketed mornings. I will, on my knees, beg her to be my wife and promise her I will be faithful in my undying love.

But forgiveness? That is something I cannot give without losing more of me to the unknown of us than I can handle.

Chapter 40

False Bravado

Ruby

Forgiveness I may never get. I almost told him everything—
that's how much I need his forgiveness. Because, if he forgives me, I
will forgive me. For Opal. For everything. But the damage to him will
be too great of a burden.

I know in my heart of hearts it isn't my fault Opal killed
herself, but the guilt is so heavy most days, I can't face it. I feel like I
murdered her with my martyrdom.

Yet, had I said the evil words of my truth, I might have taken
everything from my family. Then, eventually, from him. His business.
His land. His father's grace.

And us.

"You're pretty quiet, Rebel."

"I'm thinking."

"About forgiving me?"

"About what would happen if you told me every detail about
that night and the whole next week." He scratches the scruff of his jaw
and hums low in his throat. "Every fucking thing."

I blow my cheeks out then swallow. "I'd have to make you
promise me a couple of things first."

"Like what?"

"That you would keep it between us and that you'd marry me
somewhere down the line. And I know that's a lot since I don't even

know if I can live here again, and I have a career I'm not sure I want to give up on. I couldn't ask you to move, you'd hate living in Paris. Maybe I'm putting too much out there. God, what a mind dump." I swallow so many times in a row, I choke on my reflex. Then I close my eyes and offer a stupid prayer to Opal. As if her ghost might be able to arm-wrestle his demons. What did I just say? I guess sometimes you just have to throw things out there and figure out the logistics later.

My mother myself. Jesus Lord, help me. And, now, I'm praying to God too? I have lost it.

"That was quite a mouthful. Let's take one piece at a time. Would I be breaking the law?" His eyebrows rise.

"By marrying me?" I laugh and poke him in the chest. Though, inside, I'm all jelly. What if he says yes? What if this is the moment?

"No, by keeping it between us. I'm serious, Ruby. I'm not interested in either of us getting locked up."

I scrub a hand up and down my face when my ears fill with blood, heating up. "What do you think I've done?"

"I don't fucking know. I don't want to know."

"You're lying. You have something on your face that says you think I crossed a line. Tell me."

"Did you?"

I tilt my head, hair falling across my eyes, which he thumbs away. "Did I what? Jesus Christ, Rebel!"

"It's a simple yes or no."

Looking for false bravado, I hug myself. "And if I say yes? What then? And if I say no? You think I did something criminal?"

"Don't say yes, Ruby. Don't say anything."

"You don't want to hear it, do you? The pain and guilt and the reason I can't say…can't tell you. I suppose I do have blood on my hands and I will never feel redemption for it, but was it against the law?"

"Not another word."

I grit my teeth as a lightheadedness takes over. All the tingles of wonder and lust I had become ice and knives.

"Laws were broken that week, Rebel, and—"

"Baby, stop talking." He places his hand over my mouth, and my blood boils.

I shove his hand away. "You don't trust me? I can't believe I just laid my heart on the line and you still don't trust me."

"I don't."

"How can you love someone you don't trust?" All the hope in my heart and mind shuts down as I second-guess myself and mine for answers and truths.

Rebel captures my face in his trembling hands. "You open new places in your heart and you close others off. It would be impossible to love everything about someone. We all have flaws. Love means you love… Regardless of the flaws, you still love."

"And I'm supposed to be okay with the idea that you won't forgive me and you don't trust me because you're more capable of opening your heart than I am? Where do I fit into this?"

"You fit in right beside me." Rebel wraps an arm around me and pulls me close. "We have no choice but to weather this thing, even though I don't know what it is. Isn't that how storms go? You never quite know what they are until you're in the middle of the hell?"

"And sometimes we have no choice but to forgive someone when they tell us it's important to them."

Impossible is what this is. I tell him the truth and unearth temporary sanity relief and bloodletting of my guilt. And, in whiplash response, he vanishes into a world of hate and ugly retort. I feel like the wife who had an affair then, out of guilt and need for redemption, tells her husband. And, before the news hits him like a tidal wave, he says, "Yes, tell me. Give me the truth." And, when I do, it ends everything.

So, what good is truth? What do we get from it?

Salvation? A beginning or an end?

It's a dreadful situation. Die inside of grief and guilt from holding it in, or let it out and die from regret and loss.

For everything.

Yet I did nothing wrong. I didn't cheat or take what wasn't mine.

I was stolen from.

Chapter 41

Crazy Litte Town

Rebel

Tornado sirens blare and lights around us flicker then die. Classic Wisconsin; wait a minute, and the weather will change. Hailstones ping off the windows, and Ruby works her clothes on. Again.

"Where do you think you're going?" I ask. "We still have plenty to discuss."

"I'm not staying here."

"The hell you're not," I tell her. "This building is safer than anything we could get to if we get hit. This whole side of the street is brick, Miss Dorothy."

"Let's check the weather," she says.

"Let's not." I grab the edge of her skirt and flirt with it. "Get down here."

"Rebel?"

"Listen to me, I know we're dancing around like a couple of confused kids. One minute we're angry and judgmental, the next we're dreaming about a future together. Hell, you just told me you might consider moving here. I know it's unlikely with your career and all, but still. You said the words. That's big. We have years of time to slog through and things to make up for. And right now, I'm going to make love to you and it will feel like all the forgiveness in the world." I haul Ruby onto my lap and, for the third time tonight, strip her clothes off.

As I'm unfastening her bra, she cuffs me in the jaw with her cast. It's all play, and silly fun, but I know where it's going.

"I want the words," she tells me.

"Shhh," I say as I grip her face. "Give me your tongue."

"No tongue without words."

"You stubborn, sassy cuss." I kiss her hard and messy.

And her moans, her arching neck, and her gyrating hips are all the answers I need. I want to take her on her back then on her belly, but she's pulling away. And I give up. At least she's not running out into the storm.

"You want me to feed you something besides my cock? You hungry?"

She grins. "Starved. Are you going to make me a first-date omelet? I might stay for that."

"I'm going to make you some eggs, and then I'm going to make you come again."

"Not without words, you're not."

"Fine. Then let's eat and talk." I snap my jaw shut before I give in and instead whip up an omelet. "Are you really thinking you could live here? Not sure I believe it."

"That depends," she says, a fat smirk on her face.

She's fucking stunning, crawling around the floor in her underwear and bra with a dust pan and a brush as she picks up our earlier mess. I'm half tempted to screw the eggs and fuck her on her knees.

"On me?" I ask.

"You are brilliant."

"What if I give you one of Gilbert's puppies? I'm willing to bribe you. I hear a man with puppies can do no wrong."

She stands and nestles against my back. "I don't have a house for a dog. Mom is allergic. I have to figure out what it means for my work and my life there. And I need more than a puppy to convince me to stay. But nice try."

After plating the eggs and pouring wine, we sit at a candlelit table.

"What if you moved in with me and we took it from there? You stay the summer. Then decide." I tap the tines of my fork on Ruby's plate and grin.

"You'd want me living with you? I'm practically a criminal according to you."

"Knock it off."

"I'm serious. Plus, I don't want to disrupt your family thing. Seems like you guys have it figured out. And I should go back to Paris when I planned on it anyway. It might be better for me to figure this out from afar."

"I disagree. If you leave, you might not come back. I don't want you to leave."

"This town is a little crazy. I don't even know if I could handle living here."

"It is crazy. But I'd be here to protect and love you. We could get our own place if you don't want to live at the farm. Want to hear a crazy secret?" I ask.

Her eyes lift like I asked her if she'd streak naked through my hardware store. *Hmmm.*

"That depends," she says. "Will it incriminate you?"

"Ruby, I'm warning you. I will paddle your ass if you don't cut that shit out."

"Tempting." One corner of her lips lifts. "Fine. Tell me a secret."

"Etta and Dick Kline are an item."

"Lovers?" She laughs and claps her hands. "Holy shit!"

"Yup. Apparently since high school."

"Talk about a closet of skeletons. No one in this town knows, I'll bet."

"I would have heard by now. This town is stitched together with gossip and secrets."

Ruby scoops my chambray shirt off the table and slips into it, confirming she absolutely *will* be moving into my home. She begins to button it, but my view is too good for it to vanish.

I shake my head. "Don't touch another button." I undo the two she buttoned.

"This is fun." She grins. "I hope we have to sleep here."

"We're grownups. We can sleep wherever the fuck we want. I plan on sleeping with my cock buried in you."

"Words...and it's all yours. No words and you're sleeping over there." She points to the far corner where a mop and a bucket reside.

"The hell I am." I curve my hand behind her knee and pull her toward me.

"You think I'm messing with you?" Ruby takes a sip of wine and waits for my answer.

I mouth one word, "Yes."

"I'm not. I can't be with a man who won't offer forgiveness I've begged for."

"I think you're lying, but I'll make you a deal."

"I'm all ears." She leans in and opens her eyes wide as she pulls at her ears.

"You move into my house and sleep in my bed every night and forgive me for not showing up that night. And I'll forgive you."

She sits back, crosses her arms over her chest and taps her chin. "How about this." She smirks. "You forgive me, tell me you're sorry for the name calling, and promise me I'll be your wife someday, and I'll move in. We'll call it a trial run and take it from there."

"You will?" I practically fly off my chair, haul Ruby off hers, and whirl her around. "Holy fuck, promise me!"

"In one month," she says when her toes touch the ground. "You have one month to prove you can do all that. I'll extend my stay to give you the wiggle room."

"One week." I kiss her hard on the mouth. "We can do this." Hope for us is suddenly a promise of our life together.

"You don't know me anymore. Two weeks. I need courting."

"Courting? Two weeks. You got it. And, Ruby? I know you. I still know you even though shit has gone down. You aren't that different."

Except for the part where she might be a murderer. Other than that, she's not so different.

Chapter 42

The Boy

Ruby

A week passes with Rebel courting me like I'm a queen. Not one fight. Not an ounce of guilt. Just fun and the pure bliss of navigating the new us. We do old things, like skinny dipping in the river and picking cherries at my favorite farm. The very farm I will someday own *if* I decide to stay. And we do new things too. Rebel fucks me in the tape and rope aisle of his hardware store, proving to me he is no longer a teenager. And we hang out with the Valentines in their crazy castle, along with the Cox family. All of us playing a role in their Sunday circus event.

Our week is reassuring. So much so that I consider moving into his house earlier than proposed because I sleep there most nights anyway. The only thing I'm still working through is the idea of living here. I know full well it's the only way we'll have a future together. So, can I do it? Give up my other life, which on the scale of simple to over the top is WAY over the top. It's champagne, caviar, first class from Paris to New York and everything in-between. Versus skinny dipping in the river, fish boils on Friday nights and a local band at the Tincat for a real zinger of a time. Amazingly, the simple life sounds appealing. Under one condition. Rebel and I can continue to work toward trust and forgiveness. Time will tell.

On the following Sunday, Mom and I prepare for the deads day potluck like it's Thanksgiving. She even buys a turkey and names it

Fred. She felt naming him Fred would be of great importance to all the guests and set the tone for the dinner. Who could argue with her logic? Her *new* logic.

At six on the dot, Rebel, Rifle, and Etta arrive with armloads of food. Pies, casseroles, and something covered in puff pastry. Everyone sets their wrapped re-gifting gift on the table, where Mom made name tags out of macaroni and sequins. A craft project she and Echo worked on for the last few days. She keeps calling them maniacal. I've been trying hard not to correct her use of words, but I'm dying to know if she means magical.

Etta travels across the room to come face-to-face with Mom. I shouldn't be nervous, but I am when Mom's gaze drops to Etta's crotch and she purses her lips.

"Those are form-fitting pants. I like the floral pattern, though I prefer dresses to avoid camel row," Mom says.

"Camel what?" Etta asks, smoothing one hand down the front of her pants.

"It's why schools are banning tight pants. Boys simply cannot concentrate around camel row. I read it on Yoogle."

"Google. Mom, slow down." I bite my inner cheek and throw a look at Rebel, who's rolling his eyes. "Camel toe, and everyone here is an adult." So much for trying not to correct her. I had to make an exception.

"Opal isn't." She motions to a chair.

I nod. She is dead serious, no pun intended.

"I wanted to thank you for the solarium housewarming gift." Mom points to the center of the table, where she positioned Etta's creation. "It's quite a feat of artistry."

"Terrarium," Etta says. "You're most welcome."

After an awkward silence and quiet sips of our beverages, which Rebel was smart to serve seconds after arriving, Mom clears her throat. Three times.

"Shall we sit?" she says, gesturing toward the table. "I'll get Fred." Then she marches toward the kitchen.

I nab her arm as she passes me. "Don't forget you were going to *make some men* with a certain someone today."

"Make amends, Ruby. You should have gotten a college degree."

I growl and grind my teeth. "Rebel can get Fred."

"Who's Fred?" Rebel asks as Mom and I enter the kitchen.

"The turkey. He's in the oven."

"You man the crew out there," he says. "I got Fred."

I rise to my toes and kiss him on the mouth. "Thanks for indulging us today. You're a good man. This is kind of crazy, right?"

"Isn't that the definition of family? Crazy. And fun. It'll be fun, Ruby."

I nod and cross my fingers. Fun? Okay, sure.

Rebel carries Fred out on a large platter and sets him at the head of the table, where Mom placed his name tag. I never asked if Fred was considered one of the deads. I suppose the name tag answers that.

"After we say grace"—Mom clears her throat three times—"I'd like you to cut Fred, Rebel."

"Whatever you want, Mrs. Rose. It would be my honor."

I steal a long look around the table. Person. Deads. Person. Deads. And so on. I have to believe we aren't the only family who has made-up holidays. Then I lock eyes with Rebel.

"Lenny's going to say grace," Mom announces, tapping her spoon against her crystal wine glass like we're at a wedding.

We sit in silence for about a minute. Then Mom nods, smiles, and has her own moment with Lenny. After she thanks him, everyone introduces their deads guest upon her urging. It gives awkward and funny a new name.

Opal is my guest. Lenny is Mom's. Etta introduces Rocket, who died when…well, back then. Rebel—ever the good sport—introduces Jesus and scores big time with Mom. Echo introduces Santa. And Rifle, bless his soul, introduces Bob Marley.

Then the *real fun* ensues.

"What parts do you like to eat, Etta?" Mom asks. She passes a bowl of squash to Etta, a tight smile gliding across her face.

"What's the topic?" Etta asks.

Rebel hands a plate of Fred to Etta after she's passed the squash to me. A heaping mound of dark meat covers her plate.

"Turkey parts. What else would I be talking about?" Mom says.

I scowl at her.

She looks toward the ceiling, cupping a hand at her ear. "Okay, Len… I'll try harder."

I know she's trying to make amends. But her way of connecting makes unique appear ordinary.

"Dark meat," Etta says.

I take a sip of my wine and cheer her inside. Etta is my spirit animal. Her grace, calm, and ability to deal with Mom makes my insides form row after row of rainbows.

"I prefer the breast," Mom says.

My gaze ping-pongs between them.

"Speaking of, what parts do you have now? Now that…you know." Mom waves a hand up and down her body.

The rainbows in my belly swirl into a black tornado. *Please pick me up and take me to Oz.*

Rebel pins his lips between his teeth, and I pray that a food fight ensues before some other ugly hits the fan.

"I have lady parts, just like you." Etta doesn't flinch.

And I want to shout out her Olympic score: TEN! I can't look at Rebel or I will die laughing.

"What did they do with your reproduction parts?" Mom asks like she's a librarian needing to account for lost books.

"They saved them in formaldehyde for the high school science classes to dissect," Etta says, not a hint of a smile cracked. Then she sips her wine and follows up with a World Series home run. "I got a tax break for that donation." She's smooth and cool as freshly Zambonied ice.

I burst out laughing, a mouthful of Fred and wine glazing my cloth napkin. *Family.* Dear God. Is there anything better? Is there anything odder?

"That's very thrifty," Mom says.

Rifle coughs a laugh into his fist. Then he slides an arm around Etta's shoulder and squeezes her. It's such a sweet moment to witness that my eyes well up.

"What's the corpse?" Etta asks, continuing to hold court, pointing to the puff pastry.

"Meatloaf. Was trying something new and going with tonight's theme," Rifle says. "Would you like some, Mrs. Rose?"

"I would love to try some," I say.

"Me please," Echo says, holding his plate up.

"There isn't any dog in it, is there?" Mom asks.

Everyone quiets.

"No dog," Rifle confirms.

I want to strangle her, but instead, I smile.

"How about rodents?" Mom asks.

My spine stiffens.

"No rodents, either," Rifle says flatly, laying a thin slab on my plate.

Mom grins and holds her plate out. "I would love some too. Thank you." Then she tilts her head and focuses in on Etta. "What about you? Do you like rodents?"

"Only if a snake is chasing them." Etta raises her wine glass to Mom, who smiles merrily.

I realize she's sure she's making some serious amends. She's proud of the conversation they're having. I blush for both of us.

"Is that what the gays do? They release the rodent then a snake? That is rather inventive."

"Excuse me?" Etta covers her mouth with one hand.

Shit. Mom has crossed a line. An ugly line. A tripwire.

"Don't play coy," Mom says, patting her mouth with her napkin. "You know what we're talking about. Gays have fascinating habits."

"I'm not gay." Etta's lips thin when she enunciates each word.

I want to crawl under the table then inch toward the back door and evaporate.

"And even if I was," she says, "that's quite an assumption to lump masses of people into boxes the way you do. It's offensive."

Pin. Drop. Silence.

I pitch a death stare at Mom. Then I roll my eyes as I push my chair back from the table and begin clearing plates.

"I'm sorry," Mom says. "Lenny tells me I stepped over the rind."

"Over the line, Mom. Line," I say harshly at her ear as I stand behind her. "And yes, you did." I snag her plate then move down the table to gather the others. There might be steam coming out my ears.

"Thank you for your apology," Etta says. "It's quite all right."

After the table has been cleared and everyone's nerves seem settled by another pour of wine, we move to the screened porch overlooking the lake. The wind whips at a mighty rate, but it's refreshing considering the stale air that hung around the table. Mom asks the deads to join us for our re-gifted exchange, calling each one out by name. She's always had a thing about re-gifting stuff. Even if it's offensive, she feels the truth will set everyone free. I'm not convinced.

Mom opens a gift first, because gifts and winning are the most important things in the world to her.

"A squirrel mask!" She cheers. "What will Father H. say when I wear it to church on Sunday?"

"He'll probably want one." Rebel snickers.

Mom puts the mask on and urges us to continue. Echo opens a box of bacon mints, pops one in his mouth, then hands a gift to Etta.

"I made it," he says, rubbing his hands together as if he's given Etta a kidney. "Because you're my best friend."

Rebel scoops my hand in his when Etta tears up. And the sweet look she offers him when she holds her shaky hand out for his forces my tears to surface too. I'm a sucker for beauty, and this just happens to be a memory I will never forget.

"What a kind thing to say, Echo. Thank you." Etta stares at the tinfoil-covered box in her hands. Then, as if opening something worth a small fortune, she peels the foil away and removes the top of the box. Her face, though, is the furthest thing from appreciative when she peers in at the contents. She gasps then bites her knuckle, her face flooding in crimson. "Thank you, Echo, I will treasure this." She closes the box and tucks it into her purse.

"But…but…but…" Echo whines, his eyes watering like a child who's been told no. "Put it on. I made it."

Etta stares at Rebel, panic racing across her face.

"You okay?" Rebel asks. "You look like you might pass out."

"I'm—" Etta pauses, her wet eyes meeting mine in a haunting stare.

"What did Echo make for you?" Mom asks. "Put it on!"

"I can't," Etta says softly. "It belongs to Ruby."

Chapter 43

Heart & Soul

Rebel

Etta reaches into her purse and pulls the small box out. Then she stands and walks to Ruby's side.

"Ruby, sweetheart. This isn't a conversation we can have here." With a trembling hand, she places the box on Ruby's open palms. Then she leaves the room without another word.

Holy fuck, it's gotta be the box of jewelry.

Echo bursts into a full-blown piercing cry that includes a dive onto the floor, which has him kicking and punching everything within reach.

Ruby's face becomes ghost white and shock filled when she peeks inside the box. Then she slams the top closed. She stands and glances at her mom then me.

"I… Excuse me." She floats out of the room as if a ghost is carrying her.

And I'm certain one or two are.

Monday flips her squirrel mask up onto her wig then canvases the room with a bewildered sneer. "She always needs to be the most important one."

"Mrs. Rose?" I say. "Let her be."

"It's true," she says in a childish whine.

"It's not true. Don't do that to her." Words scrape my teeth as my jaw tightens. "Rifle, you coming with me? I need to find Ruby and Etta."

"You need help, Dad?" Rifle stands and grips my arm.

My pride for the young man he's becoming swells. "Nah, I've got a pretty good guess as to where they are."

"You go ahead," Rifle says. "I'll be at Bubble's place. Call me if you need anything."

"Mrs. Rose," I say to her, "thank you for including us today. This was... Well, thank you."

Looks like shit's about to get real.

With the Jeep absent from the driveway, my mind races with anxious thoughts. I travel the easiest route home in my truck, assuming I'll see Etta, unless she and Ruby went somewhere together. As I pull into my driveway minutes later, my stomach knots. No Ruby.

Etta's comment that they couldn't have a conversation earlier is worrisome. Why couldn't they? Etta told me exactly where she found the ring and that the crosses had never made it to the twins. I know that second part is a lie. But the other stuff? I have to assume that the only reason she would lie to me this much is to protect someone. But who?

Unsure of how to proceed without being point-blank, I knock on Etta's bedroom door, which is closed.

"Come in," she says.

An eerie awareness coats my gut. I don't know what I'm walking in on, and I'm scared as fuck I'm not going to like it. Etta is seated on the edge of her bed, her back to me. Her jewelry box has been emptied onto the quilt next to her.

"What's going on?" I ask.

"Rebel, there are things... Dammit." Her voice cracks, and her shoulders slump. Then she sweeps a hand through the mess of gold and silver on the bed, driving it off the edge with rapid force.

Objects ping and bounce off the walls and the floor. She howls a sound I've never heard come from her or anyone else before. I can't even name that sort of pain, even with what I've gone through.

I take a seat next to her. "Whatever it is we're going to be okay." I clutch her hand in mine and twist our fingers as fat tears roll down her powdery cheeks in long rivers.

"Etta…breathe."

"I'm sorry, Rebel. I'm sorry for everything." Etta covers her face with her hands and sobs. My stomach swirls. *Everything? What does everything include?* "It's all my fault. Everything that's happened is my fault, and there isn't a thing I can do to fix it."

I toss an arm over Etta's shoulder and tug her to my side. Her slumped body holds a defeated sentence that's making my pulse race. "Sounds to me like you've got the weight of the world on your shoulders. You want to unload some onto me? I'll help you carry it."

"If I do that, it'll only make things worse, because too much of the weight will shift onto you. I can't do that. The burden… Jesus. The weight of it is too much for anyone."

"But you're not going to tell me what it is?" I ask. I grip her hand and search her face as she stares at our twinned fingers. Her gaze moves to my eyes. Shock and revulsion are all I see when she takes her free hand to her mouth and bites her knuckle.

"Hey, I promise you can tell me anything. I'm your kid. That means we're locked for life. We've been through a lot. How bad can it be? Tell me what's got you all choked up and scared-lookin'."

She shakes her head. I haven't seen her look like this since way back, when she told me that she was going ahead with the operation and everything that went along with it.

"I would if I could. You've been the kind of son a father could only dream of having. You've supported me through some of the hardest things I've gone through. I'm not sure who I'd be right now if it weren't for you." She wipes her face with her sleeve. "Have you talked to Ruby?"

"No. Thought she might be here with you.

"I don't know where she is. Rowdy saw me walking and gave me a lift. Might want to go to the cemetery."

"And why's that?" I ask, gripping the back of my neck as it tenses.

"That's between you and her, son."

"Seems more like it's between you and Ruby."

"She has no idea what's between us. And, truthfully, she never may." Etta struggles through a shaky breath.

"There is a truth hiding somewhere dark in this town about the Klines' murder-suicide and Ruby. Why do I think you know something about it?"

"Rebel, I will say this one time. Don't ask me anything like that ever again. For you and Rifle and for Ruby." She walks to the window. With her fists full of curtains, she yanks them apart then leans her forehead onto the glass.

"But not for you?"

"Let's leave me out of it." Her tone is grim, everything about her stance hopeless.

I stand and amble to Etta. I lean my back against the wall as I wait and watch for clues. But the silence hangs, so I ask the obvious question.

"Is this a police matter?"

Etta mumbles something under her breath then backs up one step. Her shaky fingers land on her equally trembling chin. "This is more than that... It's a matter of the heart and soul."

"Etta, you can trust me with your life. I love you, and it doesn't matter what happened."

"It does matter, son." Etta paces a line back and forth, wringing her hands and sighing every so often.

"I need to find Ruby. Need to get to the bottom of some things."

She perches her hands on her hips but speaks to the floor. "Let me tell you something about Ruby. She is brave and courageous, and you need to let her share her story in her own time. Don't push her."

"Her story?" I take two steps and close the gap between us. "You know something?"

She tips her face up. "I know everything. Every motherfucking thing. Wish I didn't, but I do. I know more than anyone what happened that week. If only I didn't." She muffles a sob in her sleeve.

I'm rattled and unsure how far to push her. But I need to find Ruby.

"You gonna be okay if I go find her?" I ask.

"I'm going to be fine." Though her voice betrays her promise. "You are too. We are all going to be okay. We have each other."

"Yes, we do," I say, hugging Etta and knowing that my search for Ruby might be a long one. "Remember that... Got it?"

"It's gotten me through everything. I got it."

Chapter 44

Set Me Free

Ruby

I tear out of the driveway in the Jeep, knowing full well where I'm headed: Rebel's farm.

Bile swims in my belly, hoping for release, which could come any second.

I thought that damn ring and those crosses would turn up at some point, but not like that. Not in the form of a necklace made by Echo for Etta.

I'm clocking seventy-five on the road Rebel lives on, needing to beat him to his farm. I press harder, metal meeting metal. Eighty-five…ninety. My heart beats are flying as fast. Shit, I didn't think the Jeep had it in her. I glance at the speedometer, and in that blur of a second, I get an eerie sense that my life is about to change again.

The sound of glass is what I hear first. Then I feel it—the pressure on my skin. Next comes knives. Then weight on my chest. Must be ten thousand pounds. I'm upside down, I think. Warm liquid runs over my body and down my throat. Gasoline? Blood? My mouth fills and I choke. It smells like burned rubber and something I can't distinguish. It's okay. I'm almost to Rebel's farm. I need to get there… I can clean up there.

Dizzy. So dizzy and tired. Are you tired, Opal? I can see her, but she doesn't answer me. I'm coming to see you. I'm coming to tell you I'm sorry. It's all my fault and I'm coming to take your pain away today.

"RUBY!"

Rebel? I can tell him the truth now because I'm almost free from my body and my soul will now be free too. The truth… Yes, it will set me free. Mom was right.

There's so much pressure on my chest. And yelling. Why is he yelling at me? Is he angry I told him the truth? I don't remember telling him anything. But he won't stop yelling.

"Leave me alone. I'm tired."

"Ruby Mae…you fucking listen to me. You are not tired. You are… You fucking wake up. Ruby…open your eyes."

I turn to find him...the man who keeps yelling. Is it him? God. So, now, you're here? He sounds mad at me. Mad like those boys were a long time ago when they hurt me and Opal. What did we do to deserve all their anger?

So cold and numb. Full, heavy, and hot. How can I feel all these things?

"Ruby, we're gonna get you out of here, and you're gonna be okay and then you're gonna be my wife and we're… We'll live happily forever and…RUBY! Don't do that, baby. Fucking stag... You fucking piece of shit, if you killed my girl… RUBY!"

Who the hell is Stag? Must be one of those boys who hurt me and Opal. Stag is hairy and heavy. And jabbing me hard. Yes, it's them again. Why now?

"Ruby, stay with me. As soon as they get here, they'll haul this piece of shit stag and Jeep off you and... Fuck, baby. Ruby, I hear 'em coming... You hear that? The sirens—that's for you. They're gonna save you now... Hang on another minute."

It's so quiet here...sleeping.

"Rebel, we need you to back up. Back the fuck up so we can get at her," someone says. Someone loud. God?

"RUBY!"

Things happen fast, in blurs and blinks. I'm jostled around and then the weight is gone. I hear cursing and crying and I can't tell if it's Lenny or Opal or Rebel. Who is crying? Is that my baby? I couldn't keep you, baby. They gave you to me without a spine, and then I gave you freedom.

I open my eyes and someone is talking to me. Hands touching me. Too many hands. Too much pain.

"Leave her alone," I say. "You're hurting her... She doesn't understand... Let her go!"

They let Opal go and they take me.

It's better in the bright light. Calm. Peaceful. Painless. Pretty sparkles and sleep. Goodbye, Rebel... I'm tired... Too tired. Need to sleep...

Forever.

Chapter 45

Helpers

Rebel

I haul ass out of the driveway. This fucking mystery is mounting into something fierce. More people…more questions. And what now? What in Sam Hill does Etta have in this whole thing? Apparently, plenty. I'm scared shitless to find out what went down that week between Ruby and Etta and the possible murders. Damn, I'm at a loss. What next?

I might be taking the curve a little fast, but my nerves are devouring me like some flesh-eating disease I can't control.

What was in that box? The crosses and the ring? Had to be. Unless it was some other clue to this crazy mystery.

I round the curve, and my eyes trick my mind. My heart tricks my stomach. I slam on the brakes as I fly at a vision of holy hell.

"Ruby! NO!"

I grab my phone and finger in 911. Then I yell something at the person on the other end of the line about a car accident and death and fucking who knows what else.

There's no air coming into my lungs, but vomit spews from my throat at the horrid sight. Her Jeep is flipped and partially flattened, and coming out of her now missing windshield is the biggest fucking buck I've ever seen. He's thrashing through his death call, and he has my Ruby pinned under his massive rack of antlers.

On my stomach, I crawl to her. "Ruby…baby…talk to me."

"Opal? I'm coming." Her whisper is drowned in a gurgle of blood.

"No! You're not fucking going to Opal. You're mine and we're going to get married and we're going to… RUBY! Come back to me."

I have never felt more helpless in my entire life. Not even when Paris was in a coma. Nor when Rocket was standing in the mirror in his red lingerie. Or when Ruby told me that she'd lost her virginity to the Kline twins. No. Not ever…more than now. My Ruby is dying before my eyes. And this fucking stag is going to kill her.

I kick the sonuvabitch everywhere I can, trying to kill it. If it dies, she might live.

"Ruby!"

"Leave her alone…take me," Ruby mutters. "She doesn't understand. Don't hurt her."

I crawl in next to her, as close as I can, and grab the stag's antlers, trying to still him. I'm too fucking weak to save her. He's pierced her to the seat, antlers stabbing through her in multiple places. Shredding her right before my eyes.

"Ruby…listen to me… Don't you leave me. You here that… Those are sirens, baby. Those are sirens for you." I can't stop sobbing, and my heart? My heart is gone by default. Because, if she leaves me now, I will not survive. I cannot lose my woman twice. I need her.

Hands force me back. I'm swinging, punching…a feral animal out of control over love and promise. My future is dying in front of me and I'm gonna kill death before it kills her.

"Rebel, back the fuck up!" Someone restrains me. Pins me to a tree and yells in my face. Someone angry and red-faced... Someone crying and howling...and holding me.

Who is it? I can't see straight. Dick Kline? My godfather is here?

"RUBY!" I push him away.

Another person grabs me and fucking ties me to the tree like I'm crazy. Maybe I am. Ruby is blood-covered and that fucking stag is killing her.

"Get off me! I need to help her!"

"Somebody give him something. He's going to kill himself. Give him a fucking tranquilizer!" an EMT shouts.

I know him, but I'm so frazzled I can't name him.

"Rebel, calm down. You need to be able to understand that I'm giving you something."

"Yes, I understand. I think I'm having a panic attack... I think..."

I think I just died of a broken heart.

Because, when they pulled my Ruby from that wreckage, she wasn't moving. She was spurting blood like a stuck pig and there weren't enough hands to cover those leaking holes on her body.

"Ruby Mae Rose, you will not die today. You will not DIE TODAY," I say. Then I say it again. I say it again... I say... I...

I love you, Ruby Mae... Please don't leave me again.

Chapter 46

Bright Haze

Ruby

So, this is Heaven? Yes. I knew when I was hugging Opal again that I'd arrived. I thought I would feel light and free. Except I'm not. I feel strapped in and suffocated. Where is my voice? And why can't I move? And why is everything pink? Non-fucking-stop pink! I hate pink. Are those my eyelids? Who is that talking? I know that voice. And I know that one too. Someone who loves me.

"Is she ever going to wake up?"

I think it's Rebel. I want to tell him I am awake. All he needs to do is help me open my eyes.

"We're seeing positive reactions. We can't promise anything. She's not out of the woods, but she's closer to the edge."

The edge? What the hell? The edge of what? This is crazy. And where is Opal? She keeps coming…then leaving. Everyone is talking at me. They all seem familiar. But no one shows their faces. Why are they hiding from me? Do they finally know my secret and they don't want me to see their disgust?

"Ruby. Please come back to me. Why does this keep happening? First, Paris was in a coma. Then Bubble. Now, you? Not you too," Rebel says. Then he sobs.

Why is everyone crying when they're near me? What have I done now?

Opal shows up less and less. And I understand everything everyone is saying, but they don't seem to understand me. I can hear them around me all the time now. Sometimes there are so many people that the voices blur. Then they cry and hold my hand and squeeze it. They squeeze it too hard. So hard that I want to scream.

It feels like years have gone by. I have no idea what day it is. At times, I feel heavy and tired. Exhausted. Then I'm wide awake, trying to answer questions, but no one seems to hear me. Still.

"You ought to tell her. Even in her current state she might understand you."

This is the same voice I hear many times every day. I think he might be my doctor.

He and Mom have lots of conversation. She's the only one who hasn't said anything to me yet. She never talks to me. But she does talk about me. She's mad about things. Mad that I have everyone's attention again. Mad that Opal and I are seeing each other. Mad that Lenny might tell me something she wants to tell me herself. Her words are more mixed up than ever. Or is that my mind playing tricks on me?

"How do I tell her?" Mom asks.

"Would you like me to help you?" The doctor—or God or whoever the person is—answers.

"No. I'm not ready."

"I'll be down the hall. You can have the nurse find me if you'd like."

"I don't need pulp."

"Help?" the doctor asks.

"Don't correct me all the time. You sound like Ruby. Do you have a college degree, for God's sake? Leave me alone. I need privacy with her."

A warm, shaking hand rests on my cheek. Then kisses dance across my forehead.

"Ruby Mae. I don't know if you can hear me, but I want you to know something. I never say it…but…I'm proud of you. And I hope you decide to stay here for good. I would like that. I missed you when you were gone. I'm sorry I never told you that. But it's true, I missed you so much."

Mom has never told me this. *I'm proud of you.* It was always something else. "You're not such a good girl." "You're pretty, but I'm the prettiest." "You aren't as smart as you think you are." "Those girls are better." "They have more money." "You got an A, why not an A+? Work harder next time."

I know she loved me. Loved? But she cracked her whip and I jumped for her hoping I'd hear the words every child wants to hear. *I'm proud of you.*

"Ruby. Do you hear me?" Her voice is sunk in fog. Then it rises. "I'm proud of you." She cries.

I do too. Because her words are so special. And needed. I don't know if she can tell I'm crying, but it hurts everywhere in my body like I am. Hurts like I'm being ripped into a thousand pieces. I'm crying hard, and then she starts yelling for a nurse and sounds beep like crazy, making my head spin. Rebel is yelling and Opal comes to my side and tells me we're okay. We're both okay.

We're together again.

We're laughing.

We're having tapioca.

Then Opal leaves, and I follow her vanishing form into the bright haze.

Chapter 47

On My Knees

Rebel

"Ruby Mae, I forgive you." I dust kisses across her hand then draw circles on her palm, knowing she's the most ticklish there and can't usually stand it. But nothing comes of it. Not a flinch. "Please, sweet thing. Please know I forgive you. I love you. And I want to marry you. I want you to live here. Please. Baby, do you hear me? I don't care about anything else… I only…"

Everything I say is a plea. An offer of forgiveness. Another promise. To Ruby. To God. To the devil. To any spirit who gives two fucks and might want a portion of my soul in exchange for her to come back. I'd give anything. My limbs. My sanity.

What will I do without her? It was one thing to know she was somewhere in the world without me. But that she might leave this world forever? No. I can't entertain the thought without every cell in my body dissolving.

She's alive. That's all I'm hanging on to. I've been cursed by comas like I'm a fucking coma magnet. First, Paris. Then Bubble. And, now, my Ruby. Maybe it's this town. The same fucking curve where I found Bubble wrapped around that tree with her boyfriend, I found Ruby. The same curve where five drunk football players from our varsity team in high school died one week before state.

Ruby's hospital room is flooded with flowers. So many flowers that Monday Rose is losing her shit daily. Monday is the only person who won't talk to Ruby. The doctor keeps telling us to include Ruby in conversation because she may hear us. He wants us to share stories with her. But Monday has refused to include her at all.

I think she's grieving the idea that Ruby might never wake up, but in her grief, I give her credit. She's trying to reach the rest of us. Even Etta is touched by Monday's new compassion. It's almost like Ruby's accident has softened Monday. Impermanence has a way of doing that. Not that Monday hasn't seen her fair share of death. Opal, then Lenny not long after from a heart attack. And, now, Ruby's situation. Sometimes I think she's going to say something to Ruby's still form, but then all she does is walk to her side, whisper to the deads, then slump into a chair next to Ruby's bed.

Etta, Monday, and Rifle disband for coffee, and here I sit consumed with Ruby. Everything's haunting me. Her shine and sparkle. Her laugh. Her emerald eyes, which she hasn't opened in so long that it makes me ill. The darkness she was hiding in, shadows she couldn't move past. And where is my Ruby now? Where is she hiding?

"Rebel?" Etta pokes my shoulder. "I brought you coffee."

"Thanks." I drag my fingertips down my jaw. Jesus. I don't remember the last time I shaved. "Rifle okay? Did he go home?" I take the coffee from Etta, yawn, and sniff the full-bodied scent, amazed one of my senses isn't numb.

"Rifle is fine. He's going to Bubble's house. Monday is down in the chapel with Father H. I'm amazed she doesn't sleep down there."

We both chuckle. A rare thing these days.

Etta dusts the hair off my forehead, her worried gaze dancing across my face. "Are you okay?"

"As long as she's breathing. But take me to the river and shoot me if she dies. Because I will not survive her."

"Rebel, please don't." Etta drags a chair next to mine and sits.

"You think I'm kidding?"

"I think you're terrified you're going to lose her, yes. But you will go on. God forbid she doesn't pull through."

I shoot off my chair and stomp to the other side of the room. "We're not having this conversation."

"It's been two weeks. It's better to talk about it than not."

"The hell it is. I'm holding on to hope. It's all I've got."

"You've got me too." Etta comes to my side and begins rubbing my back. "And you've got Rifle."

"And I've got Ruby!" It's a shout. An angry, we're-not-putting-her-in-the-grave shout. "I've fucking got her and I'm not losing her… I'm not…" And then I'm on my knees. A force kicked my legs out from under me.

Weeping like a child, I'm hunched over, trying to stop the feeling that she may never come back to me. She may need to have the plug pulled. Jesus, help me.

The hospital door creaks open, and I look up to Monday, who's staring back at me. Her face crumples when she holds her hand out. I grip her shaking fingertips and stand. She might be going through something harder than I am now.

"Rebel. Promise me you'll take good care of her."

"Of course I will. You say it like you're leaving."

She hugs me. Monday Rose isn't known for showing any sort of affection, so the hug knocks me flat.

"Monday, what's going on?"

"I need to speak to Ruby alone." Tears coat her face, and she weeps. "I told Ruby I was proud of her earlier, might have been the first time I told my daughter those words. And I now I have some more confessions to share with her."

Chapter 48

I Loved The Devil

Rebel

Etta and I leave Monday alone with Ruby so she can make her confessions. Not that we have an inkling what she might want to confess. But she was dead serious about something. So serious that Etta starts chattering like a squirrel on crack the second we exit the room.

"Rebel. We should sit."

"I don't want to sit. Let's keep walking."

"Walking? Okay, fine. I can do this. Walk."

"What are you so goddamned nervous about all of a sudden?"

She wraps a hand around my bicep with a death grip. "I need a cigarette."

"You haven't smoked since you were Rocket. The fuck's going on?"

"Maybe a drink too. Let's walk to the bar across the street." Etta struts in marathon mode ahead of me like she's chasing after her lifeline.

I jog and catch up to her, planting myself in her way. "Are you literally ill? It's ten in the morning and you want a smoke and a drink?"

"Liquid courage and then some," she answers, pushing me aside, marching on.

"What's gotten into you?"

Upon arriving at the bar, we order drinks, and I go along with the whole shebang because Etta looks like she's about to barf. After one martini, two cigarettes, and more silence than I can take, she speaks.

"I heard her yell. Then I saw them out there. I begged Dick to let me help her, but he barricaded the door." She dabs her eyes with the soaked cocktail napkin. "They would have found out about us...and, worse, about him. He couldn't... It would have ruined his career and his life."

I love her. But, right now, and after what she's told me, I may strangle her. My hands form a circle in my lap, my fingertips pressed so hard together that my nails cut into my skin.

"His life?" I crash a hand on the table between us. "His fucking life? Where is that motherfucker? I'm going to kill him. I am going to hunt him down and gut that cocksucker then bury him in the sewer."

"He's gone."

"Gone? You loved the devil? I'm gonna be sick." I want to believe all love is on the right side. But I'm having doubts.

Then it crosses my mind. Had Ruby confessed to their murders, I would have kept on loving her. People can do a world of wrong and there will still always be someone who loves them. There is a lover or a mother or a father to each of those people, and still...though that person has committed the unforgivable and heinous, they will be loved by at least one person.

"I loved the devil, yes." Etta lights her third cigarette, her eyes rimmed in red, her cheeks sunken low like a basset hound. Sad as fuck.

Maybe as sad as I am pissed. "He lost too. Lost both his boys," she says, staring at her unsteady hands.

"He committed a crime. They all did. They deserved to die."

"I did too. But I couldn't get to them, and then I said nothing. Dear God. I said nothing. The guilt ate me inside out. I did the wrong thing, and then it felt too late." She reaches across the table, her shaky hand edging toward mine.

"Have you ever done something like that?" she asks. "It's a horrible feeling to know you could have helped someone and you didn't for fear of your own situation."

I don't answer her. Instead, I ask the unthinkable. "Did you kill them?"

Chapter 49

He Was There

Ruby

Mom has been crying for the longest while. And, for the first time in I don't know how long, I see her. Unless I'm imagining it. One second, I was trying to form words to tell her to stop bawling. The next, I'm focusing in on her shuddering form.

Maybe she thinks I'm dead. But I wouldn't be seeing so many things if I'd died. Except the flowers? And I'm lying on something so soft and white that I'm creeped into believing it's my coffin. I'm dead?

Now, I can tell her what happened too. Wow. I had no idea being dead would feel so real. All of my senses are intact. But no question, I'm dead. And hungry. How the fuck am I hungry?

I open my mouth to speak, and like magic, Rebel and Etta come into focus at the end of the bed, a small painting of Jesus hanging on the wall between them.

Rebel is crying. Etta is crying. Mom is crying. And I haven't said a word. The only one who seems to hear me now is Mom. For once, I'm thrilled she talks with the deads.

"Mom, tell Rebel the Kline boys raped me so he doesn't hate me forever and think I cheated. Tell him I'm sorry I died and took away our future. Tell him I love him more than I loved myself and it's why I couldn't tell him."

"Ruby!" Rebel practically throws himself on me.

This dead thing is wild. I can even feel him touching me. Unless my powers are greater than other deads? I wonder if Opal can feel people touching her too? This might be weirder than anything I've ever been through.

The explosion escalates. Etta yells for doctors and nurses. And Mom screams about miracles one second. Then she's condemning the Kline boys the next and calling for Lenny seconds afterward. There is so much commotion that I'm a little freaked out. And, when the doctor shines a light in my eyes, I scream, telling him to fuck off before he blinds me. Then I ask Mom why she hasn't told Rebel that they raped me. The room goes dead silent.

Death is noisy and quiet. Interesting.

"Am I the only one of the deads you can't fucking hear? Ma! Tell Rebel what they did to me. Tell him they raped me." Maybe she didn't hear me before.

"Ruby." Etta's face is so close to mine I can smell her minty, alcohol-soaked breath.

This concerns me because, when I start rotting from the inside out, I'm going to smell that stench. Maybe the deads would be better off without their senses.

"Ruby, honey," Etta says. "He knows because I was there."

Chapter 50

Rumors

Ruby

"You were what?" I ask.

Dear God, who is your ruler? Satan? Is the master of hell guiding your true north? I'm convinced God and the devil are in it together as of this very moment. My hands travel to my heart then my neck, my pulse flying at Mach speed, my heart pounding so hard I'm sure it's going to burst through my rib cage.

"I'm going to throw—" I twist, and as I do, Rebel slides a plastic container right where I need it.

He wipes my mouth with something then sternly addresses everyone. "Guys, let's give her a moment. This is too much."

"No, this is not too much… This is too late... Tell me."

"I was there," Etta says. "I couldn't get to you. Couldn't save you."

"Am I in Hell?" I ask.

"Ruby." Rebel inches his face close to mine. His bloodshot, fatigued eyes flood with tears.

"Rebel? Is this real? Am I dead or alive?" I reach up to touch him, certain my fingers will push through his skin like he's made of air.

"Alive."

That one word is a prayer wrapped in distress, the whole thing dipped in hope and joy.

"You're alive, sweet thing."

Etta's form comes into focus, her face consumed with remorse. The lines on her forehead and the wave of her eyebrows undulate as she speaks softly. Slowly. Each syllable marked with discomfort.

"I was locked in the janitor's office with Dick Kline, he and I in our"—she looks around the room then pinches her neck skin in a twist—"ladies underwear." She shutters out a small cry then stands tall, wiping tears. "He blocked me from opening the door… There wasn't a thing I could do. But I should have after. All I could do was gather up the ring and necklace and crosses when everyone left. I was in shock. I'm sorry I failed you. All of you. I committed a crime too." She hangs her head, her face cupped in her palms as she moans.

Her angst wraps around my deepest wounds. The scars no one has been privy to. My thoughts are scattered. I'm furious. I'm other things too… I just can't pin a name on them yet.

"And you killed them?" I can't focus on what happened that night. It's done. But, finally, I'm face-to-face with answers. I'm able to connect dots. Some.

"No," she says. "But I know who did."

A whoosh of anxiety whirlwinds from my lungs. Why do I need to know? I can't change history. What will it bring me? Comfort? Peace? Anguish? My morbid curiosity is uncontainable.

"I did it," Mom says.

Every ounce of air sustaining my lungs leaves.

"You're lying." Etta's aggressive tone scores everyone's attention. "It's very noble of you to protect him."

"You don't know what you're talking about." Mom glares at Etta.

"I know damn well what I'm talking about," Etta answers.

"He's not capable of understanding."

"Echo?" I ask. God, this is hell. "Echo killed them? Ma?" My throat burns. I need something... Water, air…

"I'm going to jail to pardon his sins. I have a rumor and it's time."

"What are you talking about?" Etta asks. "Get ahold of yourself. You're going to scare Ruby."

"A rumor!" Mom yells. "In my head, been there for twenty years."

"A tumor?" I ask as bile crawls up my throat.

The room spins slowly at first. Everyone floats in and out. I ask them to stop moving. The tunnel shrinks. Tumor? Oh God. I trace my cracked dry lips with a finger.

"You're going to die?" I whisper.

"I'll be with Lenny and Opal and the worm buffet. We've been talking all about it."

"I don't understand. Are you going to jail or are you dying?"

Chapter 51

Fragments

Rebel

I threw everyone out of Ruby's room after she fainted. We'd collectively barfed a hell buffet on her until she'd passed out. I fucking thought we'd killed her. And then I nearly killed Monday Rose for her inexplicable drone of nonsense.

"Ruby, sweet thing."

Her eyelids flutter along with my heart.

"Rebel," Ruby whispers. Her hoarse voice matched with her furled brow weighs on me. "I couldn't tell you."

"Baby, we don't need to talk about anything right now. Just rest." I kiss her palm then draw circles there.

When she squeals, and pulls her hand away, I know she's coming around. And I don't let her pull away. From here on out, she's all mine. Every piece of her. Her past. Her pain. Her healing. Her future. God, what she's been through. A lifetime of hell.

"I'm still alive?"

"Alive and kicking." My eyes well up when she touches my lips and traces her fingertips across my face like she's double-checking her thoughts. "Almost lost you."

"You could never lose me. You never will." Her eyes twinkle, melting my resolve. "My mom?" Her fingers wrap around my wrist.

Everywhere on her rail-thin form, spaghetti-like tubes crisscross. My sweet thing. They tried to ruin her, but she made it through an abyss, and here she's asking about someone else. She made it through a netherworld and tried to protect me while she was getting eaten alive by my accusations and her guilt. I wish I had known. What a twisted fucking nightmare.

I want to dial time back and rescue her. I want to jam my hand through a black hole and run to her. And I want to thank the one man who took those fucks out. Thank him for serving justice where it never would have been served. Was it wrong he took the law into his hands? Yes. But, sometimes, wrong feels right. Sometimes fate hunts ugly and torches it with pure morality. Eat it, you fucks. You're six feet under. And she's sunshine through a blizzard. She can survive anything after them.

"Is she in jail? Is she okay?" Ruby's a rambling jumble of questions.

All I want to do is soothe her, and all she wants are answers. Understandably.

"No one is going to jail, baby. She was stressed out and kind of lost her shit. Got confused. Typical Monday."

Ruby's eyelids droop. "She might be crazy, but I love her," she whispers.

Yeah. I get it. Family can be batshit crazy, all right. But, still, you love 'em. Still you root for 'em. Still, you pray in your silent hours, the ones when you can't sleep or wake, that they're okay.

"I heard her talking to me. I don't know when, but she said she was proud of me." She nods, and a lazy smile finds her lips along with tears. "She's never told me that before. How long does she have with this tumor thing? I need to talk to her doctor," she says like she's the band leader and ready for action right damn now from her hospital bed.

"Beat you to it. She let me have at her doc." I lean over and kiss her on the forehead.

Her whole demeanor relaxes.

"First," I say, "she's okay. Has had this tumor in her head for years. It's not gonna kill her. It's just pressing on things that make her a little off. The word mix-ups, talking to Lenny…"

"No shit?"

"Yeah. No shit."

Ruby grabs fistfuls of my T-shirt and pulls me toward her, my lips pressing to hers when I arrive.

"I love you," I tell her softly. "I fucking love you. Have always loved you. You've been my little Red Hot since that first day we met in shop class."

"Still?" she says, her eyes glittering. Is it hope and confirmation? Or relief? Both, I imagine. "With all you know about everything?"

"More. Didn't think that was possible. I'm so sorry, baby. So very sorry I never showed. Everything is my fault."

"No. Don't do that. I can't feel guilt for your guilt. That's too much. It's why I hid it. It's why I ran. Part of it, anyway."

"I know. And I was so mean to you when you came home." I trace a line down the side of her face, her porcelain skin perfect and unmarred.

Ruby grabs my shirt and tugs me to her, our foreheads meeting. "Yeah, nice work on that. You were a primo dick. But don't quit your day job."

My girl. I kiss her hands. Her chest. Her hidden pain, guilt, and remorse. I kiss her hoping my kisses hold healing power. More than anything, I need her to know she is loved. She's loved no matter what. Everyone, no matter what they've gone through or done, deserves love. Hard as it is to say, it's true. Pain causes some to hide. It causes others to be cruel. I never understood the power of it, but I'm beginning to grasp fragments.

Pain is born of many pieces, some of which she still doesn't know about.

Chapter 52

Redemption

Ruby

When I wake up, Rebel is slumped over my bed, snoring. I must have dozed off midconversation because I still don't know the whole story. Part of me is afraid to know all of it and anxious of what might happen to my family members now that things are out in the open.

"Hey," Rebel says, rubbing his half-closed eyes, his voice hoarse with exhaustion.

"Hey."

"You fell asleep so long I worried you slipped back into a coma. Scared the shit out of me. Knock it off." He yawns and stretches across my body. "When they let you out of this place, you're coming home with me.

"So we're done courting?"

"Nope. I'm planning on courting you for the rest of your life. You can laze around like a queen and I'll be your manservant."

"I don't want a manservant unless he's donning a skimpy loincloth that includes a string up his sexy ass so I can ogle his gorgeous man buns."

"Man buns?" Rebel bursts out laughing. "Not gonna happen."

"Then I don't want it." I chuckle.

Rebel frowns and straightens, his hand still on my body like he'll never let me go. "What do you want, baby?" He swings a tray on my bedside table over my chest then adjusts my bed so I'm sitting more upright. After eyeing up the food, he points to the pudding.

I nod, and he feeds me. I think about his question as I roll the sweet faux-banana pudding over my tongue. It's simple, really. I know exactly what I want.

"A husband."

Rebel smirks and bites his plump bottom lip. Even though the man looks like he's been dragged behind a truck, he's still the sexiest guy I've ever laid eyes on. Some guys are born to wear old ripped T-shirts, unshaven faces, and bedhead like they're on a magazine shoot. Rebel the cover man.

"What kind of husband you looking for?"

"The naughty kind." I open my mouth for another spoonful. "I want a dirty fucker."

"I know just the man." He sneaks a bite of pudding then grins. "He won't do that loincloth thing you're jonesing for, but he will get naked and toss you on your back, legs spread. He'll keep you damn busy, girl. Dirty, filthy busy."

"I figured as much. I want a busy husband like that."

Rebel locks the door and climbs onto my bed. He places his hand over my heart then walks his fingertips down to my breast. As much as I want to be groped by my man, there's still unfinished business. Maybe he's protecting me from pain, but it's high time I know what happened to the Kline boys.

"I need more. And don't play Clue with me. Who did it?"

Rebel exhales a long sigh and my stomach knots. "Lenny."

"Dad?" I swallow hard then sigh. Holy shit.

"The Kline boys had stolen a baseball from Echo, and Lenny went to their house to get it. Sounds like he walked into a fight the boys were having over you and Opal, lots of trash talk about what they'd done to you girls. Not sure how it all transpired, but Etta came upon a nightmare. A fucking fluke nightmare. Twice in one week. You and Opal, then the redemption."

"Jesus." My stomach sours as I think about what Dad must have felt like after that. Bittersweet. "His heart attack, oh my God."

"I'm sorry, baby. I wish I had known. Wish I had been there to protect you."

"I'm sorry I was so freaked out that I couldn't tell you. I was terrified of everything that week. I've never had fear take me over like that. Not until I came home to you."

Rebel props onto his elbow, his head tilted to the side, his free hand threading through my hair. "That gave you fear?"

"Okay, I was sort of exaggerating, but yeah. It hasn't exactly been a smooth transition."

"It has kind of been a shitstorm." He kisses me on the nose, and I honk his to receive a wonky noise in return. "I'm gonna make it better. Gonna make everything better."

"So you're not going to sell your farm or the hardware store? That was one of my biggest fears."

"I'd like to talk to you about what *we're* gonna do. Because that money, it should've been yours, not mine."

Chapter 53

Hornets By The Dozen

Rebel

"Oh my God, it's huge." Ruby blushes, places one hand over her lips, and then strokes away.

I grin. God, she's beautiful. And healthy and out of the woods. Three weeks ago, her doctors told her she could go home, and I loaded her into my truck and took her there. To my place. And, today, on Ruby's birthday, I'm taking her on another ride into our future.

"Isn't this what you begged for in high school? The biggest, darkest ride you could score?"

"Yeah, but—"

"No yeah buts. Now, get on and ride the sunovabitch like he's yours, 'cause he is."

Ruby grabs hold of leather reins in one hand and, with a small boost from me, rises onto her Percheron stallion's back like a rocket headed to outer space.

"Happy birthday, baby."

"Rebel," she whispers as her horse dances beneath her. "How could you have possibly remembered?"

She has no idea the things I remember. Sure, her fantasies about horses and a farm spread over rolling hills and family are written on all the places in my heart, which she owns. But they aren't the things that fused us together. So many things did, though. The way we swam naked in the river, a couple of country kids exploring each other with kisses, lust and eager anticipation. Hours of fishing on the lake, which always ended with me sneaking into her bedroom when everyone was long asleep. Ruby sauntering down the school halls, her head high, pirating looks from everyone, her eyes glued to mine, only mine. The list is endless.

Women get butterflies. But men? Hornets is what I always said. She gave me hornets by the dozens. That girl made my insides buzz, and I wanted to sting her hard from day one.

"He's so smooth, nothing like Rambler was."

"Rambler had the choppiest gallop ever." I laugh, remembering her old gelding. "I'm amazed you could ride that mess of a horse."

"I loved Rambler."

"I know you did. But you wanted something more like this guy. A Lamborghini."

"So you bought two?" I rise onto my horse as Ruby turns her stallion in a circle.

"You needed a riding partner. I'm your man."

Ruby clucks and takes off in a gallop, the thunder of her horse's hooves mirroring my heart. I chase, then gallop past her, heading down the path flanking the cornfield.

She races next to me. "You certainly are fun to ride with…ahem and on." She winks. "Race you to the cherry farm?"

"You're on, sweet thing." *And playing right into my plan.*

Philomena Clancy called me the day Ruby was released from the hospital. Her ninety-nine-acre cherry farm is the one I wanted to buy back when those trusts were awarded to me. I was sure, if Ruby got wind I'd bought it, she'd come home. It was the one farm she'd set her sights on when she talked of someday getting married. Someday living here in our small town.

Philomena, though, wasn't going to budge back then. Not ever, as far as I was concerned. But, when she called recently, her voice rising high as she asked if I was still interested, I knew that it was a done deal before she'd gotten all of her words out. Some things and timing are simply meant to be. Hopefully this'll convince Ruby to stay here in Snowvale like we've been discussing. She doesn't want me to leave my life, but she's not one hundred percent sure she's ready to give up everything in hers. So, I decided to go balls out. I have nothing to lose but her. And that's not an option.

"Looks better than ever." Ruby grins when we trot down the cherry orchard's long, winding gravel driveway. "Want to go pick a few buckets? I could make you a pie later…or just some cherry sauce we could drizzle over something else sweet." She licks her lips and waggles her brow.

"Cherry sauce? That sounds dirty. I'm in."

"You're easy, Rebel." She laughs, and all I hear is my next sixty years. And they're as gorgeous as she is.

"Truth is, I'm pretty hard right now with all this talk of cherry sauce drizzled on you, sweet thing."

My heart beat picks up pace the closer we get to the farmhouse. I tried to plan everything out so she wouldn't catch on. A few times, though, I was sure Monday was en route to spoil the surprise.

"She painted it red with white trim just like I always said I would if it were mine."

Oh, fuck, her smile. It's kind of happy soaked in sad. Sort of like her dream idea was stolen.

"And that old blue truck... Shit. Remember?" Her eyes water, and my pulse zips. "It's like Philomena read my mind."

When we turn the corner, heading toward the orchards, Ruby bursts out crying, sharp gasps punctuating her sobs of joy. The swooping hand-painted banners welcoming her to our new farm ripple in the soft breeze, our family members beneath them, clapping their hands and hollering out congratulatory shouts of joy.

"Rebel...oh God."

"Welcome home, baby."

Chapter 54

Stay

Ruby

"You're driving a hard bargain, mister," I say as Rebel and I wander through each room of the farmhouse now that everyone has gone home. I'm still pinching myself that he bought this place, the one farm I dreamed about since I was a little girl.

"I'll show you some hard driving, baby, come here for a little more birthday love."

Rebel pulls me into his arms and slow dances us down the hall, across the wide planked creaky floor into the master bedroom. The only room in the house all set up like we already live here. I don't how he pulled off everything he did, but his wooing me to stay in Snowvale has paid off.

"Sit on the edge." He backs me onto the bed. I sit, then flop onto my back. Twisting my head around, I admire the old barn wood planks and how he artfully pieced them together into a headboard.

"How long did it take you to build this bed?"

"I've been working on it since you got to town." He pulls me upright, winks, and threads his fingers through my hair, sending goosebumps scattering.

Wind whistles through fluttering white linen curtains, dust whirling in the last remnants of the now setting sun. Rebel looks down at me, his hands cupping my face as he bends and places a soft kiss on my lips. Gentle and comforting, his tongue parts my mouth open with ease. He deepens the kiss, a groan vibrating from his mouth to mine as his tongue plays across mine. "Ruby," he says quietly. Kneeling in front of me, he fingers the edge of my T-shirt then lifts it up my stomach and over my head.

"Why do I still feel like a teenager around you sometimes?" I ask.

"Same," he answers while unfastening my bra and removing it. "That is until I see these gorgeous tits that are all woman. Then I feel all man and wolf." His smile devours me, so handsome and pure that I blush. He pushes my breasts together and licks from nipple to nipple, flicking my wet peaks with his thumb all the while.

"Rebel." I arch into him, and he sucks my tips taut, then nibbles on them. "Oh God."

"Need you naked," he says. "Take your jeans off, leave your underwear on."

"A man with a plan?" I smile.

"Always. I've had years to fantasize about you in every damn position, I intend to follow through on every last one of them."

"I'd like that." I excitedly work my jeans down my legs with Rebel's help.

"Would you now?" He lifts my now bare ankles to his lips and kisses them then moves to the arches of my feet where he licks and tickles me.

"Very much." I giggle when he splits my legs, gently pushes me onto my back and places my ankles on his broad shoulders then proceeds to nibble my calf muscles.

"It's gonna take lots of time."

"I have lots of time."

"Years and years on this bed." His wet kisses travel up the insides of my thighs. "And on the kitchen table I'm going to build for us out in that old barn."

"What about that claw foot bathtub in our bathroom?"

"That too. Lots of things we can do in that big tub. I like you wet." He plays his fingers across my belly, as he licks along the edge of my underwear, making me insane for his tongue to travel where I need it most. With his teeth at one side of my lacy underwear, he pulls them down an inch.

This is it. Now is the time to tell him. My heart races as I suck in a breath then let it rip. "Okay. I'm in."

He stops what he's doing, much to my dismay. Leaning over my body, he places his hands beside me, his eyes wide and filled with emotion and something I'd call hope. "What's that mean? Tell me it means what I think it does." His voice cracks, melting and filling my heart in one quick whirl. "Spell it out before I have a heart attack waiting."

"I'll stay. I'll live here on this farm with you. I'll love you for the rest of my life and forevermore. I've put a lot of thought into it. I can still travel for the big jobs. The rest of it, I can let go. I'm ready for something else. A different life."

Rebel's eyes water, sending my pulse flying. I did it, I made the right choice. "A life with me?"

"You're the only man I want Rebel." His tears drip onto my face and I lose it right along with him. "That's never changed."

"Jesus, I love you, Ruby." He kisses me hard, then does it again, a grin forming against my mouth. "You're staying?"

"That's what I said. I'm staying. And I'm really happy about it."

"You're happy?" Rebel lifts me off the bed, wraps my legs around his waist and spins us, all the while laughing his deep guttural happy laugh. It's so beautiful I cry harder. "I'm out of my fucking mind! All my life...all my damned life this is what I've wanted...to be with you like this," he says, peppering my face with kisses.

"I thought you had other plans?" I smirk, horny as hell after all the teasing. "Something about positions you wanted to try? No time like the present to start exploring."

"I love you, sweet thing."

"I love you more, Wishbone."

Rebel gently tosses me onto the bed. "Get on your knees." I eagerly scramble into position. "Come here, you gorgeous thing you." With his hands gripping my thighs, he pulls me to the edge of the bed and eases my underwear down to the top of my thighs. "Head down, baby." He rubs one hand up my spine, pressing my face into the soft downy bedding.

I'm so turned on I might burst into flames when he spreads my thighs, then opens me wide and blows across my skin. "Well, I guess you like that," he says when I moan.

And while I like the way his hot breath blows across me in a sexy intimate way, I might like the way I'm picturing him exploring me with his eyes—while in this position—even more.

His wet tongue touches lightly on my inner thighs, his hands there too now, causing me to squirm. Then he spreads me open again. And God, what he does with his tongue and where he puts it nearly sends me to the center of the bed. "Rebel."

"Yeah, baby?" His fingers join his tongue, which is tracing and entering me everywhere. He licks, sucks, and blows on me so tenderly, so exquisitely, I'm seconds away from coming. And when he presses the wet pad of his thumb to my ass, then presses in the tiniest bit while treating my clit like the queen she deserves to be, I shatter.

"Oh God, Rebel! Oh God, yes!"

He doesn't for one second stop what he's doing and it turns that one orgasm into another one seconds later. I didn't realize I could have back- to-back orgasms but, holy hell, it's happening. And when I come down from the second one, drool on the spot under my mouth, thighs aching, body sated, Rebel works his jeans off and positions his thick length right there ready to enter me.

"Something about this," he says, voice deep and gruff. "You on your knees, head down, underwear still sorta on. It's really fucking sexy, baby."

"I kind of like it too."

"I noticed." He chuckles.

After dragging the head of his cock up and down my core, from my clit to my ass, he presses himself into me, inch by inch. And

God, he fills me. Deep and full, until his balls slap me with every movement. "So wet and tight." He groans. "Made for me."

Gripping my hips, he pulls me onto him, my body accommodating his girth with each thrust. He slides his hands up my sides then onto my breasts. I nearly come when he squeezes my nipples so hard I squeal.

"You okay? he asks. Too much?"

"No, I like it. I just didn't know…"

"Didn't know how good we could be playing around like this?"

"Yeah." I can only imagine what he has in store for us. I know it's going to be crazy good.

Rebel pulls out and I whine. In seconds, he has me on my back. Then he's yanking my underwear off and tossing them aside. "Open your pussy, Ruby."

Rebel's eyes are dark and sexy as hell, his muscles bulging as he presses my thighs apart, waiting for me to do what he's asked.

"Show me how you touch yourself."

He licks my fingertips and places my uncast hand between my legs. "And don't tell me you don't do it."

"Of course I do it," I say softly, the smallest smile on my lips. He catches my almost grin and bites his bottom lip.

"To me?"

"All my life. Only to you."

"Fuck, Ruby." He grips his bobbing cock and places it at my opening while I play with my clit as he watches. "You like this, baby? Me watching you?"

"Yeah." I close my eyes as he presses his head to my wet core and nudges against me without ever entering. *Wishbone.*

"You okay if I'm inside you while you do that sexy shit you're doing?" I open my eyes, our gazes locking and filled with need. Rebel grabs his T-shirt at the back of his neck and jerks it off in one movement. And there it is. The sexiest chest ever. Sweaty and muscular, nipples tight and dark.

"I want that. Want you in me."

Rebel nods, and with one hand resting at my side and his other guiding his cock, he pushes inside me. "Not gonna last while you're doing that." He looks down to where we join and stares at my wet fingers as I play.

"Give me eight seconds, Wishbone," I say, then giggle. Rebel grins and together we count to eight. And my God, when that number arrives we come together in a union filled with love and forgiveness. And also, a future I'm certain is filled with trust.

Chapter 55

Magically

Ruby

One thing I've learned in life is, you will never know exactly who someone is. You think you have people figured out by the things they say or do. You give them labels. She married for money, knew she could get away with it. Has an Ivy league law degree framed on her den wall stating she accomplished enough. Still, she's a trophy wife. Or is she? You have no fucking idea who she is. You never will. Neither will he.

It goes on and on, the way we make up stories about people. From family to friends to people we follow on social media. We think we know who they are. We think we know what they've been through. We don't. Not by a long shot. Because most people have something hidden behind their smiles or their stormy, sassy retorts. Or the way they jab at others. For many, it's pain, guilt, or shame.

I was that girl. And, while I still harbor guilt and struggle with it now and again, my running away and then coming back home to Rebel has given me freedoms I didn't think I'd ever find.

Freedoms to see in new ways, with a gentler opinion of others. Maybe the Kline boys had been through their own hell. I'll never know. And, though I can't forgive or forget what they did, I have come to the realization that maybe something damaged them too. Something awful that made them want to hurt other people. No one is born a monster; people tend to be molded by something fierce.

"Do you wear Franks? You have no panty lines showing," Mom asks Etta as they clear the dishes while Echo and I play with Gilbert's four puppies.

"Spanks...yes. I do. Helps me keep my figure and lessen the jiggle." Etta smiles back at me and winks.

Etta and I have found a new level of friendship. She thought, once I knew her side of the story, I'd leave Rebel. She thought I'd come at her with devil-soaked vengeance. Instead, we talk a lot and about so many things it blows my mind. We're more similar than I could have ever imagined. We've both gone through our own version of despair and we've both evolved. The way I've come to see it, you evolve or you die.

"You wash, I'll dry," Mom says, taking a plate from Etta. "I was wondering..." She gulps a sip of her boozy slushy. "I had read..." She slugs the rest of it down.

I brace myself for a big one. I shouldn't because she too has turned quite a corner. Well, more than a corner. She admitted to knowing that Dad did what he did. Echo told her via a cartoon he drew, and he gave to Mom for her reminders box. He told her he needed to forget but she should remember. In that same box is the cartoon Opal drew and gave to Echo the night she died. She couldn't speak that night and lots of their communication was done via cartoon drawings anyway.

"You can ask me anything," Etta says, a slur in her voice from the old-fashioned cherry slushes we've been enjoying since four this afternoon, one week in at our new farm.

"You didn't get it cut off, did you?" Mom points to Etta's crotch, and my cheeks burn. "That wasn't true that you donated your…"

"No. I was just joking with you." Etta waves a hand around and chuckles.

I sigh in relief, like I'm helicoptering two naughty toddlers who made it across a treacherous river.

"I read they turn that part inside out," Mom says, proud as a peacock. "Like a sock."

"The penis, yes. Something like that." Etta nods and shrugs. "Close enough."

I scoop my glass off the floor and stand for a refill. Truth is, I'm fascinated by Etta and Mom and my excuse to get closer to eavesdrop is my empty cocktail. They've become something new. Friends. The most unlikely friends ever, but the beauty blossoming between them is as exquisite as spring rounding a corner post a tired gray winter.

"Monday?" Etta says then stalls for an oddly long time.

I busy myself but peek up for a take on her body language. Nervous with a side of interest.

"I was wondering… Would you care to go to the movies with me?" she asks.

Mom stretches her neck tall then gives Etta a once-over. *Please say yes.*

"Are you asking me on a date? I couldn't date a woman who has an inside-out penis up inside her. I couldn't date a woman at all. I'm not a thespian."

"Lesbian. I realize." Etta's lips thin, and I get all butterfly nervous for both. "Not a date. Just…friends," she says. "Girlfriends."

Rebel waltzes into the kitchen with two puppies snuggled in his brawny arms. I shoot him big eyes. Big pay-attention-this-is-really-good-stuff eyes. He nods and winks.

"Girlfriends? Oh." Mom practically squeals.

I do too. *Girlfriends.*

"That's so…kind of you. I haven't gone to a movie with a girlfriend in a long time. Come to think of it…I haven't had a close girlfriend in a while. Most women are such foods."

"Like french fries?" Rebel asks. "Ruby though—she's sweet like a cherry."

"Prudes," I say, helping Mom out. "Not foods."

"The rumor." Mom rolls her eyes and scratches under her wig with a fork. "What about Lake and Echo…and Lenny and Opal?"

"They can stay here, Ma. You girls go. Have fun!"

"They can join us," Etta says. "And I'll drive. There's room for everyone."

When Etta and Mom stroll out of the house, Etta toting Lake, Echo trailing behind them, and Lenny and Opal drifting across the heavens somewhere or another, I realize some beautiful things. And every fiber in my body overflows with happiness. Family comes in more shapes and sizes than I ever thought possible. Imperfections and oddities you're better off embracing than judging. We may be a strange bunch with bizarre and rather damaged history, but we're us. Each of us is unique and truer to ourselves than ever before. It warms me and makes me chuckle. And then my knees buckle, previous thoughts vanishing when Rebel dances kisses down the side of my neck, reminding me of other things. Namely, that we're alone.

"That was pretty sweet, huh? The whole girlfriends thing?" I say.

"Etta mentioned it to me earlier. I think those slushy old-fashioneds gave her the courage to go for it."

"Sometimes all you have to do is ask." I laugh when Rebel spins me in his arms.

"Then I'm asking." He waggles his brow.

"Blow job?" I say, since he's been hinting at one all day.

"I was thinking hand in marriage." He scoops me up in his arms and spins. Spins my whole world.

Tears flow, and my heart beat zips, my one needed word stuck in my throat.

"It never crossed my mind to ask, 'Will you marry and blow me?' Seems like an odd combo."

I snort out a laugh, and he kisses tears off my cheeks.

"Will you be my wife and blow me for life, sweet thing?"

"Rebel." I shake my head and crack up all over again.

I love him more than life. I guess that's just one of the reasons I left him in the first place. Sometimes you love someone so much that the only thing you can do to protect them is get out of the way.

"Was that a yes?" He presses his forehead to mine, nodding.

"Yes to being your wife." I swallow hard and grin like a fool who just drank an ocean full of sunshine. "And we can rock-paper-scissor for the blow job."

We play our hands, and Rebel laughs then kisses me so deeply that I'm lost in him again. Seconds become an eternity of moments like this. All of it unfolding magically in my mind. It's sexy and perfect and everything Rebel.

"Guess today's my lucky day." He grins. "Rock beats scissors."

The End xxx

more…

Please take a moment to sign up for my newsletter:

awildingwells.com

Acknowledgments and About this story

Dear Scrumptious Lovely Reader!

Thank you with all my heart for reading this story. I hope it gave you big feels; I hope all my books do. This is Book Three in the Wild Things Series (Standalone).

If you did like it, I'd be so grateful if you'd consider posting a review. And, I've written a couple of other books you may also enjoy.

~ *How To Tame Beasts And Other Wild Things* (Book 1 of The Wild Things series, a standalone)

~ *Mastering The Art Of A Three Ring Circus* (Book 2 in The Wild Things series, a standalone)

~ *A Mess of Reason*

~ *A Field Guide To Catching Crickets*

~ *Of Winged Creatures & Nesting Grounds*

Big thank-yous to my many awesome ARC readers + blogger friends! I adore you for embracing my work and for sharing it with the world. You are lovely generous souls! I cannot thank you enough for embracing my creations. Oceans full of kisses xxxxxx

Mickey and Rahab, I bow down with appreciation. Your editing is truly so appreciated!

Thank you BEXHARPER DESIGNS for the amazing cover you created and the sexy stunning edits! Love the pants off you two!

To my darling husband, and family, I love you more than cake.

On Pinterest (www.pinterest.com/awildingwells/) you will find my inspiration board for this book. I do love building worlds—you might want to check it out. Also, please consider following me on social media if you'd like to be notified about my upcoming books and cool giveaways, which are plentiful.

About This Book

The idea of this book came to me when I was running the backside steps of the bleachers at the high school in the town we used to live in. My husband and I typically ran them together, but on this particular day he had been busy, so I was running them alone. I'm not sure why I got creeped out at one point, but I did…and in came this novel. I ran to my car and started writing it the second I got home.

If you've read my books, you know I have a fondness for the following:

- Quirky characters that are so real they become a part of you.
- Chemistry between my characters, especially the H/H.
- Family stuff. All of it.
- World painting, and especially small towns.
- Twists. Dark bleeding to light. The unthinkable. And of course, the HEA.

I also pluck a bit from my own life. Now for some rambling.

Like Ruby, I left high school a few days after graduation, and moved to Paris, France with a modeling contract in hand.

My reason was not to run, but rather, I needed to see what was going on in the world outside of the small town I grew up in and that contract was my ticket.

While I was there, I had a few scary run-ins with guys. Nothing that scarred me for life, but no question things that put me on the defensive anywhere I am. I pulled plenty from those chapters for Ruby Mae and embellished them with layers. Unfortunately, Ruby got the horrifically raw side of the deal as too many women do.

Ruby playing Martyr came into play when I was early on in this book and we decided to move from California to Nicaragua. Everyone seemed to have some sort of opinion about our move and while most were supportive, so many poked the oddest questions at us. Sort of like this: "How dare you do this to your children…steal their high school years from them for your own wanderlust." It blew my mind that anyone would first think so narrow mindedly, and second, have the balls to say it to a person they don't even know.

So yeah, when I write, I charge on no matter what's going on in my life because no matter what it is, there is a story inside it.

Rebel came about naturally once Ruby was formed in my mind. Plus, he had played a small role in *Mastering The Art Of A Three Ring Circus*, and I was already smitten with him and his rough-and-tumble sexy ways. One of my favorite things about Rebel is his vulnerability and how he loved with such intensity. I do so adore a man who loves like this but is still so human and imperfect. Etta gave Rebel so much in terms of depth and growth. And Rifle, though he didn't play a huge role, still helped define parts of Rebel that I wanted to shine.

Monday Rose might be one of my favorite characters in the book. She was easily inspired by the very idea of family holidays. In particular, one of my own family's Thanksgivings when I was in high school and my great-grandmother, who was in her late nineties and rather deaf, blurted out at the table a most unfortunate blunder about another family member. Thank God that individual laughed, because it could not have been more offensive. Deads day was inspired by that moment.

I realize what I write is a bit out of the box when it comes to romance novels. But I love...truly love how you guys reach out to me and share your feelings about my stories. I love that you appreciate how wonky my books can be at times. I write what I love, what pours out of me. Thank you with all my heart for appreciating my words and for continuing to read them.

xxx,

Made in the USA
Lexington, KY
26 May 2017